Oct 2011

ST. MARTIN'S

MINOTAUR
MYSTERIES

continued . . .

CROSSROAD BLUES

BLUES

A NICK TRAVERS MYSTERY

★ ACE ATKINS ★

St. Martin's Paperbacks

Lyrics from the following songs are reprinted by permission:

"Cross Road Blues" (take 2)
"Cross Road Blues" (take 1)
"Hell Hound On My Trail"
"Me and the Devil Blues"
"Me and the Devil"
"Stones in My Pathway"
"Love In Vain Blues"
words and music by Robert Johnson
copyright © (1978), 1990, 1991 King of Spades Music
All Rights Reserved. Used By Permission.

"Rock Me" a/k/a/ "Rock Me Baby"
Written by Muddy Waters
© 1957, 1985 Watertoons Music (BMI)/
Administered by Bug Music
All Rights Reserved. Used by Permission.

CROSSROAD BLUES

Library of Congress Catalog Card Number: 98-19416

ISBN: 0-312-97192-3

Printed in the United States of America

St. Martin's Press hardcover edition / November 1998
St. Martin's Paperbacks edition / February 2000

10 9 8 7 6 5 4 3 2

for the zen poets of mississippi

Acknowledgments

My greatest thanks to my writing mentors: George Plasketes for teaching me the fundamentals, Tim Green for teaching me how to build a novel, and Warren Ripley for teaching me how to sell my work.

I would also like to thank my mother for her support and friendship; my father for showing me how to work towards a goal; the Hudgins family for constantly entertaining me; Tammy Trout for being an incredible friend and Elvis fan; Art Copeland for always being ready with a full tank of gas for another blues adventure; Jim Purifoy for putting me in touch with the right people; writer B. F. Vandervoort for books, bourbon, cigarettes, and a great inspiration; Lynn Hartman for being my first reader; Moby for always coming through with his 1,001 sources; Wayne Moss for his sleazy but true tales of the music business; Kurt Nauck for his descriptions of 1930s recordings; Stephen LaVere for his knowledge of Johnson's early years; Peter Golenbock for sharing wonderful details about being an oral historian; Jay Nolan for making an abstract vision art; the Blues Ship for allowing Jay to do his thing; Gabe Navarro for sharing dozens of tasteless New Orleans stories; and the Sack family for taking me in while I was down and out in the Big Easy.

Special thanks to: Lindy Wolverton for introducing her husband to the South and the blues; to my editor, Pete Wolverton, for his direct and insightful comments; my agent, Andrew Pope, for his great speed; my Jack Russell terrier, Bud, for his immense wisdom; and my kindhearted woman, Shelli, for everything.

And, of course, Blind Willie's, where Travers's soul dwells.

Nick Travers would like to thank the following people for their great work in the blues and the background they provided for *Crossroad Blues:* Rudi Blesh, Peter Guralnick, John Hammond, Alan Lomax, Mack McCormick, Robert Palmer, Robert Santelli, Gayle Dean Wardlow, Pete Welding, and Jerry Wexler.

Additional thanks to *Living Blues* founder Jim O'Neal for drawing the road map to search for Robert Johnson.

I went to the crossroad
fell down on my knees
I went to the crossroad
fell down on my knees
Asked the Lord above "Have mercy
save poor Bob, if you please."

Mmmmm, standin' at the crossroad
I tried to flag a ride
Standin' at the crossroad
I tried to flag a ride
Didn't nobody seem to know me
everybody pass me by

—Robert Johnson,
"Cross Road Blues"

Travers: dweller at a crossroad
—New Dictionary of American Family Names

Prologue

August 13, 1938
Leflore County, Mississippi

ROBERT JOHNSON laid down his battered six-string, took a seat at the juke joint's bar, and wrapped his long fingers around a jar of corn whiskey. A layer of dust covered his creased suit like fallen sugar and his throat felt like cracked mud. It'd been a long walk to the crossroads, a few miles outside Greenwood, where the juke's owner picked him up. Man made him ride in the back of his truck all the way to Three Forks.

Johnson needed the money. He'd spent his last five dollars in an old boarding shack, two dollars for the room and three for the whore. It was worth it though, all that smooth, brown skin next to his tight and sore body. Almost forgot what that final loosenin' up felt like. Only a woman could pull those red demons from a man.

The juke's owner refilled the dirty jar to the rim. *Ain't that nice.* Johnson tipped the brow of his fedora and took a big sip. Nothin' like free whiskey. It tasted like sweet gasoline goin' into his empty stomach, all fiery and warm. Bringin' your guitar to a juke was as good as bringin' cash. And besides, they all knew him 'round here. Wasn't like it was in Texas, where they treated coloreds almost as bad as Mexicans. Here they respected blues.

"Whay you been, Bob?"

"Travelin'."

"Heard you made another record."

"That's right."

"They pay somethin' big fo' that? Fancy suit. Fancy hat. Man oh man. You doin' jes fine fo' yo'-self, Bob. Jes fine."

"Yeah, jes fine."

Johnson pulled the fedora lower over his bad eye and glanced down at the whiskey-soaked two-by-fours. Man must've gone crazy bein' so nice. Or maybe he'd just forgot about him sneakin' out with his wife las' time. His gray eyes didn't show nothin' though, so Johnson turned and watched a young guitar player pickin' out an old Charley Patton song. The metal plank of the player's high, tinny notes made Johnson cringe. He'd been there. Son House used to laugh when he heard him play.

But Johnson learned.

The blues came from all he knew. All he was. He put that lonesome feeling in each note. The longing. The losses. He rubbed his callous black hands together and thought of the place in his heart where the blues dwelled. Every day he'd worked on the farm. Every time he was beaten by his stepfather because of his smart mouth.

And his wife, his dear sweet wife—he could feel the edges of his heart open like a parched flower and tears well in his eyes. That's when the devil came into his life, and evil been followin' him around ever since. Sometimes when he was high, the world revolvin' all around him like the blades in a fan, he saw Satan. Watchin', followin', and waitin'. The devil wanted him. Johnson shook it off and walked outside.

It was coal black in the woods where the juke joint stood. A Dietz lantern dimly flooded light a few feet from the beaten steps and into the tall grass waving in the summer wind. He took a deep breath. Inside, it'd been like bein' high up in a loft throwin' hay—heat thick as cigarette smoke hangin' all about his head.

Johnson found a tall bank of grass under a pine tree and unbuttoned his pants. He felt a cool breeze as the crickets and cicadas played a show around him. Lookin' for lovin'. He laughed at that, letting the last few hours of whiskey go away as he rocked on his heels.

A dry, dead branch snapped behind him.

He looked over his shoulder and buttoned back up. Nothin'. The crickets and cicadas had gone silent around the juke, only the pluckin' and wailin' of the man inside. He began to walk back. Maybe he'd play a little more for the folks. Give them a few songs he'd been workin' on as he made his way back from Texas. And if Honeyboy came later, they'd show them folks a thing or two.

He looked to the edge of the pine forest. Couldn't see nothin'—only the deep blackness of the woods at night and the flickerin' tails of fireflies. Two clicks of the yellow neon tails. Another branch broke and he heard the shuffling of feet on dry pine needles.

Johnson could feel his heart pump and his arms quiver. He spun around in a circle searching. He never should've come back to Mississippi— should've just kept on movin'. Could've gone any-where...Chicago, New York.

"Psst, R.L.? R.L.?"

Out of the woods walked a young boy. Small and stoop shouldered. Skin white. Features of a black man with pale blue eyes.

"God-damn! What you doin', boy?" Johnson asked.

"Sorry, R.L. Mista wanted me to be quiet. Tole me to wait 'til you left the juke."

"Don't you eva sneak up on a man doin' his business. I 'bout wet all over myself."

"Sorry."

"Where's he at?" Johnson asked, glancing into a cotton field.

"Just up the road there."

The boy's light eyes looked away from the woods and down the dirt highway. There was a full moon and its light shone off a black Buick Roadmaster, a silver Indian pointed proud on the hood. Johnson turned and walked down the road. Get this shit over with. He'd been runnin' from this man since Austin. He was tired.

He could see the tiny red-yellow glow of a cigarette and a fat hulking shape in back of the car. Fat man couldn't drive. Shit, couldn't even fit behind the wheel, had that boy do all his work.

Johnson tromped on the dirt highway toward the car. The crossroads were bare. The front of the Three Forks store was closed with a padlock on the sun-faded door. A rusty Coca-Cola sign creaked in the wind.

The car's window was rolled down and smoke floated out like hot, gray mist on the north road's shoulder. Inside, a deep, white voice said, "Thought you'd left me behind huh, Bob? Thought you could leave our deal? But you and me keep together."

Johnson was silent.

"When you sign a contract with me, I own your soul....I own your ass. Now listen here. Takin' off with those records wasn't too smart. It takes money to make those things. I could find any nigga' in Mississippi to make those poor old sounds."

"Those records are me."

"You're not listenin' to me, Bob. I captured that sound you made and I own it."

Johnson could see the little albino boy trottin' down the dirt road like a dog. He heard the groan of windblown signs at the old grocery store and a rustle of cotton in the fields. Some bits of sandy dirt got in his eyes and he turned away from the fat man.

"I got your records, Bob. Got 'em right here in my trunk. All nine of 'em. Hidin' them in that nasty old boarding shack in Greenwood wasn't too smart. Not too smart at all. But I don't hold a grudge, Bob. 'Cause startin' tonight, you gonna be bigger than all of 'em. Blind Lemon Jefferson, Charley Patton. All of 'em,...yessir, you gonna be a legend."

The fat man shifted his weight on the squeaking leather of the backseat. "Boy, get me and Mr. Johnson a drink."

Johnson turned to leave.

"I offered you a drink, Bob."

Johnson kept walking.

There was a sharp click, an explosion, and a thud of dirt at his feet. Johnson stopped but did not turn around. *This man was crazy. Get away from him. He used you, but bigger things are comin' up.*

The little albino was out of breath as he brought Johnson a shot glass of whiskey. Filled to the rim

with some spilling on the boy's shaky white hands.
His lower lip poked out and his eyes wide with
fear.

"Finish the deal, Bob," the fat man said. "Finish
the deal."

Johnson tossed back the whiskey and threw the
glass far into weeds sprouting along the country
highway. He turned and walked down the dusty
dirt road. Grit swirled all about his feet as he whis-
tled a slow tune.

1

last night
New Orleans, Louisiana

JOJO'S BLUES BAR stood on the south edge of the French Quarter in a row of old Creole buildings made of decaying red brick, stucco, and wood. Inside, smoke streamed from small islands of tables, drinks clicked, women giggled, and fans churned. Black-and-white photographs of long-dead greats hung above the mahogany bar—images faded and warped from humidity and time.

Dr. Randy Sexton stared at the row of faces as his thick coffee mug vibrated with the swampy electric slide guitar. He tapped one hand to the music and held his coffee with the other. The buck-toothed waitress who had brought the coffee shook her head walking away. This wasn't a coffee place. This was a beer and whiskey joint.

Order a mixed drink or coffee and you felt like a leper.

JoJo's. Last of the old New Orleans blues joints, Randy thought. Used to be a lot of them in the for-ties and fifties when he was growing up—but now JoJo's was it. The Vieux Carre now just endless rows of strip joints, discos, and false jazz. Unless you counted that big franchise blues place down the street. Randy didn't.

This bar was a New Orleans institution you couldn't replace with high-neon gloss. The blues sound better in a venue of imperfection. A cracked ceiling. Scuffed floor. Peeling white paint on the bricks. It all somehow adds to the acoustics of blues.

Randy was a jazz man himself. Studied jazz all his life. His passion. Now, as the head of the Jazz and Blues Archives at Tulane University, he was the curator of thousands of African American recordings.

But blues was something he could never really understand. It was the poor cousin to jazz, though the unknowledgeable thought they were the same. Jazz was a fluted glass of champagne. Blues was a cold beer. Working-class music.

His friend and colleague Nick Travers knew blues. He could pick out the region like Henry Higgins could pick out an accent: Chicago, Austin, Memphis, or Mississippi.

Mississippi. The Delta. He sipped some more hot black coffee and watched the great Loretta Jackson doing her thing.

A big, beautiful woman, a cross somewhere between Etta James and KoKo Taylor. Randy had seen the show countless times. He knew every rehearsed movement and all the big black woman's jokes by heart. But he still loved seeing her work— her strong voice could fill a Gothic cathedral.

Her husband, Joseph Jose Jackson, pulled a chair up to the table. A legend himself. There wasn't a blues musician alive who didn't know about JoJo. A highly polished, dignified black man in his sixties. Silver-white hair and mustache.

Starched white dress shirt, tightly creased black trousers, and shined wing tips.

"Doc-tor!" JoJo extended his rough hand.

"Mr. Jackson. Good to see you, my friend, and"—Randy nodded toward the stage—"your wife.... She still raises the hair on the back of my neck."

"She can kick a crowd in the nuts," JoJo said.

Loretta sweated and dotted her brow with a red lace handkerchief to some sexy lyrics and winked down at JoJo.

> *"Rock me baby,*
> *rock me all night long.*
> *Rock me baby,*
> *like my back ain't got no bone."*

They sat silent through the song. JoJo swayed to the music and smiled a wide, happy grin. A proud man in love. The next song was a slow ballad and Randy leaned forward on the wooden table, the smoke making his eyes water. JoJo cocked his ear toward him.

"I'm looking for Nick. Isn't he playing tonight?" Randy asked.

JoJo shook his head and frowned. "Nick? I don't know, he's been tryin' to get back in shape or some shit. Runnin' like a fool every mornin'. Acts like he's gonna go back and play for the Saints again. No sir, he ain't the same."

"He's not answering his phone or his door."

"When he don't want to be found," JoJo said, nodding his head for emphasis, "he ain't gonna be found."

"Could he be out of town? Maybe traveling with the band?"

"What?" JoJo asked, through the blare of the music.

"*Traveling with the band!*" Randy shouted.

"Naw. I ain't seen him. 'Cept the other day when we went and grabbed a snow cone. Started talkin' to some gap-toothed carriage driver 'bout him beatin' his horse. Nick said how'd he like to be cloppin' 'round wearin' a silly hat and listenin' to some fool talk all day. Skinny black fella started talkin' shit but he back down when he got a good look at Nick. I'm tellin' you man, Nick gettin' back in some kinda shape. Not much different than when he was playin'. You think he's considerin' it? Playin' ball again?"

"I doubt the Saints will take him back," Randy said, raising his eyebrows.

Nick had been thrown out of the NFL for kicking his coach's ass during a *Monday Night Football* game. He knocked the coach to the ground, emptied a Gatorade bucket on the man's head, and coolly walked into the tunnel as the crowd went crazy around him. Nick once told Randy he'd changed his clothes and taken a cab home before the game ended. He never returned to the Superdome or pro football again, and Randy never prodded him for the whole story.

A few months after the incident, Nick enrolled in the master's program at Tulane. Later, he earned a doctorate in Southern studies from the University of Mississippi before coming back to teach classes at Tulane.

"JoJo, tell him to call me if you guys talk."

"His band ain't playin' till...shit...Friday night," JoJo said. "What chu need Nick for?"

"Got a job for him."

"Yeah, put his sorry ass to work. Soon enough

he'll be back to the same ol' same ol', drinkin' and smokin'."

At the foot of the bar, an old man watched the two talking. A cigar hung from his mouth as he brushed ashes from his corduroy jacket lined with scarlike patches. His gray eyes darted from JoJo to Randy, then back down to the drink in front of him.

"If you talk to him, tell him to call me," Randy said, getting up to leave and offering JoJo his hand. He knew JoJo would find Nick; he was the man's best friend.

Randy took another sip of coffee and stood watching Loretta. She had a drunk tourist on stage and was getting him to hold her big satin-covered hips as she sang the nasty blues. The old man at the bar watched her too, his face flat and expressionless. His black, parched skin the same texture as the worn photographs on the wall.

Randy and the man's eyes met, then the old man looked away.

"One of our colleagues left for the Delta a few weeks ago," Randy said. "He's disappeared."

"The Delta? Lots of things can happen to a man there," JoJo said, looking him hard in the eye. "Nick'll help, he's a fine man."

"Yeah, I think a great deal of him. He's a good guy."

2

NICK TRAVERS was drunk. Not loopy, hanging-on-a-flagpole drunk. But drunk enough to find simple enjoyment in the soapy suds churning in the Laundromat washing machine. It was two A.M. on St. Charles Avenue and he sat sideways on a row of hard plastic seats—baby blue with flecks of pink. Three loads now in the machine as heat lightning shattered outside like a broken fluorescent bulb, a tattered Signet paperback of *The Catcher in the Rye* in his hands.

"Goddamned phonies," he muttered, thumbing down a dog-eared page, waiting for his clothes in white boxer shorts and battered buckskin boots. His white T-shirt and faded jeans in the wash. No one around except a homeless man drinking whiskey from a bottle in a brown bag. A classic wino. Even missing a few teeth.

"You know what I mean, they screw it up for everybody," Nick said.

The wino nodded.

Nick liked the hard sixties decor of the place. Perfectly round stainless-steel rims circling the glass of the washing machines. No standard elevator music like during the days. Just the sound of the dry summer wind blowing Spanish moss on oaks. Outside, the ancient trees canopied St. Charles Avenue like the knurled fingers of an old man in prayer.

A black woman with her hair tightly wrapped in curlers walked through the open front of the Laundromat and saw Nick in his underwear and boots. She immediately turned and left. The wino watched her butt as she walked by him.

"Get me a piece of dat," he said, his head bobbing as if he had no neck muscles.

Nick turned to the washing machine. So this is what it had come to, washing clothes for enjoyment and talking to derelicts for a social life. Jesus, life changes in five years. Not that life was crappy now and all that sorry-for-self bullshit. Just different. Apples and oranges. Yin and yang.

Sometimes he could hear the deep resonating cheers echoing from the Superdome and wished he was still in there. Grabbing some sissy quarterback by the jersey and slinging him down. But then he thought about lacing up his cleats for a five A.M. practice and would smile. Yeah, life was simple now. Teach a few classes on blues history, play some harp down at JoJo's, and just enjoy life.

Watch the bubbles as the world pulsated in an electric vibe around him. Not quite in, not quite out. Somewhere in the middle. In his mid-thirties and getting soft mentally and physically. No challenges. No immediate goals. He needed to get back on it.

He reached down to the plastic chair beside him and grabbed a handful of quarters from a pile of keys and Dixie beer caps. He tossed the soggy clothes into a double-load dryer and walked next door, to an all-night convenience store. He bought two quart bottles of Colt 45, one for him and one for the wino. The Vietnamese woman never blinked at his pantlessness.

"Hey pal, here you go," Nick said, handing him the water-beaded beer.

"Tanks, chief," he said.

Nice of the guy to say thanks. Proved he was all right. Didn't matter that he was homeless as long as he had some manners. Nick had seen some rich bastards not even thank a waiter for bringing them a meal at Emeril's. "You from here?" he asked, unscrewing the cap.

The man jerked his head back, giving him a double chin. "Naw man, dis ma' summer home. Just on a vacation from France."

"Well, you don't have to get all surly about it, you could be just passin' through."

"Naw. From New Awlans. Stay in New Awlans."

"Yeah, I know what you mean. It's like I can't leave. As much as I hate this fuckin' city sometimes."

"Yeah, I know man. Listen I know. Twenty-nine, ninety."

"What?"

"That's the degrees this city sits on, man. Like a big magnet, it draws folks in." He set his hands a few feet apart, then crashed them together. "Smack. Just like that, your ass is stuck and you can't leave."

"I could get out if I wanted to," Nick said.

"Reason you hangin' out here is you ain't got a woman."

"Had one."

"Had me a meal yesterday but my stomach still empty."

"Brown hair and eyes like morning coffee. Voice

kinda raspy like a jazz singer and a comma of hair she constantly kept out of her eyes."

"I ain't ask you to unload on me. Jus' sayin' you need a woman."

"I need to get back on it."

"On what?"

"Life."

"Life is easy," the man said, gathering his rags and a dirty plastic bag of crushed aluminum cans. "Livin' is hard." He winked at Nick and disappeared into the thick night as a streetcar clanged past.

3

THE NEXT MORNING, the Warehouse District streets were empty, just a couple of parked cars outside the art galleries and handful of restaurants. The old district had changed a lot since Nick bought his 1922 red brick warehouse on Julia Street. Back then, it had just been a few crazy artists who needed the space to work. Now, there were restaurants and renovated apartments for the Polo shirt crowd. But God love them, there were still plenty of weirdos left.

Nick bought his dilapidated building on the advice of JoJo, who was good friends with the former owner. A stocky Italian who just wanted to unload the place, he'd been using it to store stolen goods—from televisions to mattresses.

It was a great deal for the district, but the old building needed a lot of work.

Nick kept the bottom level a garage but added a new metal staircase to the second floor, where he created a loft apartment. He installed an open kitchen and an enclosed bathroom. The deeply scarred and water-stained red maple floors were sanded and resealed. When he uncovered the stamped tin ceiling and brick walls, it was like taking a pound of makeup off a naturally pretty woman.

Nick did most of the work with his ex-girlfriend but left the dangerous stuff for the pros. It was still a work in progress, but the warehouse had certainly come a long way.

He admired the brass intercom system he'd reworked as he walked out the side door onto Julia Street and toward Louisiana Products—the only grocery in the district. He walked under a warped awning and past a flophouse hotel where the yellow marquee twittered like Las Vegas, beckoning patrons to AIDS and weekly overdoses.

A block over, he tramped into the general store's tall, bleached doors and bought two blueberry muffins, orange juice, and coffee. He ate at a checker-clothed table, waking up and watching his eclectic band of neighbors doing the same. They included a sculptor who worked only in old Harley-Davidson parts, an artist who painted his pet chicken, a massage therapist from another planet, a bodybuilding lesbian couple, and an eighty-year-old woman, still in her nightgown with her imaginary friend.

As he sipped on the chicory coffee, thick as motor oil, he tried to stare away from the old woman scratching the scabs on her head as she read the *Picayune* to the chair beside her. He knew he should feel sorry for her, but instead he squashed the second muffin in his napkin, feeling sick.

He thought about offering her some Head & Shoulders from the rows of toiletries Louisiana Products kept for the district's residents. Instead, he filled up his Styrofoam cup again and walked back to his pad.

He took a shower, heated the coffee in a blue-speckled pot on his gas stove, sat at his desk, and just stared through the dirty panes of industrial glass. But the work wouldn't come.

He sipped on more coffee and glanced back down at his notes for the biography of Guitar Slim he was working on. It was the same pain from last night. The feeling of being out of the loop, like a fat kid at a basketball court. He put on a record from Slim's Speciality recording days to jar his thick head into the fifties.

Back when Slim would wear his outrageous red suits with white shoes and prowl through night-clubs with his two-hundred-foot guitar cord. His preaching-soulful blues, a forerunner to soul and rock and roll. A sound that came from singing gospel music back home in the Mississippi Delta.

Nick couldn't find out much about Slim's early life other than that his real name was Eddie Jones and he was a ladies' man around the local jukes in the Delta. He'd conducted four interviews with people who knew Slim before he joined the army in 1944. However, the bulk of the biography would be about when Slim came to New Orleans in 1950 and formed a trio that included Huey "Piano" Smith.

It was in the Big Easy that the tall, skinny flashy dresser gained his nickname. JoJo had already told Nick some stories about Slim that made Elton John seem demure.

But more than his panache, Slim was known for his soul-powered blues number "The Things I Used to Do," which sold a million copies. "I'm gonna send you back to yore mama and Lord I'm goin' back to my family too," he sang, backed by a young Ray Charles on piano.

Some have even said Slim's blues lyrics in a gospel bar structure heavily influenced the young blind percussionist. But just obsessing over patterns and similarities in music wasn't the fascination for Nick. He never cared to be a desk professor theorizing about recordings. He wanted to know about the men and women who made the music. It was far more interesting to know about Slim's first recording session for Atlantic Records with producer Jerry Wexler.

As Wexler tells the story, they were waiting for Slim the day before and were worried the performer wasn't going to show. But soon, a tidal wave of people poured down the streets announcing, "Here come Slim! Slim on the way!"

Slim rolled up with a fleet of three red Cadillacs and a harem of women in matching red dresses. A throng of others surrounded him as if he were a king holding court. One of the ladies in red explained to Wexler that the performer had picked her up in Las Vegas just three days before. "You know that two-thousand-dollar advance you gave him?" she said. "Well, I got most of it now—at three hundred a week."

That kind of story was what it was all about—the reason Nick became a blues historian. That was the gold nugget after sifting through mountains of dirt and hundreds of hours of tape. It brought a humanity to a man who felt life like a lightning bolt.

But Slim's role in the big blues picture ended quickly. His hard drinking and living caught up with him and he died in New York from pneumonia in 1959—he was only thirty-two years old.

Listening to Slim's music just made Nick more depressed. He stared back out the warped win-

dowpanes and sighed. The coffee tasted over-
brewed and bitter. Above him, he saw a spreading
dark spot on the ceiling he'd just painted.

Then JoJo called. He said Randy Sexton was
looking for him. Even came to the bar last night.
Probably wanted him to teach that Postwar Blues
class for fall quarter, instead of waiting until winter when he rolled back on.

Nick had thought he'd have the fall to finish the
Guitar Slim book, but hell, the funk he was in
wouldn't do the master justice. So he started his
old black Jeep and drove down St. Charles Avenue
toward Tulane University.

On the way, mottled shadows of oak leaves fell
over him like jigsaws.

4

OPENING THE DOORS to the Jazz and Blues Archives building was like taking a hot shower and getting thrown into a meat cooler. Felt good and human. Randy's office was down the corridor and to the right, next door to the office Nick kept during his rotations. The head of the department had no anterooms or secretary. Just a small, simple office with sagging bookshelves filled with magazines and biographies. There was not a man alive who knew more about the development of New Orleans music than Randy Sexton. Author of more than a dozen books on early jazz and the roots of African music. From Congo Square to Satchmo.

However, his knowledge didn't come from genetics. Randy was a short white man who squinted through his round glasses like a cartoon mouse staring at cheese. He had a head of curly brown hair and talked in excited sentences flowing from an information-flooded head.

At his desk, Randy wore a black T-shirt from the 1981 Jazz Fest and black jeans. A stack of papers marked with a red felt-tipped pen sat on his desk and one finger was stuck up his nose.

Nick knocked on the outside door.

The finger shot out of Randy's nose and behind the desk.

"Catchin' anything good?"

"Shut up, man, it was a scratch."

"Right. Hey, JoJo said you were drunk last night at the bar. Said you had a hooker with you and she was dancing on the table."

"Yeah. That's right. How you been, man?"

Nick plopped down in the chair across from him. "Fine. Life's one big exciting party."

"You want a cigarette?"

"I quit."

Randy shook one loose from the pack of Marlboros, lit it, and threw the pack at Nick. "Just in case."

"Thanks." Nick shook another loose. Most of the trackers he knew smoked. Long hours in clubs, cars, and conversations. Smoking was just something to do while waiting for an interview that would be cataloged in the patchwork of music history.

Blues experts could be sociologists, anthropologists, historians, or psychologists. But to Nick, if you really got out there to find the folks who lived it, you were a tracker. To set up interviews with someone who cut a record fifty years ago for a now defunct label wasn't like looking in the phone book—although sometimes it was that simple.

Tracking usually consisted of running names through driver's-license checks in all fifty states. Cultivating sources in the business, making hundreds of phone calls and writing dozens of letters. But most of the time, finding the subject wasn't enough. Sometimes they didn't want to be found. They sold their guitars, let go of the rambling lifestyle, and settled down. To them, the lonesome blues highway was just a tattered memory. Many had found religion and remembered their musical accomplishments as that "ole devil time."

Many nights, Nick had waited outside a clapboard shack somewhere in Mississippi or a snow-covered home in Chicago only to be ignored, insulted, or threatened.

"So what's up?" Nick asked Randy, as he leaned forward resting his elbows on his knees. "You want to show me those dirty shadow puppets again?"

"Michael's missing."

"Haven't talked to the guy since June. Course, I never talked to him much then anyway."

Michael Baker, a tenured professor in music history. A real jackass. Nick couldn't stand listening to his pompous lectures or erroneous facts based on his political ideology. Guys like Baker took the stick and muddied the waters of a diminishing river of information.

"He was in the Mississippi Delta looking for some blues performers from the thirties and stopped checking in with his wife."

"Blues? He doesn't know shit about blues."

"I know. I think he was freelancing for somebody. Anyway, he seemed excited. Talked all about how great it was taking pictures of these abandoned clapboard jukes in the woods."

Nick laughed. "That's bullshit. He'd be afraid his Gucci loafers would get a speck of cowshit on them."

"Last time we talked, he was in Greenwood. He wanted me to look up a few things and I haven't heard from him in over a month."

"Did you call the police in Mississippi?"

"Yeah," Randy said, leaning back in his chair

and tossing a pencil into the corkboard above. It didn't stick. "Nick, how many times have you been to the Delta?"

"Oh no."

"Please. Just drive to Greenwood, talk to some people. Have dinner at that restaurant you like... Lucky's."

"Lusco's."

"Whatever. You know how Michael is. Sometimes condescending and rude."

"If he's condescending in the Delta, they'll string him up by those pleated slacks and make him a life-size piñata."

"That's what I'm afraid of. Please?"

"Will you recommend me for a two-year grant on that Babe Stovall project?"

"Uh, no. Remember, I don't like Michael that much either, he came with the department job.... I'm sorry, that's terrible. His wife is really upset."

"I guess I can take off Friday from JoJo's. But I've got to be back in two weeks for a gig at Tipitina's. We've planned it for a while."

Randy smiled. "Thanks, man."

"What'd he want you to look up, his ass?"

"Impossible, too tight. He had me fax him a list of living performers from the thirties and forties who lived around Greenwood."

"You mean all I have to go on is an outdated contact list? Half of which I wrote?"

"Yeah."

"I guess it's time to get back on it then," Nick said, squashing the cigarette in a plastic ashtray.

"What?"

"Words to live by, my friend," Nick said. "Why didn't you tell me he was snooping around? That's all I need is him pissing off my contacts."

"Academic cooperation? You scratch my back..."

"Shiiit."

Randy said as he fished around his desk that resembled a rat's-nest. "Here you go," he said.

"Thanks," Nick said, taking the wrinkled coffee-stained sheets. "I have a dozen copies in my office."

"Probably won't help anyway."

"Why's that?"

"I think he spent the most time with an old man in his seventies. He's not listed....Interesting thing is, the man claims he knew Robert Johnson."

Nick laughed. "Everybody in the Delta claims they met Johnson."

"I know, but Michael believed him. Said the old man lived like a hermit out in the woods. No electricity. Nothing. Said he hadn't much contact with anyone in years."

"Where's he live?"

"Somewhere in Leflore County, I think. Can't tell you his name or how to find him. Can't be too hard though."

"Why's that?"

"The old man is an albino."

5

IN MEMPHIS, Jesse Garon honed his switchblade knife on the rough concrete edge of the Heartbreak Motel's empty swimming pool. He sat and watched the Sri Lankan manager tossing handfuls of wet, molded leaves onto the mildewed diving board above and thought, What a waste of time. No one comes to this end of Elvis Presley Boulevard anymore. Only the devout. But E would appreciate the effort he had made to live close to Him.

"Oh sir, it is hot. Yes?" the little guy asked him. His bare feet stuck in the brown, oozing muck with his black trousers rolled to the knee. The man's scraggly mustache dripped with sweat.

"Uh-huh," Jesse answered.

"You do not talk much, sir, for such an energetic young man."

"Uh-huh."

"I have told you I left my country when I was only twenty. Now I work so that I may bring the rest of my family to the United States. Might I ask what has brought you to Memphis?"

Jesse stopped in midscrape of the knife, looked down into the empty cracked pool, and simply said, "God."

He stood and walked back to his room, only

one of three with a working toilet, where the red shag carpet deeply covered his toes. He winced. The damn musty smell was like ghosts from a hundred pukin' guests. He opened a window as an eighteen-wheeler roared past.

No television, no "Kool AC," like the neon sign advertised out front. Just a room and a hot plate at the Heartbreak Motel. He grabbed his last two pieces of white bread, smeared butter on the spongy pair, and placed them on the plate. The smell of burning butter made his mouth water as he changed into a black T-shirt with the sleeves cut out and blue jeans. He sat on the edge of the bed and rolled the crisp new jeans into a two-inch cuff. Perfect, he thought, running a hand over his bare upper arm to make contact with a stenciled black tattoo. He'd paid a hundred bucks for it on Beale Street.

The tattoo was of a young Elvis Presley wearing a crown of thorns, a simple inscription below: "He died for our sins."

EVERY AFTERNOON WAS the same. After eating supper and getting dressed, Jesse would leave the Heartbreak Motel and walk two miles to Graceland. There, he would stroll through the gift shops at the Elvis Mall and sit for hours in the darkened car museum. He could watch clips from E's films in '57 Chevys cut in half and turned into seats.

Sometimes when no one was around, he would slip under the velvet ropes and slide into E's cars, feeling the leather where He'd sat, the steering wheels and the gear shifts He'd touched. A vehicle to that connection he'd always felt with E. Jesse would sink low into the floor of the backseat and smell the holy air that E had breathed. Sometimes, he'd stay there until the following day. Sleeping in E's cars.

Today they showed *Viva Las Vegas,* and he thought about that incredible chemistry between Ann-Margret and E. They did everything but touch each other. It was like they were so damned close to tearing each other's clothes off, but it was like there was some kind of force field between them. Somethin' holding them back. All she could do was coo and purr the whole damned film. *Man, oh man.*

Jesse shook his head and walked next door to the gift shop, a buzzin' in his loins like a snapped electric cable. Out of all the official shops, this one concentrated mostly on T-shirts and small tokens of love. The pencils, coffee mugs, buttons, necklaces, postcards, and toenail clippers. Icons of affection.

Inside, he watched two middle-aged women— one short and dumpy and the other trim and athletic. Frizzy hair and big boobs. Jesse massaged a hand over a dusty porcelain head of Elvis. He smiled and walked toward them, pushing back the jet-black pompadour that cascaded over his forehead. He ran his fingers over the back of his neck, real modest-like, and gave the trim woman with big boobs a good two-second eye contact. He knew he had it. That confidence E had. The way of working the eyes and body. A way of showin' that you were a little shy but the devil sure did know where you lived.

"Afternoon, ma'am," Jesse said.

She nodded her head and gave a little grin. "Do you work here?"

"Ah, no, ma'am. Why do you ask?"

"Well...you look just like him. I guess you know that though," she giggled.

"Ma'am, I can show you all Memphis like you've never seen. I can take you to some of the places not on the maps. Where He worked. His high school."

"Actually...," she said, laughing, "we don't even like Elvis." She and her friend both kept snickering out of the store.

Jesse could feel the heat in his face. It wasn't that they were laughin' at him that made him mad, it was how she did it. Like he was some kind of freak. Well he wasn't.

He turned and walked down to Rockabilly's malt shop and waited until he saw an old couple leave. Before the busboy could clear the table, he sat down, finished half a cheeseburger, and gulped down a melted chocolate milk shake. He belched as he stared through the plate glass and across the boulevard at the grand house. The damned center of it all.

It wasn't until two hours later that he saw another target. She stood at the wishing wall around Graceland. Seventeen or eighteen years old. About his age. She smoked a cigarette and doodled a message to E on the wall. Short dark hair, tight blue jeans, and a short, black baby-doll shirt that showed a pierced belly button. He just stood and watched.

She leaned on the wall and stuck the pen in her mouth, twirling it around. Her lips were red and puffy. On the ground next to her was a tattered, brown teddy bear, some kinda weird purse. She stopped working the pen and stared.

"If looks could kill," she said, putting her hands on her hips and looking at him with the greenest eyes he'd ever seen.

"No," Jesse said. "If eyes could fuck."

6

THAT NIGHT, Jesse snuck the girl inside Graceland. A few months back, he'd made himself seduce this nasty, alcoholic-hag employee so he could learn the back-entry code. He already knew where to hop the fence behind the meditation gardens where E, Vernon, and Gladys were buried. And E's twin brother—the one they said died at birth.

The girl was a German tourist. Said she quivered just thinking that E had once been in her country. She could imagine feeling the stubble of His army haircut and the way He smelled after basic training. She worked nights in a McDonald's in Frankfurt just for the airfare to New York City. After arriving in the States, she'd hitched all the way to Memphis. There was a little trouble with a trucker in Kentucky, but she grabbed his balls until his eyes bulged. Gutsy little piece.

The girl thought she was psychic or something because she knew this was where she would meet another E. It was a vision that told her she'd find that missing part of her soul at Graceland to make her a complete woman.

Her hands tousled Jesse's black hair as he popped the back door.

Jesse and the girl made love all over the holy

estate: in the deep, green shag carpet of the Jungle Room, on the stairs leading to the basement TV room, and on E's pool table. She was on top mostly, but sometimes he would get behind her. It was what he needed.

He worked her until his body rolled with sweat and his chest heaved. About three in the morning, he took her upstairs to a place where the tourists weren't allowed. They stood naked in E's bedroom and stared around His room as dark branches from a tall oak tree clicked against the window. He took her to the bathroom where E had taken his last breath. They knelt in front of the toilet and cried as a purple dawn cracked near the stables like a ragged bruise.

Later that morning, they said their good-byes at a Hardee's over sausage-and-egg biscuits and Dr Peppers. He told her that he loved her, that he wanted her to be his girl. But she just laughed and wiped a piece of egg off his lip.

"Shh. We will be together, one day," she said in a heavy German accent. She pressed a folded note with the number of a Biloxi hotel in his hand.

Then she was gone.

JESSE TRAVELED SOUTHBOUND in a Greyhound bus on Highway 61 to Hollywood, Mississippi. The old man had said to meet back on Wednesday. So there he was, his pelvis aching from working all last night, and his head hurting from the lack of sleep. A copy of *The Prophet* rested on his knee, along with an old Captain America Junior comic book. Too tired to read though, so he slept the rest of the way, until the driver yelled at him to get off at the gas station.

He walked a few miles along a dirt road until he

saw the sign for Puka's Appliance Repair. Actually, it was just a junkyard where Puka sold parts off old refrigerators, stoves, and washing machines. Must be thousands of them baking in the hot August sun behind his shop. Rust runnin' down their white sides like blood. Little pine trees taking root in the eroded red clay.

He banged on the old screen door. Nothin'. He walked back outside through the weeds to a concrete staircase that led to the cellar. The bottom door was open. He could feel the cool, moldy air as he reached the last step.

The cellar was filled with all kinds of crap: old furniture, rusted car parts, a 1971 *Playboy* calendar, and a long workbench. A light was on.

"Puka?"

Through the back door, he could see the rusted rows of appliances. A weird graveyard. Mixed with the mold and grease, he smelled something. Smelled like somebody had shit all over himself.

He walked over the sawdust-sprinkled floor to a storeroom door and opened it. Inside lay a black man twisted at a weird angle. The man's head slumped down to his chest like a doll's and his leg twisted clear in back of him. Jesse spit on the ground.

"Shit," he said.

"Had to," Puka's weak voice called behind him.

He turned to see the dim outline of Puka standing in a bare corner the sun had yet to touch. A thin rod of light hit a bottle of Old Grand-Dad in his shaking arthritic hands.

"You promised, Puka. You done told me he was mine. I'm the one who found him."

"He tried to run out of here. He was halfway to

the row of pines out there. Didn't mean to. All I had was an old twenty-two to scare him a bit."

"He's been shot more'n once."

"Can't leave a man squirmin'. I know you know better than that."

"What are we gonna tell Keith?"

Jesse looked back down at the dead man. A Polo shirt with pocked, dried blood lay over what had once been his face.

"Already called him. Said he wanted it done anyway. And there's somethin' else too."

THEY SAT ON the porch and drank sweet tea. An AM radio played old country music inside the store as a few cars whizzed by on the back highway.

"Maybe it was better that I killed him anyway, Jesse. Your mama wouldn't wanted you to have that on your mind."

"I've killed before."

"When?" Puka said, scrunching up his nose.

"Plenty of times."

Puka bent forward in the nylon sun chair and spat on the ground. One of the straps on his bib overalls unbuttoned and Jesse could see the two long, thick scars where Puka had one of those heart surgeries. Triple somethin' or other. Too much fried catfish.

"Keith's got another deal for you, son. Said he likes you. Maybe if you do good at this he'll get you workin' in New Orleans with him. He's a big man there."

"What's your son want?" Jesse asked.

"You found this uppity nigra down in Greenwood, didn't you?"

"Yeah, at the motel where Keith said he'd be."

"Well, he wants you to go back. There's an old nigra man that this dead man was workin' with. Well, I guess he's a nigra, he's got white skin and pink eyes. Keith wants him too."

"Yeah, I seen 'em together," Jesse said. "Can I kill 'im?"

"I reckon that's what he wants," Puka said, spitting on the ground again. "I tole your mama I'd look out for you."

"You mention my mama again and I'll kill you too, Puka."

7

WOODSMOKE HUNG *heavy in the air as he emerged from the thick trees near the highway. In a rumpled black suit, he walked along the uneven ground, sweat rolling off his face. He opened a tattered black umbrella and adjusted dark sunglasses to shield his eyes.*

It had been the same routine for many years. The suit. The flowers. The long walk, a few miles from his place back in the woods. He had found the umbrella like most things, something someone had thrown away, that he had made work again. As he did with everything he owned.

He turned onto the highway that led to the tiny Zion Church. A simple white building in the middle of endless cotton fields. A weathered doll's house on a piece of wedding cake.

When he approached the church, he reached inside a brown grocery bag and pulled out seven purple flowers—the kind he used to call shaving brushes when he was a kid. Growin' up in Texas, seventy-five years ago.

Breathless, he cautiously stepped around the headstones to a tiny plot in the church's dark shadow. He knelt at a pointed granite monument, laid the flowers at its base, and said a short prayer, hands laced in front of him.

And as he stumbled to his feet, bracing himself with a white hand on a knee, he mumbled the penanced words he had said for so many years: "Forgive me, R.L. Dear Lord, please let him forgive me."

8

EARLY THE NEXT MORNING, Nick slept away the Highway 61 trip in a Greenwood motel room until a dull yellow light leaked through the brittle curtains and onto the flowered bedspread. It was the kind of place they used to call a motor court before the superhighways destroyed the character of travel.

Nick stayed there out of sheer hatred of the new cracker box chains. The Dixie Motel advertised outside with a neon rebel flag and had about twenty units, a chain-locked coffee shop, and a swimming pool filled with acrid chlorinated water.

His head felt thick with the smell as he crawled out of bed and changed into a gray Tulane Football T-shirt, shorts, and a pair of running shoes. He hooked his feet under the bed and counted a hundred sit-ups, then rolled onto his stomach and counted four sets of twenty-five push-ups.

After stretching, he walked outside and started a slow jog down the four-lane highway, trucks blowing by him and scattering grit into his eyes. He continued, and smiled remembering the last piece of advice JoJo gave him: "Watch your white ass."

It wasn't exactly Oriental wisdom, but it was real. Typical of JoJo, to grab the point right by the throat and not fuck with a long explanation.

That was the reason he liked blues and blues people. They all hated bullshit, not a phony bastard among them. Of course, there were the white guys who sang "Mustang Sally," wore fedoras, and snapped their fingers on Bourbon Street. But that was like comparing an artist to someone who worked with paint-by-number kits.

The Delta was the soul and the heart. Mother blues. Sacred, fertile ground for the most influential music of the twentieth century. At that moment, Nick felt like he was in the center of the world. It was good to be back. Didn't matter if the story Randy fed him was crap.

Johnson was the holy grail of blues. For years, no one even seemed to know how the twenty-seven-year-old died. Some said he was poisoned, others said he was stabbed. But the murderer was never caught. Only through some hard work by Stephen LaVere, Mack McCormick, and Gayle Dean Wardlow did a shadowy picture of the man slowly emerge.

Johnson probably didn't want to be found. The phantom of the Mississippi seemed to like playing the elusive and mysterious stranger. When McCormick went searching for Robert Johnson, he found a handful of recollections of a blues singer that met Johnson's description and repertoire. Sometimes the name was Spencer. Sometimes it was Dodds. Both were surnames of Johnson's stepfather in Memphis, and soon McCormick was able to trace his route.

When Alan Lomax, one of the first blues historians, went looking for Johnson in the 1940s, he didn't even know Johnson was dead. There were no press releases or radio tributes. Johnson was mainly known by southern blacks and by a few white collectors who recognized his brilliance. But by searching for Johnson, Lomax discovered Son House and Muddy Waters, who spoke of Johnson with awe. Johnson was the link between those two men. House was old-school blues and Muddy Waters would later leave Clarksdale, Mississippi, to become one of the greatest and best-known musicians in the world.

Decades after Johnson died, more clues surfaced. Stories from traveling partners, photographs from his family, and, after a four-year search in four states, even a death certificate from Greenwood. No cause of death listed—no doctor present. Even his grave site disputed. Two cemeteries still claim his burial. But through the tales of men like Honeyboy Edwards and Johnny Shines, Johnson became more human.

Shines said he met Johnson in Helena, Arkansas, while they were playing on opposite street corners "cuttin' heads." Head cuttin' was a battle of street musicians over tips. Johnson drew a larger crowd and soon Shines started tagging to learn his secrets. He later told stories of a man almost Mozart-like in brilliance. He said Johnson could carry on a conversation and remember details of what a radio played in the background. Even though Johnson didn't seem to take note of the music, he could play the same song weeks later. It was almost like Johnson could pick music out of the air. "Chord for chord, lick for lick, note for note, word for word."

Others have said Johnson would sit silent by a window at night and finger guitar frets to himself. No sound. Just the internal music, only he could hear.

Johnson didn't play blues. He was blues. To Nick, Robert Johnson would always remain the sallow-faced figure from the dime-store photograph. Drooping eye and dangling cigarette. A man who made music like "chilled rain with iron chords that intermittently walk like heavy footsteps."

Nick stopped jogging, his breath coming in steady gasps, as he looked over the banks of the Yazoo River.

THE DINER WAS in a crumbling brick building sided by an appliance store and a defunct law firm. Pickup trucks and dusty sedans parked along the railroad tracks. The bell above the glass door jingled when Nick walked in, and a peroxided woman smiled at him from behind a broken-spined romance novel.

He ordered eggs, grits, bacon, pancakes, and coffee. As he ate, he scanned through the living blues contact list and marked five names and addresses. Most of them were remnants of a better time for Greenwood's music scene. The blues had left the southern town long ago. Most modern music centered around Clarksdale or Oxford. Greenwood was unfortunately a place of history, not action. But there were signs of a rebirth, like other Delta towns that now saw blues as a marketable asset.

When Nick finished eating and drained a second cup of coffee, he paid the check, used a Greenwood map, and started the tracking of Baker.

Greenwood was a classic *To Kill a Mockingbird* town: richly restored antebellum homes, a decaying downtown unchanged since the 1930s, and endless rows of poor living in shotgun shacks. The Leflore County Courthouse dominated a business district full of churches, feed stores, flower shops, used-car lots, and a Chinese restaurant.

Outside the grand courthouse stood fat magnolias and a statue of a stone woman cradling a fallen soldier. An inscription read: "A testimonial of our affection and reverence for the Confederate soldier."

Nick drove past the monument to the have-not part of town, listening to the song "I'm a Steady Rollin' Man" on the radio. No one was home at the first address, and the second was a washout. Could've been for Baker too—the former occupant died two years ago.

The third address was a woman's. Well, he hoped it was a woman's—Blind Lilah Rose. She lived in a shotgun cottage not far from Lusco's restaurant—train tracks ran right through her backyard. She was a piano player for an obscure bluesman in the forties by the name of Little Tommy. She stared at Nick through cloudy, unblinking brown eyes.

Lilah couldn't have been more than five feet tall. Her hair wrestled into black pigtails all over her head like worms sprouting from their holes. She invited him in and offered a "Co-Cola."

"That's okay, ma'am. Thanks."

"Don't be all nice and shit 'cause I'm blind. You think I can't find it?"

"Thank you, a Coke would be nice."

In about five minutes, she shuffled back into the room with all the speed of a windup toy that needed recranking. "So yo' from the inshorance compney?" she asked, holding the bottle in the opposite direction of Nick.

He took the bottle from her and sat back down. She felt around for a torn cloth chair and sat down

too. The floors were wood and coated with a layer
of dust as smooth as vanilla icing.

"No ma'am, I'm looking for a friend of mine.
Do you remember talking to Dr. Baker?"

"Doctor? Ain't nothin' wrong with me."

"I mean professor. He talked to you about playing in Little Tommy's band."

She paused and cupped a shaky hand to her ear.

"He talked to you about Little Tommy!" Nick
said louder.

Her dead eyes stared at the wall behind him.
"Shore, I remember Little Tommy. That motha-
fucka!"

"Yes ma'am. Do you remember talking to a
man about Little Tommy?"

"He'd shake all around the stage playing his
harmonica. Tellin' the band we couldn't keep up
with 'im. I wanted to kick his skinny little ass. We
all did. When he finally cut a record in Chicago, he
jus' left us behind and didn't send us shit. And
most of the songs we wrote. If he'd come back to
Miss-sippi, he'd be dead."

"Yes ma'am. Has anyone asked you about Little
Tommy recently?"

"Yeah, I tole him the same thing. If he sees Little
Tommy, tell him Blind Lilah's gonna cut his balls
off."

Nick coughed.

"Sorry. You ain't used to an old woman talkin'
that way. Is ya?" She cocked her head. "Is ya?
Well, I always lived in a man's world and could
always outplay, outfight, and outcuss any one of
'em."

"Did you ever hear about a musician...well,
I'm guessing he was a musician, that was an
albino?"

"A what?"

"An albino. A black man that looked white."

"Now how the fuck am I spose to know what someone look like? Far's I know, you's purple."

"This is true," Nick said and smiled.

"What?"

"I said, yes ma'am!"

"I tell you the same thing I done tole that otha man come to see me las' week. Go see my son, he'll talk to you 'bout blues all day. Hangs out with all the ole ones when he's not workin' cotton. He can tell you this and that 'bout all the sons-a-bitches in Leflore County. Yeah, my son knows his shit 'bout blues."

"Where can I find him?"

9

MISSISSIPPI DELTA driving is about the white dots of cotton stretched forever flat like the tiny points of an impressionist painting. It's about the crooked crosses of wooden electric poles that line the two-lane highway with sparse farm-supply stores, barbecue joints, squat cone-topped silos, and windowless burned-out 1930s gas stations. It's the deep maroon of a rusted tin roof above a weathered clapboard shack and the skeleton of a sun-parched tree, dead rooted in stagnant water. Or fallen cotton caught in highway gravel.

The images were clear—caught in Nick's mind's eye like a Technicolor stamp. It was good to be out of New Orleans, he thought, as he hit the beats of a Muddy Waters song on his steering wheel. He felt like a bear who'd just gotten his big ass kicked out of his cave. There wasn't a neon sign or strip joint in sight. Not that he had a Baptist conscience toward naked women. Actually, he thought they could be quite therapeutic. But the latest therapy was just a distant memory.

His last girlfriend decided to marry a slick restaurateur with an uptown mansion. Kate Archer, a newspaper reporter for the *Picayune*. The most complete woman he'd ever known. Nick spit out the window and grabbed a fresh piece of bubble gum out of the cup holder. When the brain locked too long, it was always best to change the channel.

He needed to focus on Baker's mind-set. The man had to have been thinking about details of Robert Johnson's life. New information would gain Baker instant fame on the lecture circuit. Maybe books. Almost every blues history devoted almost an entire chapter to the legend. Nick had read so many he could recite the details like a twisted mantra.

Being in Mississippi, it wasn't hard to imagine Johnson rambling down these same highways. Cutting across railroad tracks and dirt roads with Johnny Shines or Honeyboy Edwards. Thumbing a ride deep into a muggy Mississippi night. Their stomachs grumbling from hunger with rich mud caked to their shoes.

It had to be exciting to live in what Johnny Shines, a highly eloquent man, later recalled as an "exploratory world." Johnson traveled all over, to places like St. Louis, Detroit, Chicago, and New York, sometimes deciding to hop a train at a whistle's notice. His trademark was leaving a room without ever saying good-bye. Perhaps because permanence was seldom known by his family. His mother, Julia, was married to a wicker-furniture maker in Hazlehurst named Charles Dodds. But a few years before Johnson was born, some prominent landowners ran Dodds out of town. He left Julia, a mistress, and several children behind.

Dodds started a new life in Memphis, where he lived under the name Spencer, and eventually sent for his mistress and some of the kids. Not Julia. Four years passed before she gave birth to Robert in 1911 by a field hand named Noah Johnson.

Julia worked migrant labor camps in the Delta to support the new baby and his sister. Back-breaking work. After a couple of hard years trying to make it on her own, she decided to go back to her husband. But by now Dodds had even more children with another wife and his mistress.

Julia was desperate and left her kids in Memphis anyway.

Nick wasn't sure how Johnson adjusted. But for a young child, about seven, it had to be tough. The mother leaves. New authority figure. And Johnson didn't exactly become the model step son—after a few years Dodds sent him back to his mother in Robinsonville.

Johnson didn't listen. Was troublesome.

When he rejoined Julia, she'd also remarried. To a man they called Dusty because of his dust-flying work ethic. The short, very dark-skinned man probably gave Johnson lessons on how to please the white bosses and become a good worker. For awhile, Johnson went to school near the local plantation but dropped out. He blamed a bad eye.

Didn't really matter. Johnson wasn't interested in farming or an education.

He'd already found out how to string baling wire on the side of their house and pick out Leroy Carr's "How Long, How Long Blues." Soon he took up Jew's harp and harmonica and was sneaking out late at night to watch the great Charley Patton.

The blues was edging into his life.

It was a time of late night jukes, whiskey, and women. Though that all stopped when he met a young girl who took his life into a big U-turn. As hard as it was for Nick to believe, Robert Johnson, the laid-back arrogantly neat musician, started plowing behind a mule.

He'd married the girl, all of sixteen, named Virginia Travis, and settled down to become a farmer. He was a proud man when she became pregnant. Once he even got on his brother-in-law for driving too fast—"Careful man," he'd said. "My wife's percolatin'."

The happiness didn't last though. Virginia and the child died during labor. People blamed Johnson because he was into what they thought was the devil's music. Rather than fight it, Johnson cloaked himself in the stigma. It shrouded him. Maybe even made people fear him in a weird way. Johnson wasn't a big man. He was small-boned, with delicate hands and wavy hair. And back then, a bad mojo was better than a gun.

The superstitions remained. Mississippi was in many ways a time capsule. So much of the sameness that dominated America hadn't dawned on the Delta. Nick loved the region for it. That was the important thing about grabbing all the folklore before the strip malls and franchises leeched the color from one of the last cultural frontiers.

Nick never fully understood blues until he started his fieldwork. Each time he returned to New Orleans loaded with more interviews and Delta stories it all made even more sense. Like a man who returns from Europe with a broader view of art and culture. It was very much the same.

There was something simple and Zen about going into the Delta with his Jeep loaded with a box of blank tapes, an old duffel bag, and a carton of cigarettes. There, the songs and lives from textbooks became real.

The blues got the railroad and levee camp workers through a life that was as bad as the serfs' in medieval England. They gave roots to an internal rhythm of the spirit that beat as steady as the human heart. Beyond the pretentiousness of Mozart and jazz. A riding though the bullshit that grabbed the listeners by the balls and said this is what it's all about. It was a baring of soul, a soul raw from a deceitful woman, being broke, and a painful loneliness of a man living in sensory deprivation. Cut off from sound and human contact.

That was surely what Johnson felt when he sang "Cross Road Blues."

> *Standin' at the crossroad, baby*
> *risin' sun goin' down*
> *Standin' at the crossroad, baby*
> *risin' sun goin' down*
> *I believe to my soul, now*
> *po' Bob is sinkin' down*

No one was there for Johnson. Right there in that X of dirt roads waiting for something, anything, to happen. Nick could imagine a deep orange ball of sun sinking below the cotton and darkness sweeping over the Delta. Nick believed the crossroads were a destination for Johnson. Johnson perhaps reached the best he thought he could ever be. He'd practiced until his fingers bled and gained admiration from his mentors.

Once you've reached the final crossroad, where do you go?

Perhaps Johnson couldn't see beyond those clapboard shacks. In his world, there was nowhere else allowed. That reaching of the final destination was a universal human dilemma.

Nick had sweated his ass off to become a professional athlete, he'd studied until his mind throbbed, and now what else was there? *Were there no more goals? Nothing more to obtain?* The stagnant feeling sat in his stomach like a jagged stone.

DARNELL ROSE'S DUSTY Oldsmobile was parked next to a mound of rich upchurned soil that resembled a spilled chocolate ice-cream scoop. Nick parked next to the car and waved to the form on a John Deere tractor as it plowed under a row of harvested cotton. After a few minutes, a sinewy black man asked what he wanted above the sound of a chugging motor.

"Just need a second of your time!" Nick shouted.

Darnell squinted at Nick from under a tightly scrunched baseball hat, turned off the motor, and hopped down onto the soil. He wore a faded flannel shirt cut off at the sleeves—biceps corded like hemp rope. Tall and lean frame with a gaunt face.

"My name's Travers. Your mother told me I could find you out here."

"My mama? What fer?"

"I'm looking for Michael Baker. You know him?"

He squinted at Nick again. Nick smiled and slacked his shoulders so he wouldn't seem aggressive. "I work with him in New Orleans."

"Yeah. He come to talk to me 'bout some blues players 'round here. Paid me hunnard dollars to give 'im a tour. Just was with 'im a few days and he left."

"You know he's missing?"

"Deputy Brown axed me when I seen 'im las,"

Darnell said. "But that's all I know. What chu lookin' for 'im for? Did he do somethin' wrong?"

"He's an arrogant bastard but legally he's probably okay."

Darnell laughed. Must've been a casualty of Baker's charm.

"Where'd you take him?" Nick asked.

"Jus' to some jukes. He was real interested in the ole-timers. Wrote down almost every word they said. Yeah, the man was doin' research for a project."

Darnell's mouth curved with vacant light in his eyes, like he wished Nick would get in his Jeep and leave him alone. He was lying.

"If I paid you, would you take me where you took him, so I can talk to the same people?"

"Sure, but it ain't gonna be 'til this weekend," Darnell said, tucking leather work gloves into his back pocket.

"I can double what he paid," Nick said.

"I appreciate that. But ain't nothin' open 'cept the Purple Heart tonight. We only went there once."

Across the highway, clapboard shacks intermingled with trailer homes. Faded wash hung on lines like old flags, not moving in the breezeless air.

"Did he ever say anything to you about an old albino man?"

Darnell nodded.

"What?" Nick asked.

Darnell toed the loam with his work boot.

Nick reached into his wallet and handed him a fifty.

"Thought you said a hunnard?"

Nick sighed and handed him another fifty.

"Yeah, I took the professor to see the ole man.

He's a crazy ole son of a bitch. Says a lot of weird things when he talks. Which ain't that much, 'cause he don't like people. In fact, I don't even know his name. Everyone jes' call him Cracker."

10

NICK DROVE back to the motel and slept for an hour. He'd tried to squeeze Darnell a little, get him to hint where Cracker lived, but it didn't work. He just kept on saying, "Talk to Deputy Brown." Yeah right. The local cops would enjoy Nick's presence about as much as a mangy dog at a cocktail party.

But Darnell did promise to take him to see Cracker tomorrow—said it took a while to get back into the woods to the albino's shack. The old man was apparently a little Robinson Crusoe, a lot of Kurtz.

After Nick woke up, he showered and stretched. His legs ached from the long drive and the morning jog. Too much drinking and smoking had made him soft. He needed to limber up joints still damaged from years of football and numerous fights. Jesus, his joints felt like rusted hinges on an antique puppet. In his thirties with a sixty-year-old's body. He looked in the bathroom mirror at his mildewed reflection. His dark hair going gray on the sides and down on his chin, where he hadn't shaved for the last few days. Looked like Superman's badass twin from the Bizarro Planet.

His long fingers, slightly crooked from so many

breaks, turned on the water. He had a sliver of scar tissue cut through his left eyebrow and thick lateral scars on both shoulders from a probing scope.

He remembered how his shoulders felt during Saints training camp. Sometimes they ached so badly from the cracked cartilage he couldn't even raise a squirt bottle to his mouth. The trainers would shock them with electricity, rub them with heat creams, and wrap them both in an Ace bandage almost every practice and game.

Just thinking of the pain made him grit his teeth. A lot of friends thought it took a lot of character to leave football the way he did. But he didn't walk away from a very bright future. His shoulders were so pumped full of cortisone, he couldn't feel his upper body.

The reason he knocked the coach down was simple—it just felt right. Nick's specialty was pass rushing. He was pretty good at it. He wasn't the biggest defensive lineman, but he was quick and could anticipate the snap and be in the backfield before the quarterback raised his arm. He could see the ball out of the corner of his eye and sense the count in a Zen-like way.

However, starting his third season, his coach had little use for him. Even on passing downs, Nick sat there on the sidelines and watched this pile-of-crap rookie get pummeled yards off the ball. The rookie was a lazy shit-bag, but to the coaches he was a big investment—someone they must develop. Screw that, Nick thought, play who could get the freakin' job done. But game after game, he had to endure this pudgy dude's less-than-inspired play. The coaches kept on coddling the man for the future.

The only future the rookie worried about was

thinking about new ways to fuck his Oriental stripper girlfriend and hold homemade porno-movie parties for his friends.

That year was the toilet. Nick's move on the coach wasn't planned. In fact, he played a great deal of the third quarter that night, racking up two sacks while the rookie complained of some dirt in his eye. When the coach sent the bastard back in, Nick snapped. He tried to calm down, get some water, and look ahead, but the Superdome was a muffled blur around him. He could feel the heat in his face and the blood rushing in his ears as he drank a cup of water.

The coach, a freckled-faced, racist black man who thought the past tense of the word "squeeze" was "squez," walked over and said, "Sit the fuck down, Travers. We got what we need from you."

Before Nick knew what he was doing, he gripped the man's neck with his sweat-soaked glove, hooked a foot behind the coach, and slammed him to the ground. He took the ice-cold Gatorade bucket and dumped it on the man's head.

Nick didn't say a word. No catchy line. No ranting diatribe. Just ripped the tape off his wrists with his teeth and retreated to the dressing room. He got dressed, took a cab ride to JoJo's, where they all hated Nick's coach, and got loaded with a bunch of dockworkers who liked what he'd done to the bossman.

Nick returned from the memory and shut off the running water—steam had obscured the mirror.

The window air conditioner hummed and groaned. Nick could hear the pat of water hitting the old carpet. He changed into a fresh chambray shirt and a pair of jeans. He slid on his boots and checked inside, where he stored his Tom Mix boot knife.

At the front desk, he asked where he could find a juke joint called the Purple Heart.

11

THE PURPLE HEART HUMMED with hard-driving music. Nick parked his Jeep between a pickup truck and a portable sign reading, *Tonite Virginia Dare. Cold Beer. Shake your ass.* The juke was a simple cinder-block building painted purple near a crossroad of Highway 49. Orange and yellow cardboard posters advertising the weekend's music wrapped nearby crooked telephone poles.

His cowboy boots crunched on the ground all the way to a dented metal door with a sign above announcing, *Where there is dancing, there is hope.* He could only wish for such a simple answer. Inside, dozens of black faces didn't give him a glance. No mean stares in the smoky room. No phonograph skidding off the record. No switchblades flicked. Just a Little Walter song coming from the jukebox and a mass of folks dancing on a smooth concrete floor. Maybe there was hope after all.

There was a small elevated stage loaded with the band's equipment, a couple of ratty chairs, and a duct-taped table topped with a small lamp. It looked like a display from a secondhand-furniture shop. Behind was a mural painted on the cinder blocks of a huge Highway 49 road sign and a boll of cotton.

Nick filtered through the heated crowd and made his way to the bar for a beer. A quart Colt 45, ice cold from a slushy bin. He bullshitted with the bartender for a while, asking him about local acts that played in New Orleans at JoJo's. Just as he was about to start another quart, the jukebox stopped playing.

Nick couldn't see the stage but could hear the perfect-pitched guitar sounds. Guitar licks as clear as metal cylinders popping in a spinning music box. People slowly shuffled around and he finally saw her. Red hair cascaded into her face as she intently worked a slide along the frets. Her body trim and athletic under a thin white T-shirt and faded jeans. As she lifted her head and tossed back her sweaty hair, Nick could see her face more clearly. High cheekbones, strong chin, and bright red lips.

It was like one of those puzzles where you had to pick out the one thing that didn't belong. She sure as hell didn't belong here. This wasn't a place where a white person jammed, let alone a white woman. Yet here was this good-looking redhead doing her thing and being perfectly accepted by the crowd. Nothing short of amazing.

As she bit down hard on a pouty lower lip, she ground her hips and changed into an ass-shakin' song. Her guitar wailing and crying and making every damned person in the juke move their body. When she opened her mouth, a throaty voice rattled the concrete floor.

Nick took a big sip of the Colt 45 and smiled at her. She laughed and looked into the crowd before she changed into a slower song. After the turn-around, she shyly glanced down at Nick and smiled. She shook her head and put her eyes back down on her bright, pink guitar stamped with stickers like an old-time piece of luggage. One big black woman waddled the rhythm as her partner strutted to the bass.

Nick walked back to the bar and sipped the second half of the Colt 45. His body felt a little numb, but good. This is what it is all about—sometimes in life you have those times when you're completely content. Right here and right now is where you want to be, like a kid entering an arcade with all the promise and hope of a pocket full of quarters. This was the time. Man, that woman was good-looking. Nice, deep dimples when she smiled.

After the last song, she pounced off the stage and headed toward the bar as people slapped her on the back. Her T-shirt was soaked with sweat. She nodded to the bartender, who handed her a beer and a shot of whiskey. She tossed her head back for the shot and chased it with the beer. As she took another sip, she reached into her jeans and pulled out a crumpled pack of cigarettes. Nick made his way along the bar and found a place next to her. She cut her eyes over at him, lit her cigarette, and pursed her mouth. Freckles dusted around her cheeks.

"Enjoyed the set," Nick said. "You work a mean slide."

She continued smiling.

"Who am I talking to?" she asked.

"Who am I? Who are you? Does anyone truly know themselves? Hell, Miss Dare, these are all very complex philosophical questions."

"Smart-ass."

"Yes ma'am."

Nick took a sip of his beer and spilled it on his shirt when the fat black woman bumped him with her huge backside. The wet stain spread like a bib.

"Very smooth...Socrates," she said.

"You are tough," Nick said, wiping his shirt.

"Shit, I have to be." Her eyes squinted as she exhaled a smoky cloud. They fixed on his without blinking. "You smoke?"

Nick followed her out a metal door that looked like it had been pummeled with a ball peen hammer and they found a stack of concrete blocks to sit on. There was a full moon and the unplucked cotton fields bathed in a glow as clear as the street lights in Uptown New Orleans.

"You see the man in the moon?" she asked.

"Yeah, looks like Jackie Gleason," Nick said, tossing a rock into a nearby field.

"There are his eyes and mouth," she said. "They look like pools of water up there."

"Yeah, I can see it," he said. Already Nick could imagine the placement of his right arm around her thin waist. Her back would be damp and her mouth would taste like cigarettes. Instead, he gave her his best smile and took another drag.

"Do you play?" she asked.

"A little Mississippi saxophone."

"You bring one?"

"I'm always packin' heat," Nick said.

She shook her head. "You are a pistol."

"Please don't tease me. I'm very shy," Nick said, looking far into the field. Rows of battered cars were parked on its banks. The cotton made crisp, brittle sounds in the warm wind. "You know, Robert Johnson was killed not too far from here?"

"Why do you think I play Greenwood so much?" she said, leaning back and pushing her pelvis forward. She exhaled a trail of smoke. "I'm looking for the crossroads. I don't suppose you've found them?"

"The crossroads are wherever you want them to be."

She placed a lock of red hair behind her ear and one hand in her front jean pocket. "You like Johnson too?" she asked.

Nick nodded.

"You know the first time I heard his music I had to turn off the tape. It was too powerful, like all the music I heard until then was watered down. I had to take in slow sips like you do when you start drinking whiskey."

"How much can you take now?" Nick asked.

"The whole damned bottle," she said as she smirked and patted his knee. "So, are you gonna tell me your name or are we gonna fuck around all night long?"

"Nick Travers. But we can still fuck around all night long...if you want."

12

DAWN BROKE over Jesse Garon's head like a spilled blue milk shake. He yawned and started to practice tae kwon do in an open pasture where he'd slept the night before, ten miles outside Greenwood. The morning sky was hard in his eyes as two goats and a mule watched him. One of the goats even tried to ram him every time he gave a loud "*ki-ya.*" Next time the stupid old goat came at him, he should kick the thing right in those low-hangin' tits.

Inside block, upper block, step, kick, and punch. "*Ki-ya!*"

The shaggy goat trotted over to Jesse again and butted him softly in the behind.

"Now I tole you to quit. Stop it. I'm tryin' to do a form here."

The damned old goat baaed at him and shit all over his bare foot. "Son of a bitch!" Jesse yelled, looking at the chunky brown mass. "Should kick you right in your ass."

He gritted his teeth until he heard them squeak. But when he backed up to get a good start on the animal, he suddenly stopped and fell to his knees. The way that animal just turned to look at him, so helpless like, it was like...like the animal was just plain scared of him. And that made Jesse sad.

So sad that he grabbed the fetid-smelling goat and wrapped his arms around him. Poor old animal. Just sitting here chewin' his grass, doin' his business, and hell, just protecting his family. That was no different than what he would do. If someone was to come around his mama, he'd probably shit on their foot too.

All over it.

He let go of the goat's neck and wiped his eyes. He untied the black belt from around his yellowed *do-bok,* stripped naked, and carefully tucked the uniform back into his Captain America suitcase. He pulled on a pair of shorts and a tank top—the black tank top made E's tattoo stand out real nice.

The hard brown grass itched his legs as he tied his shoes staring out at the countryside. Sure was flat around here. Flat and quiet. Not a soul in the field. In the distance, he could see the green walls of the forest and a few little patches where trees hadn't been cleared. Across the highway, a section of irrigation equipment stretched like a snake on its high wheels.

This better be somethin' to Keith. Big man in New Orleans. Always braggin' about the women he'd done and people he'd met. Just like when he was in the bodyguard school in L.A., talkin' shit 'bout movie stars. Said they're people just like you and me. Mama had always tole him actors were nothin' but trash.

"See if he has the nerve," Jesse said out loud, kicking a hunk of soil skyward. Puka didn't believe he was as good as that damned muscle-bound son of his.

Jesse knew better. E lived for fifteen years in a

one-bedroom house with his mama and daddy and look what happened to him. The German chick knew it. Didn't matter if Puka was just plain stupid. He'd show that fool. "Fuck him," Jesse muttered.

"Sorry Elvis. Sometimes I need not know what I'm sayin'." With two fingers, he crossed his heart and silently mouthed: "Takin' care of business. TCB."

13

NICK WOKE UP in a twisted pile of sheets underneath the motel-room sink. His faded blue jeans hung from a lamp. A Colt 45 bottle was tucked inside a rogue boot and a redheaded woman walked out of the bathroom brushing her teeth with his toothbrush. His head pounded, his teeth ached, and his loins felt as empty as the malt liquor bottle in his Tony Lama. Nick opened one eye and said in a gruff voice, "Oh my God. There's a strange woman in my room."

Virginia laughed and spit in the sink. She had on his Tulane Football T-shirt and no underwear. Even in his sickness, she looked more beautiful than she had last night. He looked down at her calves as she raised up to look in the mirror. Rock hard.

"Do you work out?" Nick asked.

"No, genetics. My mother was built well. You okay?"

"Yeah, but I feel so used."

"Mmm-hmm."

"I think I'm dying," he said.

"You want to swim? There's a nice pool outside."

"You crazy?"

"C'mon, it'll be fun."

"I don't swim...," Nick said, grabbing the edge of the sink and pulling himself to his feet. "On the first date."

"All right," she said, reaching into the twisted nest Nick had left. She pulled out her bra before walking across the room to find her panties. She stripped off the gray T-shirt, strapped on her bra, and pulled her panties up over a thigh tattoo. It was of Earth, about the size of a small orange.

"I'll be back," she said, opening the door and walking outside.

The sunlight cut into Nick's eyes like a laser as he felt his way into the bathroom and onto the road to recovery. After showering, shaving, taking four aspirin, and draining a cold can of Coke from a vending machine, he felt a little better. Somewhat human. Still sort of animal.

Virginia came back in and shook her damp red locks like a dog. "Now that's the best hangover remedy I can think of." Her face was a bit pale but burned with a ruddy glow. It was a natural look like you would expect from a beautiful Irish woman centuries ago.

"I'm going into town, how 'bout breakfast?" Nick asked.

"No thanks. I'd appreciate a ride back to the Purple Heart though."

"You live around here?"

"Questions, questions," Virginia said. "Let's see how long you stay around before I answer any."

Nick tossed her a towel and she ran it over her tight body. "How 'bout you? she asked. You in the Delta looking for the blues?"

Nick smiled and said, "Exactly."

*   *   *

AFTER HE DROPPED Virginia off at the Purple Heart,
Nick drove back to the same downtown Greenwood diner from the day before and ordered grits,
toast, and black coffee. He'd grabbed a copy of
Nine Stories from his Jeep glove box and read
until his head hurt. He kept the book open with
one hand and massaged his temples with the other.
He put the book down, sipped on some black coffee, and looked out the window. In front of the
closed storefronts, weeds sprouted around railroad tracks and weathered flatbed pickup trucks.
The decay was symmetrical. Not depressing, more
picturesque.

He thought about Virginia Dare coming to look
for those mythic crossroads. Not too unusual. People came from all over the world to get a little
Johnson-inspired magic. You didn't have to be a
blues historian to know the story. Most teenagers
could tell you Johnson sold his soul to the devil
late one night at a Mississippi crossroads. He cut
his fingernails to the quick, waited for Lucifer to
come, and then traded guitars with him. That's
how they say the man earned his skills.

Nick knew it was a story Johnson cultivated.
One of the first music icons to know image was
everything. Hell, it worked for the Rolling Stones.
Other popular blues singers of the time almost rev-
eled in their devil's-music status. In St. Louis,
Peetie Wheatstraw, named for the evil character in
black folklore, advertised himself as the devil's
son-in-law.

Johnson's second recording session was filled
with hard, evil images that would've made Dante
shudder. In "Hellhound on My Trail," he sings of
being constantly pursued by the devil. Nick could

imagine a leafless tree creaking in the wind as Johnson made his way through a field on a dead cold night:

> *I got to keep movin'*
> *I've got to keep movin'*
> *blues falling down like hail,*
> *blues falling down like hail*

Some of the selling-his-soul-to-the-devil theory was bolstered by his mentor, Son House, who taught him some licks when they were living in Robinsonville after Johnson's wife died. Son said that when he first met Johnson, the young boy couldn't play a thing.

There is a famous story that takes place at a juke when Johnson tries to play Son's guitar and the guests complain about a god-awful racket. According to House, Johnson left Robinsonville and returned a short time later, a changed musician.

Johnson walked up and asked Son and another bluesman if he could play and their jaws dropped open at his prowess. House said he had been gone only six months, an impossible time to become great.

Nick believed the real story was less mystical.

In truth, Johnson had been gone for a couple of years. He went looking for his real father, a man he'd never known and maybe never found in Hazlehurst. While hanging out there and practicing guitar, he met Ike Zinnerman. Zinnerman was an Alabama bluesman who took over where Son House left off. He was Johnson's Yoda. A man who told his wife he gained his guitar skills by playing in graveyards at midnight. A very black, sleepy-eyed man who wore his fedora way back on his head.

Johnson watched and learned from the older man, taking notes on what Zinnerman taught him. He honed his skills deep in the woods, where no one would cringe when he hit a bad note. He and Zinnerman worked the local jukes and fish fries until the music consumed him.

It was like one of those karate movies where the student doesn't do anything but train with the master and commune with nature.

The guitar became a tool to expel the culmination of experiences that weathered Johnson's soul. Being left as a child by his mother, being berated by a stepfather who thought he was lazy and no good, and perhaps most of all losing his sixteen-year-old wife while she was in labor.

Before he returned to Robinsonville, Johnson became known as just R.L.—a damned fine player. No wonder Son House was amazed—his former student was now a master.

As Nick took the last bite of toast, the bell jingled above the door, and a large black man walked in wearing a tan sheriff's department uniform. He had a smooth, bullet-shaped head, a chest like a steer's, and biceps as large as Nick's thighs.

He nodded to the cashier and came over to where Nick was sitting.

"Deputy Willie Brown," the man said, extending his hand.

Nick shook it.

"Heard you talked to Darnell Rose," Brown said, and sat down. His massive arms crossed over his chest.

"I did."

"You want to tell me why you're harassing Greenwood residents?"

Nick didn't consider giving someone a hundred bucks harassment.

"You make it seem like I'm walking around downtown showing my privates to old ladies," Nick said.

"I know you're looking for a man named Michael Baker. Sir, a report has been filed with us. We'll let you know if we find him."

"Great."

"When will you be leaving Greenwood?"

"Not before I show my privates to a few old ladies. And I'd like to see the cotton history museum. Looks fascinating."

"I know he told you about Cracker."

Nick sipped his coffee and opened a packet of saltines. He put a little Tabasco on top. Nice little pools of red on the salt. Good hangover cure.

"Cracker's an old man who doesn't need some punk from New Orleans talking trash."

Nick leaned forward and laughed.

"You want me to get mad, maybe talk a little shit," Nick said. "Hey, maybe even take a swing at you. Yeah, right, so I can spend time in the pokey. You want to tell me what I'm doing wrong?"

"You're interfering with an investigation."

"You think he's dead?"

"I didn't say that."

"Can I see the report?"

"It's public record. Courthouse is open nine to five."

"Thanks." Nick sipped his coffee and Brown was silent. "Are we going to continue these belittling idiotic psychological games you probably read from a paperback book? We banter back and forth whacking off our verbal manhood. Let's talk, let me meet Cracker, and maybe it will help. If you were a smart cop, that's what you'd do."

"What do you know about police work?"

"I've got a good friend with the NOPD."

"I know an astronaut but doesn't mean I'm competent to do a fuckin' moonwalk."

"Don't discount Michael Jackson."

Brown stared at him. Nick looked down and noticed a purple-gemmed football championship ring on his thick finger.

"When were you at LSU?" Nick asked.

"What?"

"When did you play?"

"Back in the eighties? Why?"

"I played at Tulane," Nick said, thinking it was worth a shot to soften this guy up. Pump up his ego until he blathered all about the glory days. Eyes wide with slow-motion memories. "What position?"

"Offensive tackle."

"Maybe we butted heads before."

"Wouldn't that be ironic? I'll trust you once," Brown said.

Nick shrugged.

"Can I trust you?"

"Hell, if you knew where to find me that means you already ran my plates and did a criminal-records search. You know about me."

Brown smiled.

"So tell me about Cracker," Nick said.

"I saw Cracker when he was making the rounds, digging through trash around the highway. Told me the man talked to him and left."

"Did you ask why?"

"I know why."

Nick looked at him.

"Old Cracker thinks he knows who killed Robert Johnson. You know who Robert Johnson was?"

14

JESSE GARON DIDN'T realize how far back in the woods the ole man lived. Last time, spying on the sharp-dressed black dude trackin' through the woods like he was Daniel Boone, Jesse hadn't thought about all the shit in between. The damned kudzu, spindly pine trees, and vines. He wished he'd killed them both when he had the chance—been easier that way.

He'd followed the smart-ass nigra with a box of records back to the motel. Keith had told him the man would be waiting to make an exchange for some cash. Take the dude and the records to Puka's, he said. So Jesse put a knife into the nigra's ribs and kept it there all the way back to the junkyard. Long drive, with the man calling him a "little-dick racist."

Shit, Puka had all the fun killin' the guy.

Tonight, all the crickets, cicadas, wild animals and shit were wakin' up. It was like some kinda fucked-up safari movie. Like *Paradise, Hawaiian Style*, when E and that good-lookin' woman were marooned on that island. They acted like they were just roastin' marshmallows, singin' and shit. Bet your ass, off camera, they were fuckin' on that island.

Sure as shit, E could get pussy.

He shook his head for thinking that. That was terrible. "Sorry, E," he whispered so low all he heard was the sound of moving lips.

It was just him and the weird-lookin' nigra man. He'd get in and get out. Take care of business. No guns. He could do this himself—just beat him until he had a heart attack from fright or take 'im with a blade. Ole man was weak with the leprosy or whatever God's curse he had.

Jesse could smell the ole man cooking in the early dusk from where he squatted and waited. Smelled real wild, like a squirrel or somethin'. Must've scraped the animal off the highway with a shovel, then roasted its smelly, rotten flesh. Probably had a sack where he kept all the dead animals he found on the highway. Sure as shit, didn't hunt. Slow as he moved.

But the last thing he wanted was for the ole man to get nervous and start shootin' at shadows. If he knew someone was out there, the guy could hole up forever. Then everyone would be pissed at him: Keith, Puka, and his mama. Embarrassed 'cause he couldn't kill one ole nigra man. This ole nigra probably had an advantage on him. He could sense shit by livin' in the woods so long. Could hear an animal if it licked itself.

This time he'd be careful, he thought, slowly taking his clothes off and tucking them under a flat rock. He put the switchblade in his mouth and bit down on the handle. He'd be an animal like the ole man: no shoes, no clothes, no nothin'.

Above him, the moon was as round and perfect as the Sun God emblem on E's jumpsuit. He could feel its glowing energy giving him power. The

moon had always done that for him—given him
that strength. If E was the sun, then Jesse was the
moon. When it had all its force behind it, so did
Jesse. Tonight, killin' was easy. In and out. TCB.

15

NICK AND WILLIE BROWN traveled south along State Road 7 to a hamlet called Quito, about ten miles from Greenwood. Outside the arced whiteness of the headlights, there was nothing. A place where people once lived, all the sharecroppers and landowners gone now. Just a few lights in rusted trailers. Hard-core farmers. Men who had worked the rich Delta loam for generations.

"Did he owe the university some money?" Brown asked.

"Nope. Just stopped checking in," Nick said, chewing a wad of bubble gum and watching the weeds roll by in blackness.

"Why'd they send you?"

"Because I blend in so well."

"Yeah, like the cream filling in an Oreo."

Brown slowed and pulled into a circular, rocky lot. He stopped the car in front of a long shack with crumbling fake-brick siding and plastic sheets for windows. The tin roof had rust splotches like blood smears and a narrow smokestack like a crudely made periscope. Two black men sat on the stairs sipping quart bottles of Budweiser.

Nick considered sitting down with them and bullshitting a little. Sometimes that was the best way to get stories. Bring some beer and let the words flow. Walk out of your car with a notepad and you can hear the locks clicking.

"You wouldn't know it but this old place is a historic site," Brown said. "James's house here is the old Three Forks store. Used to be down the road a ways. But, it was moved. This is where people say Robert Johnson died. Hey, James."

"Robert Johnson ain't at home," James said. His smallish face as drawn as a hound dog's. "Don't bring no mo' damned tourists 'round here. This is my house."

James's buddy laughed, beer foam running down his chin, "Willie, tell him the part how he was howlin' like a dog when Satan took him."

"No. I think this man is too sharp for that," Brown said. "Why don't you tell us, Travers, how Johnson died? You're the blues man."

"I know this probably isn't the house where he was killed. Three Forks could've been anyplace. His old traveling partner Honeyboy pointed out a completely different spot where he died. Same as the Zion Church where they say he's buried. There were over a dozen Zion churches in Greenwood in the thirties."

"Shut his ass up, Willie," James said. "Just made me fifty bucks yesterday from some Japanese. They thought I was Robert Johnson's son."

"You can't even play with yourself let alone a guitar," Brown said.

"Now, hold on," James said, tossing Nick a bottle. "Listen, what happened to the son of a bitch? I live in this goddamned ghost house and I want to know."

The bottle was lukewarm and the label felt soft in the palm of his hand. Nick looked over at

Brown and smiled. So he ambled up on the porch, where the plastic sheeting was popping in the wind, and sat down on the brittle wood.

There was a feeling about the place, some kind of bad mojo. Maybe it was the August heat or just the possibility he was actually at the place where Johnson died. He wanted to go in and trace the layout, see how the place looked all those years ago. Listen to how the wood sounded under his feet. Wood that may have soaked up Johnson's music.

"That's just it," Nick said. "No one knows for sure. Some say he was stabbed. But most believe it was poison from a jealous husband. Police back then weren't too interested in a dead black man."

"No shit," James's buddy said. "Still ain't."

"The story fits." Nick started again, looking across the highway at the inky pattern of the cotton. "Johnson was a real ramblin' man... he loved women."

"Everyone loves women lessen you're a queen," James said.

"Not like old Robert," Nick said. "A friend of his said he used women the way some do hotel rooms. He had them in every town."

"Fine lookin'?" James asked.

"No. Actually, butt ugly. Worse off they were, the more attention Johnson would show 'em. I'm sure he had his share of some fine ones but Johnson liked comfort. He liked women to take care of him, cook for him, mend his clothes, and shit like that. And ugly ones were a little bit more willing."

"Sound like a smart man," Brown said.

"Keep goin'," the buddy said. "Our TV broke."

"When he recorded in San Antonio, the police picked him up for vagrancy," Nick said. "And he—"

"Ain't that just like the po-lice," James said, giggling at Brown.

"Yeah, they picked him up and his producer had to bail him out," Nick said. "Johnson called him a few hours later from his boardinghouse. He told the producer he was lonesome."

"Lonesome?" James asked.

"Yeah, Johnson said there was a woman there and she wanted fifty cents and he lacked a nickel."

That sent all the men into a frenzy of laughter, including Brown, who broke into a smile. Nick stood up, glad to pass on a small tale they'd surely repeat on other nights. James leaned back until he was flat on his back and staring at his porch's broken roof. "Where y'all goin'?"

"To see Cracker," Brown said.

Both men laughed.

"Damn, Willie, you're the only one I know talk to that stinkin' monkey," James said. "He smell like shit."

The buddy mumbled, "He do smell like shit."

Brown walked ahead, away from the men, and Nick got up and followed. They passed over a creek and through a junkyard of old tractors. As they entered the woods, Brown turned on a flashlight, which shone onto a well-worn path leading into a smiling mouth with green teeth.

BLOOD. A GASH on the ole man's head really let it all out. Must've been that iron stove, Jesse thought. Hell, he hadn't even heard him come in. Just sat there in this ratty ole green chair eatin' beans out of a can. Turned to stare at Jesse only when he broke through the door. Up at his face, then down at his nakedness.

Hell, he'd forgotten about being naked.

Jesse let out an honest-to-God war cry. A sort of Indian thing. Didn't know what caused it—must've been the moon. Sure as shit put fear in that ole man's pale blue eyes though. He was in the middle of putting them beans down when Jesse grabbed the back of his ole neck and rammed him into that black stove. A little fat one sittin' in the middle of that shitty ole shack.

Jesse laughed when the guy fell. Then watched as the guy tried to get to his feet, only to fall back down. He walked over to him, threw down his knife, and kicked him square in the gut. Son of a bitch ole man vomitin' all over himself. Shit. That's gross. So Jesse kicked him again. Kicked him for bein' so damned nasty.

Nasty ole man. Kick. Nasty man cursed by God. Kick. Sure as shit he'd kill this guy and make everyone proud of him. Mama and Puka. He thought about their faces as he kicked again.

"You kill the nigra?" she would ask.

"Yes, mama."

Then it would be worth it all. Worth the work. Worth the effort. He'd always remembered what mama told him when he finally stopped tryin' to play the guitar. When he found out there wasn't no music in him—that he couldn't be like E.

She looked at him, huggin' him as the hot tears streamed down his face, and rubbed his back. "That's all right, Jesse. Maybe you have another talent, just as good as Elvis. Just remember, you can be the Elvis of anything you want."

And he had found it. He was the Elvis of killin'. Takin' Care of Business! He grabbed the ole man off the floor and punched him in the throat.

* * *

THE TRAIL LEADING to Cracker's house was smooth as talcum powder underfoot. Dense, high grass and weeds bordered with low-hanging vines and long, thin spiderwebs. A small rabbit froze for a moment in Brown's flashlight beam, then darted away from the trail.

"So who does Cracker say killed Robert Johnson?" Nick asked.

"I'll let you ask him. He's got a much longer explanation than I can give you."

"Is he crazy?"

"Depends what you think crazy is. I mean do you call talking to the dead and swatting at imaginary flies crazy?" Brown asked, raising his eyebrows.

"Yeah."

"Well, I guess Cracker is crazy then. Just wanted to let you know that before you think he's going to tell us anything about Baker."

"How far back does he live?" Nick asked.

" 'Bout a mile."

Rain began to drop from a few fat clouds that moved in the sky like Mardi Gras floats. Soon it came in hard, full sheets down through the pine needles. The moon still shone as the clouds passed and made the water look like silver ice on the branches. Rain as warm as bathwater.

"A mile, huh?" Nick said, thinking that Randy was going to owe him a big fat favor when he got back to New Orleans. Dinner at Antoine's, drinks all over the Quarter. As curious as he was about the old man, this was fucking ridiculous. Too much of an effort for babbling.

"Hell, we're almost there," Brown said, knocking the branches away.

Then came the sound, through the imposed

static of rain falling among the trees. That unmistakable sound that made Brown turn a walk into a full sprint. A human cry of pain.

"AIN'T YOU GONNA cry or somethin' ole man? I'm gettin' tired of watchin' you breathe," Jesse said, kicking him in the ribs again. He could hear the pasty man's breathin' gettin' real raspy. Like he might quit at any moment.

Jesse pushed the cascade of black hair out of his eyes, thinking about the punk E played in *King Creole*. He thought about all that anger and energy E must have felt when that woman told him he couldn't graduate 'cause he took a swing at a guy and brought that whore to school. Must've made him real pissed off. He thought about the ole nigra tellin' the same thing—that he had to repeat high school.

"Ain't gonna do it, boss. No way, Daddy-O!"

Before he wrapped his hands around the man's wrinkled neck, he felt a hot, sharp pain shoot through his calf. He fell to his knees, hands clutching his lower leg. A fork stuck in his flesh.

The ole man stood over him, lower lip trembling, and holding a can of beans in his hand. He threw it and hit Jesse right in the forehead. As the ole man tried to get away, he fell onto the floor clutching his chest and howling like a hurt animal.

Got 'im, Jesse thought. Ole son of a bitch is finally havin' a heart attack.

He could hear his own breathing and rain splattering on the tin roof above like a million tiny drums. Through the haze of pain, Jesse almost felt comfortable in the old cabin, woodsmoke floating in the air. But that was just his mind playin' with him. Lullin' him to lie down, lick his wounds, and fall asleep.

It was time to move. Performance or not, he needed to kill the ole bastard now. Sure it'd been a game before of doin' somethin' different, kickin' him all in the ass until he fell over, but he kept hangin' on. Maybe he was havin' a heart attack, but Jesse didn't want to wait around and see what was gonna happen.

Shit, it was time to move. His hand, covered in blood, grabbed hold of the fork and yanked it out of his leg. He threw it down and reached for the switchblade he'd brought. Nice and sharp from all the days honin' it at that crummy motel. Could probably cut a hair in two like in them funny cartoons.

He popped the release just as the front door flew open. At first he thought it was just the storm. Then he saw a big nigra man comin' into the shack with a flashlight. The nigra seemed more into goin' to the ole man. His eyes didn't even pass Jesse's way.

The shack's back door was a few feet from where Jesse crouched behind a ragged chair. The big nigra would see him soon enough. So in two shakes of a lamb's tail, he turned the knob and ran through the door. He hopped off the back stoop filled with trash and hightailed it back into the green, wet safety of the woods. Two shots rang out behind him.

NICK HEARD THE shots and saw the flash from the back of the house. He ran to the shack and knelt down when he reached the front porch. He tilted his head up and saw an old man on the floor, his skin a ghostly white in the glow of a lantern.

"*Around the side!* On the other side!" Brown yelled.

Who or what was on the other side, Nick didn't know. How about a hint. A killer? A bear? Little green men? Nick pulled the Tom Mix knife from his boot and flicked it open. He'd fillet whatever it was with a collectible.

"You see him?" Brown yelled again.

"No," Nick shouted through the rain.

Then he heard feet rustling through the undergrowth and saw a flash of skin. Nick followed. The man was fast, leaping over small trees and piles of rotting leaves and plants. He zigzagged through a trail impossible to follow without the occasional light from the full moon. Nick tried to keep an even pace, not getting too close, running when he ran, stopping when he stopped. The rain slowed to a patter, still masking the sounds.

The fat clouds rolled away and the full silver light of the moon poured into the woods. The sky was the color of navy flannel.

Couldn't be far from the highway. Not far at all. Even through the zigzags and cuts, the man stayed in the same direction. Maybe he had a car waiting for him on the road's shoulder. He crept forward and could see the man catching his breath and looking around.

The rain stopped. A quiet drip fell from the leaves. A car rumbled by and a slash of headlights cut through the woods. Nick was close enough to get a look at the guy. *He must be going crazy.* It wasn't that the guy was nude that shocked him. It was the postage-stamp image of a young Elvis Presley. Pre-army. "Heartbreak Hotel" days.

The light was gone.

Another car passed down the highway. Must be only yards from the road. Nick needed to make his move now. He broke into a full sprint so he could tackle the guy, just like a darting running back, and drag his ass back to Brown's car. No more games.

Nick moved a few feet and the moldy leaves beneath him fell into a small crevice. The creek bed from earlier, he thought, as he climbed out of its muddy walls. Dirt painfully filled under his fingernails. He found a root and grabbed tightly as his feet slipped beneath him. Finally he found a foothold, and pulled himself out of the gully. Nick scanned the woods and looked through a clearing to the highway.

Elvis had left the building.

16

KEITH FIELDS RECEIVED Jesse's phone call at three in the morning but he wasn't asleep. He was just sprawled on his black leather couch, listening to an infomercial about an ab machine. He tried to imagine it melting away his gut as he munched on a box of vanilla wafers. Little sandy crumbs bunched up between his thin roll of fat and beer-stained T-shirt.

"Jesse, just tell me where you're at."

"A gas station somewhere 'round Quito."

"Awright. Did anyone see you?"

"I don't think so," Jesse said. "I was invisible, man."

"I ain't got time for this," Keith said as he snatched his lighter and a pack of Vantage cigarettes. "Either you're a pro or not, Jesse. You tole me you could handle the job."

"I was handlin' it, Keith, and this big nigra just bust through the door as I was about to kill the ole man."

"Shit, Jesse. You weren't suppose to kill him! Goddamn, are you crazy?"

"Puka said you wanted the nigra taken out."

"You still talk like a goddamned racist pecker-wood. Shit no, you were suppose to bring him

back to Puka's and I was gonna pick him up there.
Nigra? What you gonna do if I give you a client
here that's African American?"

Jesse snickered.

"I'm serious, you gonna call him Mr. Nigra?
Like Puka would?"

"No."

"Then shut your damned hole and listen." Keith
heaved off the couch and closed his balcony doors
looking over Royal Street. A carriage horse
clopped down the road and he could see a woman
squatting in the shadows taking a piss. "I'm
comin' up there. You find a place and you stay put.
I'll be up by mornin' and take care of this myself."

"Keith...the nigr...the man just bust through
the door."

"I know, Jesse. I know."

This hit was not just for some no-name client;
this was a full-time deal. Good pay and good contacts. His boss had it. Had juice like the Mob guys
used to have. Like the old criminals in New
Orleans, only with a modern approach. Modern
methods. Keith had heard bits and pieces, how he
used to be some kind of big record producer in Los
Angeles. A little weird and freaky with the all-
black clothes and stuff. But hey, that's L.A. Everybody's weird out there. Any man who trusted him
enough to make him head of security couldn't be
all bad.

"Naw. I got this one, Keith," Jesse said. He
could hear his friend's breath go ragged through
the connection. "Just give me a few days. Need
some money though."

"Awright. Till Saturday. But if you ain't snag
him by then, you can forget about comin' to work

with me. How you want this money sent? Western Union?"

"Clickety-clack."

SIX HOURS LATER, Keith Fields locked his apartment and headed out into the French Quarter. His head ached bad from worryin' about the mess. Couldn't even go to sleep after Jesse called. Should've known that he couldn't handle somethin' professional. Keith could feel his temples throb with every bad thought. If his boss got word Jesse tried to kill the old man, then he might as well reach for his toes and kiss his pecker good-bye. Yeah, this was bad. Real bad. And this was the first thing his boss ever really asked him to do as the new head of security. Shit, Jesse. Why'd you have to mess it up?

Keith stopped walking under a rusted overhang and closed his eyes tight. He ground an index finger hard into his temple. He'd just have to tell him. Go right in, sit down in those plushy black leather chairs, and tell the truth.

Mr. Cruz, you know that old nigra man you wanted? See, I tole my friend from back home to do it. But he's kinda slow and, well, he thinks he looks like Elvis. Yes, Elvis. And he got run off before he could grab the fool.

Man, he was fucked.

As he rounded the corner onto Conti, he formulated another plan—be real businesslike. Mr. Cruz would like that. *Mr. Cruz, the target has not yet been apprehended but I'm gonna assume control of the project. Go to Mississippi myself and finish the job. After all, I am your head of security.*

Much better.

Even this early, the construction crews ham-

mered away on the new hotel. Keith could hear the
buzzing and banging sounds that came around the
site. Reminded him construction was how he first
made it in New Orleans. That was after Los Angeles and bodyguard school and a short stint trying
to be a soap actor. He'd gotten a walk-on role on
Days of Our Lives as a male nurse. But his southern accent, his acting coach said, was his biggest
flaw for ever getting a speaking part.

Keith walked farther down Conti and into the
lobby of the Blues Shack Entertainment Complex.
Its three stories contained two bars, a restaurant,
an ampitheater, an African American art gallery, a
blues museum with an actual reconstructed Mississippi juke joint, a cigar room, and a souvenir shop
right out of a tourist's wet dream. All the T-shirts,
ball caps, and beer koozies you could want with
Little Bob the guitar-playin' alligator logo.

He took the dark-stained wood steps to where
two beefy white guys dressed in black guarded a
double leather-padded door. Keith nodded to
them. They nodded back and the guy on the right
spoke into a small microphone on his golf-shirt
lapel.

He'd trained them right.

The doors parted mechanically to reveal a room
that resembled a set from freakin' Chinese epic: big
ceramic elephants, thick oriental rugs, lighted can-
dles, incense, beads, and a fat ole Buddha statue.
Mr. Cruz was into that stuff, always lightin' can-
dles and ringin' bells.

Toward the back, Mr. Cruz's secretary, Kimber,
sat at her desk amid the weirdness. Keith had to
shake his head, the woman was so kick-ass gor-
geous. Damned Hawaiian or Samoan or some shit.
Always wearin' a little flowered sundress with her

bra strap showing. Small waist, big breasts and ass. Legs like a Malibu Barbie.

"He in?" Keith asked.

"You have an appointment?"

"No ma'am. It's important though." Keith pulled his sleeves up higher over each bicep and ran a hand over his buzz-cut head.

She licked her lips and sighed, pushing her chair back like he wasn't worth the effort. Then she walked into the back office, never looking Keith in the eye. Even as nervous as he was, he still scoped the outline of her panties through that slick, satiny material. Her ass wigglin' all around in her thong.

"Come on back, Keith," he heard Mr. Cruz's bourbony voice call.

He felt like he was in his goddamned principal's office back in Mississippi. As he entered the room, Keith saw Pascal Cruz talking on a headset phone, his arms waving out some details. Dressed in all black. Sport coat over one of those collarless shirts. Long black hair and pointed beard. Black eyes with arched upside-down V's for eyebrows. A face long and thin like he was on a hunger strike. Tall and bony. Loose limbed. Cruz reminded him of Satan from all those Baptist comic books he had to read as a kid.

Kimber pointed to a chair in front of the glass-top desk, and he sat down. Keith swallowed and didn't look at her ass as she left. He needed to be respectful of Mr. Cruz. Keith was sure the boss-man took a piece on the side.

Mr. Cruz said something to the caller about "real bidness in Nawlins" and to come in the club anytime, for whatever they needed. "Carte blanche," he said, or somethin' like that. Keith took a deep breath and his broad chest filled with air as the man hung up.

"So, Keith, what can I do for you? Want a drink?"

"No sir. The reason why I wanted to take up some of your time today sir, is that the operation or business that we talked about last week has not lived up to the full expectations of what we've, I mean I, have planned.... My contact in Mississippi tells me before the business could be concluded that he, well...got sorta broken in on by two men and that the gentleman we talked about is still free.

"Shit, I'm sorry, sir. I thought Jesse, *my contact,* would've taken care of everything. I'm sorry, sir. I'm real sorry. *Shit!*"

"Slow down, Keith. Slow down. Don't get your dick twisted in a knot. Didn't snatch our man, huh?"

"No sir," Keith said, not daring to mention the fact that Jesse had tried to kill the man 'cause he was so damned stupid.

"That's all right," Mr. Cruz said as he leaned back in his chrome-and-black-leather chair and looked at the ceiling. He put a finger on each side of his nose and sniffed.

"Tell you what, Keith, let's go eat," Cruz said. "I'm hungry as hell and we'll talk about it. There's a reason for this. There is a reason for everything."

Keith exhaled. Felt like his face had been turnin' blue.

"I'll be right down. And on your way out, tell Kimber that I want her to call Floyd. Tell her I want him to meet us for lunch."

"Yes sir."

HOLY. FOR SOME reason that was the way Keith had always thought about Pascal Cruz. It wasn't just the way he lectured all his Far East philosophy—which Keith thought was total bullshit. It was more in his slow, practiced movements and the way he wore his black, the way the pope wears white. It was almost like you expected Pascal Cruz to lead you to the Holy Land or something. Or be some kind of fuckin' prophet. Whatever it was, it sure as shit made him nervous.

"Keith?"

"Yessir."

"You used to be a truck driver, didn't you?"

"Yessir. Me and my buddy Jesse both."

"Floyd's what we call a mechanic. Only it ain't engines he cleans up. Comprende?"

"Yessir."

Keith rubbed his sweating hands on the napkin tucked in his lap. He had this little piece of napkin string comin' unhinged from the rest of the material real nice. Like a piece of dental floss.

Over Mr. Cruz's shoulder, he could see the heat lamps warm the buffet's food line in the Chalmette restaurant. They were early for lunch and the cooks were still setting up the trays of food in the family-style arrangement: turnip greens, fried chicken, biscuits, black-eyed peas, and all that shit. Steam rose past the sneeze guard above the heat lamps.

"Yeah, ole Sweet Boy Floyd and me go way back. Back to Memphis and those sweet soul music days. Sweet Boy used to be a backup singer at Stax Records. Man, that was a time...Otis, Sam and Dave, Carla Thomas, Booker T and the MG's. Best music that's ever been made."

"Yessir."

"I want you and Sweet Boy to head out to the Delta and clear this mess up. I think it'd be a good learning experience for you."

"Yessir."

"Would you quit callin' me sir. Just call me Pascal. Like the painter, okay?"

"Yessir."

Keith was so intent on trying to keep eye contact with Mr. Cruz, or Pascal, that he didn't notice the big black man until he wrapped his arms around his boss's neck. Keith was too busy trying to look through Mr. Cruz's black sunglasses. See if the guy really had pupils.

The black man's forearms were huge and covered in thick gold jewelry. In fact, there was gold jewelry all around his neck and on his ears. When he smiled, all Keith could see was gold. It was kind of primitive. Like some kind of tribal thing.

The black man said in a low, vibrating tone, "I love this man." His voice somewhere between Barry White and James Earl Jones. A goddamned gold-plated Darth Vader.

Mr. Cruz patted the man's arm and pulled him over into a seat.

"Keith Fields, I want you to meet Sweet Boy Floyd."

Keith shook his hand and it was dry. Not like his hair. His hair dripped with oily jheri curl like a big-assed Jermaine Jackson wanna-be. He wore a black net shirt and slick polyester pants. Two steps behind fashion.

"This yore new talent?" Floyd asked.

"It is," Mr. Cruz said.

"Hmm. Awlright there podna. You know you hooked up with one fine organiza-shawn wit dis man? He's a class act."

"I'm proud to be here," Keith said.

A small crowd began to gather at the buffet and

girls in robes began to walk to each table. Keith knew the deal, he'd been here before. All these teenage girls would sell you raffle tickets for lingerie. They'd parade around and model while you ate. Hell, these girls weren't even as old as Keith's sister and she was only a junior in high school.

Only in New Orleans.

"Let's eat," Mr. Cruz said, as he led his employees to the buffet line. Keith let the two men go ahead as he quietly made a simple plate not to offend them. He was too nervous to eat. Cruz and Floyd bullshitted up ahead of him. He could hear Floyd's odd, high-pitched laugh from the other side of the buffet line.

"You want some chicken, Keith?" Floyd asked.

"No sir."

"Sir. Shi-it."

Cruz and Floyd laughed some more.

Keith ate some soggy sweet potatoes and washed them down with a gulp of cold iced tea. He tried to push the food around the plate to make it look like he had eaten more, but Cruz and Floyd had no problem. They shoved their food in like they were hidin' evidence or it was the Last Supper. All that southern soul food in their mouths like a couple pigs. Hell, his manners weren't the best, but these two ate like a couple of prisoners. Arms wrapped around each plate like someone was gonna steal a greasy drumstick. How Cruz stayed so damned skinny Keith didn't know. Maybe he puked it all out like them Romans did.

Cruz wiped his mouth and slurped down some tea. "Floyd, we had a little trouble in the Delta last night. I want you two to head up there today. I'll have Keith fill you in on the way. But I want this thing resolved quick."

"Tell me now," Floyd said. "I like to know the who before the what."

Cruz looked at an elderly pair of men behind him and turned back.

"Baker's dead."

"Thought you wanted it that way," Floyd said. "More of them records for you."

"The records he had on him were nothin'. Not what he promised."

Floyd snorted. "Not the lost nine, huh? Man, I cain't believe you fell for that. Ain't no such thing. His yuppie black ass was just workin' your chain like a crank."

"I still believe it, Floyd. Keith's buddy out in the Delta knows where to find a man who might know where they are. I want you to trap this wild animal and bring him to New Orleans. That professor was on to somethin'."

Sweet Boy Floyd nodded and kept eating. A moment later, he stuck a toothpick in his mouth, swiveled it to the other side, and said, "Got me some Delta pussy one time. Wasn't too bad."

Three teenage girls, two blondes and a brunette, walked over to the table wearing nothing but white, lacy cupped bras and high-cut white panties. Their faces smooth. No zits or anything. Just wide deer eyes and red-painted lips. Angels smiling painfully as a mean-lookin' old woman stood behind them pushing them on.

"Would you gentlemen like a ticket?" the brunette asked with arms crossed over her bare stomach.

"Tell you what, baby," Floyd said, as he chewed on his toothpick and tossed them a hundred. "Y'all come over to see us after the show and show us them lil ole titties of yores and I'll buy a whole mess of them tickets."

Pascal Cruz winked at Keith. "You're gonna like workin' with Sweet Boy, this man is the master. You just might learn something. Just keep your eyes open, son."

But all Keith could see was his own reflection in Pascal Cruz's black Ray-Bans. His satanic smile spreading wide.

17

TWO DAYS LATER, Nick still hadn't found out shit. Willie Brown wouldn't let him talk to Cracker, who was still in the hospital. So he spent his time at the Purple Heart with Virginia, making love, drinking, and going over the remaining names on the contact list. No luck. He drove all around Greenwood within a twenty-mile radius to talk to old blues singers or their relatives and friends.

It was something to do while he waited, like playing solitaire or working a crossword puzzle. But he knew he needed Cracker.

That morning, he lay on a musty bedspread in the Dixie Motel and mindlessly flipped television channels. Oprah. *Love Boat*. Soap operas. He threw the remote on the floor. A commercial came on from the Jamaican tourist board showing a white woman having her hair braided by a poor young girl. The young girl smiled and danced. Nick groaned and closed his eyes. Pathetic.

Why would anyone want to kill an old man like Cracker? He knew why they'd want to kill Baker—the man could've given Mother Teresa a conniption. Maybe Baker pissed off Elvis and Cracker witnessed it. Hell, it could be just a simple robbery and murder from that psycho.

Brown took down the description Nick gave him but refused to put out an APB on a young Elvis Presley. He even asked Nick if he'd been smoking some shit before the other night—he wasn't joking.

Nick reached over with a blind hand for the phone, pulled it over to his chest, and called JoJo's in New Orleans. He was already missing the rhythms and cadence of his New Orleans circle: coffee at Louisiana Products, night jams in the Quarter, and JoJo's gruff voice.

Felix, the bartender, answered the phone and told him to hold on.

Nick had known JoJo since he was a freshman at Tulane. Back then he already had an appetite for the blues and the natural place to filter in New Orleans was JoJo's. Nick used to go there at least three nights a week, sitting and watching Loretta, Fats, or the house band.

JoJo knew Nick and his friends played football at Tulane and would send them over a round of Dixies. Their friendship never progressed over a polite nod, a named greeting, or the regular "How's the team doing?" questions.

But a woman changed all that. Not just any woman but a blond-haired siren in a sundress. It was during the football season of Nick's sophomore year. Tulane had lost to LSU again and he'd gone to JoJo's for another blues-driven Saturday night.

The woman, she was actually only in her early twenties, decided to dance by herself close to the band. That night it was Chicago Bob, and he was playing some covers like Little Walter's "Dead Presidents" and of Elmore James's "It Hurts Me Too."

This blonde was moving her hands all over her body and really feeling the music. She mimicked all of Bob's licks that night. It was one of the most erotic things Nick had ever seen. Then her dreamy eyes turned to Nick and watched him the whole way through a hip thrust.

A man would've had to have medical problems not to feel something at that moment. When Bob stopped and the jukebox started back up, Nick followed her outside to Conti Street, where she dried her sweat in the cool spring wind. Her freckled chest was soaked and her hair damp.

She didn't even hesitate when Nick offered her a smoke. She grabbed the back of his head and gave him a long, sloppy kiss. She moved his hands down to her ass and stuck her tongue in his ear. They didn't even make it back to his car before she was rubbing on him.

What Nick didn't know was she'd left her husband, a gaunt, bearded businessman in his fifties, inside the bar. The man had been watching them. For some reason, he let them continue the grubbing until he met them in back with two of his employees. Two guys apparently hungry to impress the boss.

All night they'd probably drooled watching his young wife get off on the dance floor of the juke. They both grabbed Nick as he was kissing the woman against his Jeep, and one held him while the other pummeled his stomach.

Nick fell to his knees and tackled one guy, punching him in the mouth, then kicked the other guy in the stomach. The guy grabbed Nick's foot, tried to pull him close, but only got a punch in the ear for it. Nick was about to walk away when the husband tucked a gun in Nick's ribs and said,

"Junior, I think you need to stand still and just take what's comin' to you."

The woman didn't wail or say to let him go. She actually grinned at Nick as she reached into her husband's pockets, grabbed the keys to his BMW, and walked back around to Conti Street.

"The men I let her fuck, let me watch," he said.

"Can't get it up, huh?" Nick said.

About that time, two police officers wandered out back with JoJo pointing to them. Nick didn't know JoJo too well and was expecting him to get all their asses put in the tank. The husband tucked the gun inside his coat and his two young friends stood behind him as he told a story that amounted to Nick trying to feel up his wife without her permission. Of course, the two young executives agreed.

However, JoJo did not.

It could have turned out a variety of ways, most of them ending with Nick getting kicked off the football team and losing his scholarship. Any Tulane athlete's arrest would've made the news the next day.

But JoJo wouldn't let the cops take Nick. They argued for over a half hour in the crushed-shell lot. JoJo told what he saw, explained he was a property owner and wanted these men out of there, never to return. Basically, he vouched for Nick's character, because most of what JoJo told them, he couldn't have actually seen.

As Nick walked back into the bar that night he asked JoJo why he did it.

JoJo responded simply, "I know what you're about, just watchin' you. When I was your age I was so horny I would've screwed a snake. How 'bout a beer?"

There was a rustling on the other end of the line and a grumpy JoJo answered. Nick imagined him sitting on a barstool and cradling that ancient black phone to his ear, Loretta rattling some pots somewhere in the back.

"Can't make it tonight," Nick said.

"Who's this? The hooker I lined up?" JoJo asked.

"You lookin' for a male hooker?"

"Shiiit."

"JoJo, call Smoky for me and have him fill in."

"Why don't you?"

"I'm still in Greenwood."

"Sittin' by the pool, pickin' your ass?" JoJo asked.

"Looking for some deranged lunatic that likes to hurt old men.... Say, maybe I'll send him over to see you."

"Yeah. He'll get a can of whoop-ass from this *old man*."

"Will you call him?"

"Guess so...Hey, hey...hold on. Nick?"

"Yeah?"

"You found out what happened to Baker?"

"Yeah, I think Elvis killed him."

"Shiiit. Alright, don't tell me nothin'."

"I'm getting tired, wish I was home, and the whole mess cleared up," Nick said.

"Son, remember the truth," JoJo said. "You can shit in one hand and wish with the other."

"See which one gets full faster," Nick finished.

"You're learnin'."

"Alright, JoJo, I'll call before I get ready to leave."

Nick replaced the phone, reached on the floor for the remote, and turned off the television. He put his hands behind his head and closed his eyes. Imagine nothing. Hear nothing. See nothing. Take everything away, all the bullshit that overloads the brain and keeps it from really seeing. The trick was not to think or pound over details. That's when the mind would come back with the answer. He relaxed.

Someone pounded on the door, ending his moment of Zen. He got up and opened the door to see Willie Brown. The sunlight cut hard into Nick's eyes and he squinted at the deputy. Brown motioned inside.

"Yeah?"

"Can I come in?"

"Oh, sure. Sorry, I was just trying for complete consciousness."

"I won't ask."

Brown sat down on a mustard-colored vinyl chair and looked around the motel room. His eyes were puffy around the lids and his shoulders lacked posture. He breathed out his nose and stared blankly at a cheap painting of three seagulls on a white beach.

"That bird in the middle looks like it's taking a dump," Brown said. "Hey man, you ever wish you were still playing football at Tulane or coaching or something?"

"I miss playing and my friends, that's about it."

"It just was so uncomplicated, you know? You knew when you practiced, when you ate, when there were meetings. Your life was just so organized."

"That's the part I hated."

Brown laughed.

Nick was beginning to like the guy. His hard-ass shell melting. A little more relaxed and trusting.

"Why was Baker down here?" Brown asked.

"Field research."

"Do you know that?"

"I've talked to everyone I can think of. I'm pretty sure."

"I think his agenda changed."

A scrawny white woman smoking a cigarette rolled a maid's cart by and jiggled the room lock. Nick could hear her smacking bubble gum. The smoke must enhance the flavor.

"I'm naked with a small animal," Nick said. "Please come back when I'm finished."

She continued to roll.

"Man, you got a sick sense of humor."

Nick looked back at Brown. "So what was Baker's agenda?"

"I don't know. Cracker...he...shit, maybe he's crazy. He said that when Baker came to see him, he showed Baker these old records he'd kept forever. Had them in this nasty old leather trunk. Anyway, Baker got real serious when he saw them."

"And?"

"Couple days later, Cracker said the records were gone."

18

NICK AND WILLIE BROWN DROVE south again to Quito. Cracker was back in his clapboard shack in the woods. A cracked rib. A stitched eyelid. Nothing too serious. The old man even had a pot of coffee going in a blue-speckled pot when they arrived.

It reminded Nick of his pot back home.

Cracker poured them both coffee in a couple of chipped china cups. The cracked wooden floor unpainted but clean. Everything arranged: plastic graveyard flowers in rusting coffee cans, fruit jars, old license plates, washboards, worn-out stuffed animals, and wallpaper made of newspaper.

Cracker acted like any other lonely man glad to have company, his hands shaking around his own cup. Eyes the same bright blue as the mugs.

"Cracker, tell Dr. Travers here about when that professor came to see you and what he took."

Cracker nodded, slurped the coffee wincing slightly, and put the mug on the pine floor. "He took my records. I h-had 'em a long time. They was my records. I was tole to keep 'em."

"What records?" Nick asked.

Cracker looked at Willie Brown and Brown nodded back. "Cracker, he's okay. I promise."

"Them records are real ole. Almost as ole as me.

Man a-asked if he could borrow them awhile. Said he wanted to make sure they still played. I know they still play and I wouldn't let 'im. I-I's kept them in a trunk all bundled up in a red satin kimono I borrow from this woman in town after R.L. died."

"R.L.?"

"Robert Johnson, he was my friend."

"How'd you know Robert Johnson?" Nick asked, not believing him.

Cracker began to rub his pale, chafed hands together and rock. "I u-use to live in Austin and work for a r-r-record man. R.L. use to be only man who come talk to me while he was singin'. Everyone else afraid to get what I got."

"Was his name Law. Don Law?"

"No."

"Did you know him?"

"No."

"So how'd you move to Greenwood?"

"I was here when R.L. died. Willie, you know that. No one believe me. But I stayed with him all night as the poison taken to him."

Cracker's voice got shaky. "R.L. was on his knees spittin' up blood, just waitin' for the devil to take him. He never cried though. He just said it was time."

"Who killed him?" Nick asked.

"I cain't say, mista. I k-know. I just cain't say."

"Were you friends with the owner of the juke?" Nick asked.

"W-w-wasn't him."

"It was his wife then."

"I cain't say. I cain't say."

"You say you worked for a record man. He recorded Johnson?" Nick asked.

Cracker nodded.

"When was that?"

"Few months before R.L. died."

Nick knew Cracker was full of shit. Johnson hadn't recorded for over a year before he died. The old man was delusional or had a fogged memory. Don Law was the producer of both Johnson sessions.

"What'd he look like...R.L.?" Nick asked. "He was a big man, right?"

"N-no suh," Cracker said. "He was real small. B-but had big ole hands, long fingers."

For a crazy old man, Cracker had studied.

"They were just old blues records, right?" Brown interrupted, giving Nick a sharp glare.

"Yeah. I had R.L. and Charley Patton. Kokomo Arnold."

"Last year an original of "Love in Vain" sold for ten thousand dollars at an auction," Nick said.

"There you go, Travers. Sounds like Baker stole some old records and then skipped out," Brown said. "That white boy we ran off probably was coming back for something Baker left. Maybe they worked together. Baker might be in Jamaica right now drinking something with an umbrella in it. Thanks, Cracker. I brought you some food. If you run out again, leave a rag on that stick by the highway like usual."

"Thank ya sir," Cracker said.

"Hey man, wait, I need a few minutes," Nick said. "What did his eyes look like?"

"What you mean. His eye? Oh, oh yeah. He sensitive 'bout that. Ain't n-nice askin'."

"Why?" Nick asked.

"He always try to keep his hat coverin' that bad eye."

Nick's face tightened in an uncontrollable grin. He stifled the smile and could feel his fist open and close with nervous energy. Brown stood up, walked to the door, and threw the last few sips of coffee out onto the forest floor.

"I'm real sorry, Cracker," Brown said. "A man doesn't have a soul that would rip you off."

It was hot outside, but beneath all the pine trees, Cracker's house felt cool and breezy. Needles occasionally fell through the open windows.

"Make me glad I didn't show him the rest," Cracker said.

Nick and Brown looked at each other. Nick's fingers stopped moving.

"Yeah. I still got the rest hidden, where ain't nobody gonna f-find 'em."

"Would you show me?" Brown asked.

"Just you." Cracker looked over at Nick.

Brown left him and followed Cracker into the woods and around the back of the house. The shuffle of their feet was soon replaced with cicadas, birds, creaking pine trees, and scurrying squirrels. Nick poured the remainder of the coffee from the pot into his china mug and went out to sit on the stoop. For a hermit, Cracker sure made good coffee. Of course, he probably had more practice living in the woods with nothing.

Maybe he could get Cracker on tape and get him to talk about that last year of Johnson's life— 1938. Memories fade and run together; perhaps he would recall just a small nugget. He needed more time with Cracker. Maybe he could jump-start his memory. See if it contained any truth.

The solitude of the country was nice compared to the concrete forest where he lived in New Orleans. It wasn't just the green life, fresh air, and all that crap. It was also the complete absence of tension he felt anytime he stepped outside in New Orleans. No cars, no machinery. Just man. Maybe he would reach complete consciousness today.

He could hear Cracker crawling under the old shack. Secret hiding place? No wonder it was easy for Baker to steal the records.

Nick watched two black birds land in a puddle of tan, muddy water and flutter around. They squawked and flew away when Cracker and Brown came around a kudzu-covered trail. Brown set a wooden packing crate on the front porch and stood back. Cracker pried the top open with a pocketknife. Rusty nails slipped out like thick quills from an animal's back.

"Yeah, I put this under the porch p-probably thirty years ago. I check on it s-sometimes to make sure it's still there." He pulled out a handful of mildewed yellow newspaper and a bundle wrapped in a black trash bag. "Yeah, I knew this keep it nice and dry. They w-was flat too. Store 'em real tight. And it's cool under that porch."

He walked with the bundle into the house and set it on the floor. He slowly got on his knees and began to unwrap it like a precious Christmas present. Eyes intense. Hands precise.

Inside the layers of black plastic was a narrow wooden box. After he rubbed his dusty hands on his overalls, he opened the box like the top of a cigarette carton. Cracker pulled out a flat piece of cardboard covered in red satin and removed an aluminum disc covered in lacquer. The way it was marked with a black pen, it looked like a demo.

"This j-just one, we recorded 'fore he died," Cracker said.

19

JESSE GARON, Sweet Boy Floyd, and Keith Fields followed the marked police car with the cop, the ole man and the same dude who had chased Jesse through the woods. Dude was big. Taller than he was. Looked like a dockworker, wearin' all denim and boots. Short black hair and kinda scruffy.

Floyd's big truck kept a nice distance behind them. King Cab Ford with dual tires on the back axle, damned thing could've seated twenty. Inside, the Naugahyde shone smooth with an oily sheen of Armor All. It was real slick and all, especially with the nudie air freshener danglin' from the rearview mirror. The back mud flaps were custom too, with Calvin takin' a piss on one and Hobbes takin' a shit on the other.

"Y'all my boys. We gonna have a fine time killin' these dudes," Floyd said, sucking on a pink bubble-gum cigar and patting Jesse's leg.

"Take your hands off me," Jesse said. "I don't know you and you sure as shit don't know me."

"Easy there now hoss," Floyd said. "We're all coworkers here. I'm just applyin' my trade."

Keith snorted and shook his head. "He's just funnin' you, Floyd. Don't worry 'bout it none."

"Just keep him away from me and we'll be fine," Jesse said. He could see Floyd's black eyes watching him from his rearview mirror. The naked woman on the air freshener seemed to dance as wind blew through the truck.

"You ever been out of Mississippi, kid?" Floyd asked.

"Hell, I'm from Memphis."

"Then you should know when a man talks, you should keep yore punk-ass mouth shut."

"Don't go sleepin' 'round me, Floyd," Jesse said, his lip curling.

"Would both of you quit it—we got some serious work to do," Keith said.

Floyd flicked on the radio. Booming disco funk pounded the rear half of the cab.

"Feel like I'm in Africa," Jesse said. "All this damn shit. We're better than this, Keith."

"Hush up," Keith said. "And you listen to what Mr. Floyd says."

"Why we kidnappin' this man?" Jesse asked.

"Ain't none of your goddamn bidness," Floyd said.

Jesse shook his head. These guys think they're pros but they really don't know shit. They could never understand his talent for killin'. Not even his buddy Keith. Sure he was all pumped up and tough but he didn't have that feelin' for takin' someone's life. Keith wasn't even excited about a challenge like takin' down a couple men. E always liked a challenge.

THROUGH THE BRIGHT reflection of the car's window, Cracker looked like a corpse dressed in a black suit with his fingers tightly laced in his lap.

Nick opened the car door for him, letting the old man open a black umbrella over his head before setting foot into the unmerciful sun.

Across the blue sky, long strips of clouds, as black as chimney smoke, began to roll in and threaten the light. Yet Nick could still feel the August heat through the soles of his boots. Brown walked ahead into the downtown Greenwood soul food restaurant. It stood on the bottom floor of a brick building adorned with a faded red-and-white Coca-Cola mural.

Nick led Cracker through the door and over a scuffed red floor as Christmas lights blinked above the bar. Brown had already ordered three sweet teas, all served in mismatched jelly jars. As he drank, the old man's lips moved over his gums in a nervous frenzy. He reminded Nick of a dog with peanut butter on his tongue.

"Cracker, we're gonna find you a nice place to stay until all this mess is settled. All right?" Brown said, and then looked over at Nick. "Thought I'd put him up in that motel you're staying in, til we find out who that man was from the other night."

"You mean Elvis?"

"Yeah, Elvis. An ex–New Orleans Saint got outrun by a dead man."

"Ah-hah. You've been checking my background," Nick said, stretching his arm on a bench behind him.

"Been real slow downtown. It was that or clip my toenails."

"I'm flattered."

An old Johnnie Taylor song pumped from the speakers and no one spoke until a little black woman clacked in wearing a soiled apron and asked what they wanted. Brown ordered a vegetable plate and Nick got the fried chicken. It took some prompting for Cracker to ask for two pecan pies and a Coke.

Except for them, the restaurant was empty. The front and back doors were open and a warm late-summer breeze washed over Nick's face. He could feel the sweat dry on his T-shirt. Late lazy Mississippi afternoon. A kind of comfortable silence passing over them. The greens weren't salty or soggy and the corn bread was so thick, Nick drank three glasses of tea.

"I-I cain't go home?" Cracker asked.

"No sir, but you gonna have it good," Brown said. "Nice motel room and some more good food like this."

Cracker looked over at Nick as he spooned the pecan pie into his mouth until the brown muck ran down his chin.

"That man Baker. The one that took your records?" Nick asked. "What'd he want to know?"

Brown eyed Nick as he took a sip of tea.

"He wanted to know all 'bout R.L.," Cracker said. "W-What the man like to eat, w-would he let people see his fingers when he recordin', did he eva play with a big fancy band."

The questions were good ones. Johnson was known to be really paranoid about someone ripping off his style. Some have said he would turn his back if another musician watched his finger movements too closely. And some have said Johnson played with a pianist-and-drummer combo shortly before he died.

Cracker frowned and his hands shook around the shiny metal fork.

"And you didn't like that, all those questions?"

Nick asked, trying to make eye contact, to see how the man responded. Watch his breathing to see if he was lying. Nick believed people who held their breath had something to hide.

"People use that man up," Cracker said, breathing real even. "S-Still usin' him."

"I don't understand," Nick said.

Cracker laughed and looked down at his empty plate. Through the crudely painted letters on the window, Nick stared at thick, coal black clouds covering the sun.

"I need to borrow your records," Nick said. He smiled, trying to calm the old man. Make him know everything was all right. That he wasn't going to take off like Baker and swipe the last of his collection. "If Robert Johnson did make these before he died, how come the record man you worked for never sold them? Could've made a lot of money."

Cracker started rocking back and forth like a child and snorted his breath in and out of his nose. His lips worked overtime around his gums. And when he put his hands to his face, the pie plate clattered to the floor, shattering into hard-edged chunks.

"Cool it, Travers," Brown said. "I'll see what I can do about the records."

"I need to hear what's on them. Could be songs no one knows about. Johnson never recorded in thirty-eight. His last session was fourteen months before he died."

"Like I said, I'll see what I can do. Just stay the night. Besides, it's gonna become a shitstorm out there in a few minutes."

The waitress walked out from the kitchen and saw the pie plate shattered on the floor. She looked at Cracker the way Nick had seen some people observe the baboons in the Audubon Zoo, and picked up the pieces.

"So Baker ripped off Cracker, and took off for Montego Bay. That's your theory?" Nick asked.

"You got a better one?" Brown said.

"Good reason."

"Real valuable, huh?"

"More than you know," Nick said. "Unreleased Johnson tracks would be priceless. Really something too good to be true. I mean it'd be like finding out Mozart had a few more symphonies stashed away. But it's impossible another recording session wasn't discovered in sixty years. Someone would've known, a producer, another musician....There was one story a teacher of mine heard from a guy in Memphis years ago, about some Johnson demos destroyed in a poolroom fight."

Brown looked at him from over the top of his tea glass.

"It's nothing," Nick said. "Crazy professor at Oxford. He told us the story to demonstrate the unreliability of some sources."

"What?"

"He said the man called them the 'lost nine.' Said Johnson went back to Texas before he died and laid down some more songs. It was bullshit. Something we would all like to believe. A Lost Ark for researchers."

Nick looked over at Cracker, who eyed him with a mean tenacity. His fierce eyes bore into Nick like he wanted to leap on him. Beat the crap out of a pushy white boy.

"You all messin' with some p-powerful shit. Things need not be talked about," Cracker said, rocking away. "Big Earl wouldn't want it. No sir. Big Earl wouldn't have it."

"Who's he talkin' about?" Nick asked.

"Big Earl Snooks," Brown said. "Slide guitar player, doesn't live around here anymore. I'm sure he's dead. Used to be a friend of Cracker's."

"You guys want me to stay with you tonight?" Nick asked. "Help keep watch?"

"Naw, another deputy is gonna trade with me after midnight. Besides, I crap bigger than Elvis Presley."

20

FIVE HOURS LATER, Sweet Boy Floyd parked his truck behind a burned-out gas station on Highway 82, just a ways down from the Dixie Motel. The three of them had spent the day feeding off beef jerky, Yoo-Hoos, and Moon Pies. A pile of Mountain Dew cans and coffee cups littered the truck's floor as rain splattered the cab like an impatient man's fingers. A few minutes before, they'd seen the white dude peel off in his Jeep and the glow of red taillights disappear down the highway. Jesse knew it was time, and he was ready for it, as Floyd handed out three pairs of surgical gloves.

"Awright, you two boys follow me and when I say hit it...you hit that sweet spot like a black man and take no prisoners," Floyd said, his eyes wide and nostrils flared.

Sweet, maybe this nigra wasn't bad after all. He liked this dude's attitude. Take no prisoners, hit and run. TCB. Just like the life lessons E learned in the army. Shit, he could do this, this was what Jesse Garon was all about. A damned real professional hit. No more bullshit killings of thirteen-year-old crack dealers for twenty bucks in Memphis.

This was live and in concert. Damned '68 Comeback Special.

"I got two fresh Glocks here," Floyd said. "Party favors for each of you young mens. All you got to do is hit that shit when I open the door and we gonna be just fine."

As Floyd talked, his head bobbed and weaved like a spring-headed toy. Kinda like it would pop off any minute.

"How you gonna get 'em to open up, Sweet Boy?" Keith asked. "Hell, they ain't gonna fall for no room-service or maid-knockin'-on-the-door stuff. The sheriff's department will be on our ass before we get out the door."

Floyd reached under his seat and pulled out a heavy, burnished crowbar. "I don't fuck with knockin'. I'll crack that bitch open in two seconds. And y'all best be ready."

CRACKER HAD NEVER seen television. Heard of it. Had even seen the muted light patterns it made as it shone in the trailer homes around his woods. Always thought you needed one of them big satellite dishes to bring pictures in. But there it was: voices, faces, beautiful women who wore next to nothing flouncing around.

"What k-kind business is this?" Cracker asked. "It ain't right."

"You want me to change the station?" Brown asked.

"No. Dat's all right. Dey shore is pretty."

"Cracker, you ever have a woman?"

He smiled. Not many folks he would talk to, but Willie Brown was a good man. Willie was his friend. "There was a young girl I met when w-we was in Austin."

"How many years ago?"

"Nineteen hundred and thirty-six. I do believe."

All the flashing colors were making Cracker a little sick. It was like his head was bein' crammed full of stuff he didn't need. He stood up and walked over to the bathroom, ran the water, and put one foot on the commode. He grabbed a hand towel to run under the cool water.

The towel felt nice on his face. Yeah, made him feel calm. He coughed up a little phlegm and spit into the sink.

Out the little cracked window he could see the yellow glow of a streetlamp shine on a wet field of kudzu. The weeds grew over a rusted car, vines twisted in and out of the broken windows. The streetlamp, the rain, the kudzu, and the rusted old car somehow made sense to Cracker, like that's the way it should be. Familiar.

BLESS A MY *soul. What's wrong with me? I'm itchin' like a man on a fuzzy tree.* Jesse's breathing was comin' too quick, he thought. Right in through the nose and out through the mouth like his tae kwon do teacher taught him. Yeah, slow it down. Big daddy was gonna get it tonight. Make a fool of me once. Never twice.

"You two boys ready?" Floyd asked as they gathered in the motel's parking lot.

Keith and Jesse both nodded as rain filled their eyes.

"Remember, like a black man. Ain't no time for no limp-dick muthafuckas."

E wouldn't like all this bad language—he'd talk to Sweet Boy later. Jesse gripped the gun and followed to the motel's edge, where fat bugs played in dirty yellow lights.

*   *   *

CRACKER HAD HIS hand on the bathroom door
when he heard the outside door splinter. Then
there were two pops like fatback in a fryin' pan.
Willie Brown yelled his name and then there were
a couple more loud cracks.

He moved his hand away from the knob and
looked up at the narrow window. Just might could
get out. He moved his toe onto the narrow edge of
the bathtub, gripped the towel rack, and pulled his
head up through the window.

Cracker flipped out the opening and landed on
his back. All the wind crushed out of him and his
eyes watered. He had to get out of here, couldn't
trust nobody. Should've never come out of the
woods. Should've just stayed there. He rolled to
his stomach, got up and hopped into the wet
weeds—only place he could trust. Only good
friend he had. The green could cover him like a
warm blanket. Give him everything he ever
needed.

Another loud splinter came from the bathroom
and the muffled voices of two men. He limped
faster to the kudzu-covered car. Without another
thought, he dove into the rich green leaves and
crawled under the rusted belly. He tried to breathe
real light. Just be the woods, feel the green. Come
light, he'd go back to his home. Forget the blues.
Forget the past. And keep away from anything
about R.L. ever again.

FLOYD WALKED INTO the bathroom and came out
cussin'.

"I'll be a muthafuckin' monkey ass," Floyd said.
"Ole man...out the window. Damn fool dove into

some kudzu, like he's bein' sneaky or some shit. Knock that fool right in the head."

"You get 'im," Jesse said. "Can't you see my friend ain't right?"

Floyd picked up a wooden crate and hoisted it into his big arms. He didn't even say a word about Keith, who was spitting blood onto the room's shag carpet. Shot once in the throat and another time in the stomach.

"I'll get the ole man," Floyd said as he walked right past Jesse. He was almost out the door before he turned around. "You done good, boy. You shot that man before he could shoot me."

Jesse looked at the twisted, bloody sheets wrapped around the nigra cop. Shot right in the head and in the heart. It was nice work; mama would be proud.

"Appreciate that," Jesse said, his ears ringing.

Keith coughed up blood and wrapped his arms around Jesse's foot. Jesse looked down at his friend and began to cry, then looked back to Floyd.

"He ain't gonna make it," Floyd said. "And I don't care for prison myself. Make me feel a little tight."

Gut shot. That was the worst, or that's what the old Westerns said. Jesse knew what he had to do. He bent down, kissed his friend's head, and pressed the gun against Keith's temple. "See you on the flip side, brother."

21

A LITTLE PAST midnight, Nick drove through an apparition-like fog. He and Virginia had decided to cut across Mississippi highways late that night on a simple premise from a drunken conversation. They were at Lusco's, where they drained twelve beers and ate two orders of chicken and two bowls of gumbo. As they dined inside the former 1930s drugstore, the conversation grew serious. Maybe it had something to do with the headstone maker next door, the stamped tin ceiling, the weather, or the intimacy of the individual room partitioned with a shower curtain.

Whatever the reason, he blurted out the inspiration for his thesis on the "Life and Times of Sonny Boy Williamson II." He told her about this mural on the back of an abandoned building in Tutwiler. That there was a rendering of Sonny Boy rising from the grave near the spot where W. C. Handy waited for a train late one night and heard a blues called "Goin' Where the Southern Cross the Dog."

Nick wasn't trying to be cool or play the wise professor or any of that horseshit. It had just come up naturally. He told her one night he'd driven from Oxford to see about the place and was sitting there in that dead little town, when the blues began to make sense. That he could almost feel the early part of the century in a nowhere Mississippi town. Something clicked.

And it wasn't just the oppression. As a white man born in the sixties, there was no feasible way to understand that. It was the loneliness and the isolation in the center of the fertile region. Virginia held a finger to his lips and simply said, "I want to go. Now."

The rain stopped about thirty miles outside Greenwood as if they'd peeked out of a huge, wet curtain, and she was reclined like a contented cat as the wind whipped red hair across her face. A Patsy Cline song played on a scratchy AM radio station. Filled with music and alcohol, Virginia sang along.

"You know I love that woman. I could listen to 'Walkin' After Midnight' over and over," she said. "Never get tired of it. I just feel the mood, I know what she was sayin'. Too beautiful. Too beautiful."

Nick smiled. It felt good to be with a woman again. Sometimes being lonely for so long made you think you didn't need anything. Like a person who denies himself guilty pleasures.

"We're almost there," he said.

They passed a long row of one-story brick storefronts, all deserted with boarded-up doors and broken windows. The buildings seemed too small, as if they were modeled slightly less than life scale. But it didn't matter now. There was no life. Tutwiler was a real ghost town.

"This is it?" she asked, nodding toward the railroad tracks. "Doesn't look like anyone has been here since Handy."

Nick shifted into neutral, put his foot on the brake, and shut off the engine. "Sonny Boy came back. Ran his life in a complete circle. From Tutwiler, then all over the world, then back to Tutwiler."

She combed the hair from her eyes and scooted herself up in the seat.

"This is where it all began," Nick said. "The home of the blues. Over there is where Handy first heard a field hand playin' slide. He was just waitin' for a train and heard this weird music. Now it really started God knows where, maybe Dockery Farms, but this is where a man really took a good listen. Wrote the lyrics and structure down. And right there, you see those murals?"

He punched on his high beams to hit the back of the deserted storefronts. Painted on the brick walls were five colored murals. "That one right there is one I told you about. Sonny Boy Williamson rising from the grave."

It was a dark mural of the famous harp player halfway out of the ground. A Second Coming–type image. Nick remembered Wade Walton, another famous harp player, now a barber in Clarksdale, telling him a story about Sonny Boy coming back from Europe very sick. He said the legend walked around downtown Clarksdale with a gin bottle shortly before he died, his life empty. Dead blues singer, buried in a dead town.

Nick offered Virginia a cigarette. She accepted from the pack of Marlboros and Nick lit both. The air was muggy, blowing from over the railroad tracks. No houses nearby. No sign of life. At once, he felt vulnerable, nervous, and lonely.

"How long you been in Mississippi?" Nick asked, shifting in his seat.

"About three months. I was in Austin but I knew if I was going to develop a real sound, I needed to come here. Everybody told me I was crazy, said I'd get killed in these jukes out here. But I work them from Jackson to Clarksdale. I ain't ever had a problem."

"What do you think? This spot changed my life," he said. "People say if you keep real quiet you can hear Sonny Boy's harp."

"Shh." She put a long finger to her red lips. "Let's listen."

Nick flicked his cigarette out the Jeep, its red end rolling down the asphalt.

Virginia's eyes closed and she began to hum to herself. A basic blues rhythm. Hands locked together and arms stretched tall above her. Her chest rose and fell with the music.

She opened one eye mischievously. "Two white blues musicians in the Delta. What are the chances?"

Nick pulled the weight of his smile to one corner. "Who would have thought it?"

Virginia leaned over, put both hands on Nick's face, and kissed him. Hard. Her hands moved around his neck and she crawled out of her seat and onto his lap, straddling him.

"That was unexpected," he said.

"Mmm-hmm," she said, going back to kissing him.

Nick's legs began to go numb with Virginia on his lap. But all he could do was respond. His hands under her thin T-shirt. Her bra already on the floor of his Jeep. Her skin was warm and body tight. She pulled a piece of the deep red hair out of her mouth and smiled.

Her eyes reminded him of a Siberian husky's. Sky blue with a strong black edge around the iris, as if they were circled in ink. She put both hands back on his face again, closed her eyes, and continued.

She moved her hands under his denim shirt and then moved them onto his crotch.

"Whoa. What are we doing here?"

"I don't know, what do you want to do?" Her hands once again brushing his crotch.

"I, ah...," he began, looking over at a hearse parked behind the Tutwiler mortuary.

She took one of his fingers and put it in her mouth, swirling it around.

"Ya know..."

She kissed his hands.

"Be quiet, Travers, you ain't so tough," she said, unbuttoning his jeans, then undoing hers. "I've been in the Delta too long."

She momentarily went back to the passenger seat, slid down and pulled off her boots and jeans and threw them in the backseat laughing. She pulled her hair into a ponytail and crawled back on Nick's lap. She maneuvered one of his hands under the thin edge of her pink panties. As he moved his hand lower, she responded to him. They kissed hard and Nick heard her rip the panties off her legs. She brought herself up on him, sighed softly, and moaned as she joined with him. Her thighs strong.

Nick put his arms around her and held her tight. With a late-summer wind against his back and the taste of strawberry hair in his mouth, he thought he heard the fleeting sounds of a trilling harp.

THE NIGHT'S GLORIOUS alcohol glow settled into an early-morning hangover as Nick slipped a key into the motel room's door. He could still taste Virginia's sweet lips and smell her scent all over him.

As he walked into his room and flipped the wall switch, a tight arm wrapped around his throat and he was thrown onto the floor. His head thudded against the bed's headboard as he fell.

"Get down now!" a man's voice yelled.

Nick tried to fight, but one man restrained him while another clamped on handcuffs. The grip on his wrists felt like razors.

"You low-life sack of shit are under arrest for the murder of Deputy William Brown."

22

JAIL IS about humiliation, loss of freedom, and being treated like an outcast degenerate. It is the antiseptic-urine smell that permeates your clothes and lungs. It is about pale blue iron bars and a bunk that stinks of human waste and pleasure.

The only jail Nick had ever known was on White Street in New Orleans. That was only to visit his friend Jay Medeaux, a police detective, or occasionally bail out a fellow musician. It wasn't a hell of a lot different from this place, he thought. Jail is jail. They don't reflect local color.

He'd been there all day. In that time, he'd familiarized himself with the residents. A happy bunch: a three-hundred-pound pedophile named "Big Larry," a wife beater who constantly cried, a local lawyer in for a DUI, a twenty-one-year-old car thief, and a muscular man who paced the room but did not speak.

Nick had found a three-year-old copy of *Newsweek* that he now read for the third time. What he wouldn't give for a decent book or meal. He wasn't trying to be snobbish about it, but eating gray gruel wasn't even above animal standards. A dog wouldn't shit on it.

Not only was the food bad but there wasn't

much of it. He began to hallucinate about the meal he'd had at Lusco's. That chicken and beer was a vision. He could see the beads form on the Budweiser label and the juicy white meat.

"Hey shithead. You wanna piece of me?" the muscular man asked.

Nick continued reading.

"I said shithead. You dickless turd."

Nick had no idea about the ethnic diversity in Bosnia. He read on.

The man spit on Nick's arm.

Nick folded the magazine neatly and laid it on the bunk next to him. He sighed. Moments like these really enforced the theory of evolution. Just a bunch of big monkeys in a cage. No different except monkeys were much more fun to watch.

The big man stepped forward and bumped his chest with Nick's.

Nick faked his head to the right and led with a hard elbow to the man's nose and a quick jab to his gut. When the man tried to come back, Nick head-butted him, knocking the man down hard on the floor.

Nick returned to the bunk, lay down, and crossed his feet in front of him. He picked up the magazine, found his place, and went back to Bosnia.

THAT NIGHT NICK dreamed of bloodstains on the ceiling and all over the wall. That's all he could see—streaks of red all over the sheets and on the cracked headboard. He couldn't breathe; he just stood there looking at rumpled sheets just holding his breath. Bile came up in his throat.

Virginia Dare smiled at him between twirling red and blue lights. He thought someone yelled but he couldn't tell. It was outside of him. All of it was. Not a dream, just a surreal reality. He should have been there. They wouldn't be dead. He should've been watching instead of fucking.

More voices yelled. Red and blue lights spun. Someone grabbed his arm. He hit it hard, bent at the waist, and vomited. Cracker and Willie. And then he woke up.

23

"I KNEW this day would come," Wayne Cary said as he laughed and looked through the Plexiglas at Nick. Even with the smart-ass remark, it was good to see Wayne. He'd been his drinking partner in Oxford while Nick worked on his doctorate.

Man never asked him once about football. They'd just sit there all night at the bar, slamming Dixies and talking about their favorite restaurants in New Orleans. Big guy with thick brown hair and a hard southern drawl. Not country, Wayne sounded the way Nick imagined Confederate officers talked.

Wayne's heroes were Stonewall Jackson, Lewis and Clark, and professional rock climbers.

"Either this or I'd be trying to release your mother for solicitation," Wayne said, really guffawing this time. His old friend actually enjoyed seeing him in jail. Like it was some big fraternity joke.

"That's okay, Wayne, I left your mama in the back, she seems to make friends very quickly. Woman that big can really move."

The joke came up in some sick Pavlovian way, like they never left their old life routines. And that really cracked him up. Wayne leaned back in his chair and let go a revving staccato of giggles.

Behind him, Virginia Dare stood hugging her arms around her bare waist. She looked great to Nick in her faded jeans and flannel shirt tied in front. Nick smiled weakly up at her.

He leaned close to the Plexiglas wall and spoke into the intercom. "Wayne, it's really good to see you, please don't get me wrong. But I've spent the last twenty-four hours lying on a piss-stained mattress having nightmares about being arrested for a double murder. It ain't happy hour."

"Sorry, Nick," Wayne said.

"No problem. When am I getting out of here?"

"Ain't it strange? But you rousted me this way like I was some type of Gerry Spence wanna-be or a character from a John Grisham novel and you know what...didn't matter. They don't have anything on you. Young deputy kinda jumped the gun because the woman working the night desk at the Dixie Motel said she saw you with Willie Brown. That was his name, right? She gave a fairly detailed description of your big ass. But nothing to tie you with the murders. Miss Dare here came to me and told me she was with you the entire night. She's found a half dozen witnesses at Lusco's who also said you were there when the murders occurred, and no fingerprints. You'll be out of here in a couple of hours. It's all bullshit."

Nick nodded and let all the breath ease out of him. "Thanks a lot, man. I owe you big. Can I talk to Virginia?"

"Sure," Wayne said. He pushed back his chair and exchanged places with Virginia in the corner.

Nick smiled a lopsided grin at her. "Thanks."

"I just found out last night," Virginia said. "I had a gig in Oxford at the Gin."

"Thought maybe you'd hopped a train like an old-time player."

"I wouldn't do that to you."

Wayne walked forward and leaned over Virginia's shoulder. "I've scheduled a hearing at noon. You should be out by one. A deputy here said they found a witness who saw two males boogie on out in a big fat truck with Louisiana plates. One black and one white. And of course there is the unidentified body."

"His name was Cracker. An old hermit that lived in the woods around Quito."

"Says here he was a white male in his late twenties found alongside Brown. Kid was from New Orleans."

"What about an old albino man?"

"I don't know, man. Say, maybe those deputies knocked you silly. Sounds like you're chasing ghosts."

"Yeah, it's what I do."

24

PASCAL CRUZ TRACED the sharp edge of the acetate disc and laughed. They were his, finally. After all the shit with that slick college professor, he now owned the damned heart of the blues. And damned if it wasn't just the nine, but twelve discs. Paper thin, a little over ten inches wide. They looked perfectly flat, no damage to the black lacquer. *Johnson lived inside those grooves*. This was it, the thing he'd waited for all of his life.

Cruz always knew he would be something, growing up in that no-name suburb outside San Francisco. He used to play his John Mayall and Stones and read the liner notes, curious about the blues. Something mysterious and dark. After Cruz became a record producer in Los Angeles, he used to watch some of the white blues acts and ask them about the music.

They said the blues just wasn't popular enough. It needed some kind of push. Years later, Cruz knew the marketing niche was ready. He was tired of working with a bunch of ignorant rappers and sluts with grating voices. So he played up the days, only a few, that he worked at Stax Records in the early seventies and created the mystique—dark sunglasses, black suits, and spouting blues quotes.

He began to package young white guitarists who knew more about Eddie Van Halen than Buddy Guy. But they'd have the look and he'd give them stacks of old Chess Records songs to listen to and practice. They'd mimic the licks like a parrot, make their voices scratchy and deep, and he'd have a hit. Didn't matter if it was blues or mayonnaise, he knew how to package and sell anything.

Soon, Cruz became an icon around L.A. making the old music a cool trend. He'd started hanging out at this small club off Sunset Boulevard called Louie Louie's. It was there that he first had the inspiration for the Blues Shack. Louie Louie's was all wrong, the way it had mixed blues and jazz as if they were the same thing. Cruz knew if someone could present blues performance in the right way it would sell. He needed to build a high-tech juke joint. Old wood and rusted signs with video and state-of-the-art sound. Make it feel like you were in Mississippi with a little *Star Trek* mixed in.

Besides, it was time to leave L.A. anyway. The place had drained almost everything he had. At the time, he was hooked on bourbon and cocaine. He craved it like a fucked-up monkey pressing buttons for bananas. Could barely do business without thinking about that rushing hum in his brain and a warm glow in his stomach. The final act was the night he invited the wife of a record company president over to his Malibu beach house. He had the sliding glass doors open, listening to the surf and the Guess Who with the man's wife bent over.

She was biting on his fingers when her husband walked in and went crazy. The man tried to kill him with a fire poker. But the funny part was, the woman was so scared she had Cruz gripped inside her. They stuck together like a pair of horny dogs as her husband kept on swinging. Cruz rolled all around like he was on fire trying to get that bitch off him. It was ridiculous. Finally, the man swatted his wife. She started bleeding and the man started crying. Husband and wife roared out of Cruz's driveway together in a candy apple red Lotus.

It was a decisive moment.

The stereo was still jamming: "No sugar tonight in my coffee, no sugar tonight in my tea." He lay paralyzed on the white carpet until the disc switched to Muddy Waters's "Mannish Boy." Even as fucked-up as he was, Muddy's deep growling voice, the twanging of Johnny Winter's guitar, and James Cotton's harp made his blood boil. It motivated him to rake all the cocaine off the table into a Ziploc bag and stumble onto the balcony. He tossed it into the wind as if it were fake snow.

Cruz then picked up the phone, called Floyd, and said, "Gas up, we're headed back to the South." Within six months, the Blues Shack was born. A bunch of white California investors came in on the project, even though they thought New Orleans was a shit location. What they didn't understand was that the Big Easy was perfect because of all the mom-and-pop music joints. Little places that didn't look at the overall tourist dollar.

Cruz did. He knew he could corral all the tourists into one huge joint. Not leave them spread about the city in little dives. It worked, and now with these lost recordings he didn't just have a marketing tool, he had a goddamned chain saw. Robert Johnson World: T-shirts, hats, CDs, posters, festivals, and coffee mugs. The Blues Shack would become the place where the tourists came to grab a piece of the South.

This would become "Robert's place." The kind

of bar Johnson would've hung out in. Or something like that. Cruz would continue to play up his phony southern drawl and market the pale imitation of the real blues.

Cruz added a dash of Kentucky bourbon to a glass of water and cubed ice. He wanted to be alert and keep clear. As the ice clinked to the last swallow, he could taste a hint of aged whiskey. Sweet flavor. Floyd had a beer open from the minibar and drank it in about two seconds. Cruz handed him another and patted him twice on his thick arm. Floyd's loose gold jewelry jangled on his wrist.

"Good job. Good job," Cruz said. "Ain't nobody fuck with my Sweet Boy. You always hit it like it needs to be hit."

"I got that ole albino man too," Floyd said. "Man was hunkered under a car when we found him like a scared dog. Had to use a stick to poke his ass out. If you want him, we got him. If not, we can tie a block to his leg and kick his ass in the Mississippi. *See ya*."

Cruz felt smooth and comfortable in a long black kimono, his hair knotted in a ponytail. Outside the top floor of his French Quarter hotel, fat raindrops pounded his window and fell to the neon rain-slicked world below.

"Keith's dead?" he remembered.

"Ain't nothin' we could do but put that boy out of his misery," Floyd said.

"Damn shame.... We used to dream about this stuff in Memphis, didn't we, Floyd? You singin' backup at Stax. I knew it would happen."

Floyd nodded like he knew better than to try and rattle Cruz's image thing. He would never try to hold a mirror to the chuck wagon.

Cruz stroked his beard. "How's the kid doin'?"

"Awright."

"Does he really look like Elvis?"

"Son of a bitch, if he don't."

"What is he, a real fat country boy with sideburns?"

"Naw man, like the young one on that postage stamp," Floyd said. "Kid just a teenager. But he has that meanness in his eyes. Like he would put a cat in the microwave just to see what'll happen next."

"I want you to take care of him. Make sure he eats and has a place to live. You say he handled himself well?"

"Kid done good. He's sleepin' on my couch but my ol' lady don't like it none. She call me a 'no-good muthafucka with punk friends' before I shoved some Dial soap in her mouth and locked her in the closet."

"You did good with this, Floyd," Cruz said, placing his hands behind his back. "You did real good."

"Thanks man. I get that same faggot down on Royal to let us use his old phonograph like before," Floyd said. "Hope it ain't the same as Baker's tracks. Don't want you bein' too excited and shit for nothin'. You know I just grabbed what I seen in the motel, don't make it real. But I sure want to hear this man you love so much sing. Must be somethin' else."

"I appreciate your concern, but we'll be fine; I had a vision when I meditated today," Cruz said as he laced his hands together and slightly bowed. "You remember when I played that tape for you when we drove out to Las Vegas. Mozart made you cry."

"I tole you I had some road trash in my eye."

"Yeah, well this man is one of those blips in music history that changes everything. A true genius."

Cruz stuffed a wad of cash in the front pocket of Floyd's shirt and walked back into the suite's adjoining room. Even though it was still early in the evening, the darkness felt like midnight.

"What's going on?" Kimber asked.

He took off his robe and crawled back into bed. His skinny body coated in black hair.

"A job just got done."

Kimber pushed herself up onto one elbow. The weight of her heavy breasts dropped down and the neon light bathed her body in an intermittent red and blue glow. She looked like a damned perfect statue.

"Baby, I now own the best in the world," Cruz said. "A man who had guitar licks that could break your heart."

"Is he going to play at the club?"

"No, baby," Cruz said, laughing and patting her head as if she were a small child. "He was buried in a pauper's grave, many years ago."

"Oh."

"Like I always said, everything always works out when you have a plan. Come on over to papa and let him give you a little celebration present."

Kimber rolled over on her back.

25

NICK RETURNED TO New Orleans by midnight. The smell of the fetid, salty Mississippi River a homecoming as he passed the sporadic squares of light from Warehouse District windows. He liked New Orleans best late at night, when the city resonated with a nocturnal loneliness.

Maybe he used melancholy the way some use a drug.

Nick remembered rolling back into town late one night several years ago. It was after a long drive from Alabama after his father's funeral. The only sound he'd heard on the two-lane highway back to Louisiana was the prattle of rain on his windshield. He hadn't slept a solid night in days and everything seemed to come at him in a gray tattered fuzz. There was no food in his stomach and his hands trembled when he shifted down moving into the streets of New Orleans.

But when he drove into the football dorm's parking lot, there sat JoJo's 1963 El Dorado. He and Loretta were waiting in the middle of a thunderstorm. A muted radio on and windshield wipers ticking back and forth. JoJo didn't say a word, just got out, grabbed Nick's bag, and motioned him to come on.

They took him for a meal at Felix's Oyster House and didn't prod him with unnecessary conversation. Nick ended up sleeping on the couch of their townhome that night and later spending more and more time down at the bar.

For some reason, JoJo had decided to take Nick on as his harmonica prodigy. He showed Nick how to make those hard, clean licks that touched a single note at the right moment. JoJo taught him to make the harmonica beat and breathe like it was a living animal.

The way he'd learned from his mentor back in Clarksdale, JoJo said he was just passing it back around the loop. He told Nick a harmonica was the instrument that could most closely mirror the way a man felt. He said he could show Nick how to use it. But the rest would be what was inside. The harp was just a tool for bringing the soul out. Nick learned to make a harp laugh and cry. It wasn't about being fancy, JoJo told him. It was about bringing the right emotion out at the right time.

Virginia stirred in her sleep next to him, jarring him back into the night. Somehow with her curled near, he felt more settled and anchored. She was like a stray cat found in a deserted part of town—no way he could've left her. Back in Greenwood, he'd taken her downtown to the spartan room she'd rented and grabbed her canvas duffel bag and guitar case.

She slept during the whole bumpy ride south and didn't wake up until the doors closed in the garage of the red brick warehouse. The motor off, just the clicking sounds of a tired engine. He watched her for a moment, staring at her lips and red hair tucked behind her ear. He noticed the slack jaw, and freckles on a nose a little too wide.

Suddenly she jumped as if startled by a harsh dream and looked wide into his eyes.

"You okay?" Nick asked as he slid out and grabbed both of their well-traveled duffel bags and her guitar.

"Please. Let me sleep," she answered, and closed her eyes.

"C'mon."

Nick trudged up the metal stairs to the second level and flicked on the long row of industrial switches. All three thousand square feet was how he had left it. He threw his keys onto the kitchen counter, turned on the ceiling fans, and went back down where Virginia still slept. He scooped her up and carried her upstairs.

"You're a nice man, Travers," she said, wrapping her arms around his neck. She smelled like honeysuckle in the spring.

As soon as he walked in, she tapped his shoulder to be set down, her mouth agape.

"You could park an airplane in here," she said.

"I'm slightly claustrophobic."

She looked from the open kitchen to the bedroom and from the stamped ceiling to the hardwood floors. "I love it."

"Used to be a hardware storage back in the twenties," Nick said. "Sometimes you can still smell the damp lumber when it rains, but I don't charge much rent."

"I'm sure we can work something out," she said, walking toward him and putting her arms around his neck.

"Bribery with sex. I admire that."

He kissed her.

"I'm sorry I zonked out on you," she said, massaging his neck. "You gonna be alright? Doesn't feel good when people you know die like that. Makes you realize we're one step away from the long, last Cadillac ride."

"Really, I'm fine. You want something to eat?" Nick said, shaking off the comment and walking into the kitchen quadrant of the apartment.

"You cook?"

"I've got Froot Loops and Cap'n Crunch. I'm a connoisseur."

"No Frosted Flakes?"

"I'm trying to quit," Nick said.

They ate in silence before Nick went to the king-size mattress he kept on the floor and changed the sheets. Virginia followed and unknotted the front of her flannel shirt, stripped off the shirt, her bra, jeans, and panties, and fell into bed.

"Pajamas?" Nick asked.

"I'm trying to quit."

AN HOUR LATER, Nick couldn't sleep, so he eased out of bed and pulled on his boxer shorts. He grabbed a pack of cigarettes and a box of kitchen matches and quietly walked upstairs to the roof. There was a light rain like someone flicking damp hands. A warm breeze blew over the few plants, a couple of rusted chairs, and a grill.

Nick felt like he'd failed. Why couldn't he have stayed and watched out for Cracker? He knew someone had tried to kill the old man and that someone had probably killed Baker. And what did he do, but take off with a woman. It was selfish and stupid.

Cracker was dead, Nick knew it. They probably dumped his body in the Yazoo River and it would wash up in few days. Drained of all his stories and histories. But to stick around Greenwood didn't make sense. The dead kid was from New Orleans and he was the only link to what happened to Brown, Cracker, and the second set of records.

To punish himself about not being there when they were killed was to wallow in self-importance. He didn't even have a gun and probably would be dead now too. Just a forgotten shadow in New Orleans. Maybe a plaque or scholarship at Tulane or a good story or two at JoJo's.

He rested his elbows on the cracked brick wall and looked toward the river. He could see the Greater New Orleans Bridge and Algiers Point. A tugboat flashing a tiny red light passed under the bridge towing a barge.

Nick wanted to find whoever killed Willie Brown. They extinguished his life, too easily. Too cheaply. Like it was the Delta of fifty years ago. This wasn't the way it was supposed to work now. It felt like a violation or a blatant kick to the head.

Nick knew all he could do was wait for what the Leflore County Sheriff's Department found out. See if they could find a man who looked like Elvis. He felt ridiculous as he explained it was the young one, pompadour and clean sideburns, not Las Vegas. They'd have to pick up half the truckers in Mississippi.

Nick flicked a long ash over the warehouse edge.

No one would know what was on those records now. Baker had to have known what was on them. Maybe he told someone about the songs and they became so greedy that men died. It had to be something more than just a rare copy of "Terraplane Blues." Maybe they really were new recordings—a huge piece in the ragged puzzle that was Johnson's life.

Maybe Johnson did record in 1938 like Cracker said. Maybe he wasn't a confused old man.

That was an opportunity Nick couldn't miss. Men had spent their entire lives trying to find out when Johnson was born, where he'd learned to play, what kind of man he was. Nick knew about Johnson, listened to his music. But he'd never enveloped himself in the actual search. To most researchers, Johnson's life was a beautiful woman better men had tried to court unsuccessfully.

The answers were as sketchy as the few faded black and whites that existed of the man. The ultimate mystery perpetuated in the haunting music that inspired so many. Nick visualized Johnson's face, smiling in that tightly creased pin-striped suit. *C'mon, Travers. This is what it's all about.*

26

EARLY THE NEXT morning, Jesse Garon hung over a Royal Street wrought-iron balcony above Royal Street. In the eye-squinting light, the grillwork looked to him like the lace off an old woman's garter. He grabbed its rusty bars monkey-style and searched for the King Creole Club. Had to be around here somewhere.

E had turned it into a real big place in the movie. It wouldn't have just gone out of business or somethin', even though that old bastard had tried to fuck it up. 'Cause if there was one thing about Elvis—He always won. E always rose to the top to become whatever He wanted to be: a singer, a race-car driver, a gunfighter, or a goddamned helicopter pilot. E was the shit.

He pushed up his pompadour with pride and walked back into the apartment where Keith had lived. On a mirrored table, he flipped through a stack of photographs of bikini-clad women from a trip to Panama City Beach. He smiled at Keith flexing his muscles with a Miller Lite can in his hand. There were other pictures of Keith, in another stack, with movie stars and a rap singer whose name he didn't know. Jesse stopped flipping when he saw a shot of Puka. Just sittin' there in those same ole bib overalls, a fat wad of Red Man in his cheek. He needed to call that dumb son of a bitch in Mississippi. Tell him 'bout him takin' over Keith's business.

Jesse took out his switchblade and rubbed the steel along his cheek. Felt real nice and cool. Just a simple rough scrape. The knife like a microphone. Killin' his singing. When E was nine, His mama said, "Son, take this guitar, you're not going to get a rifle. Take it and play it." Well, Jesse's mama had given him a switchblade and said, "Go make us some damned money."

He tossed the pictures of Keith into the cardboard box he'd brought. Floyd said to clear out anything personal Keith had before the cops got there, especially anything that said something about the Blues Shack. Told him he'd come by in a few minutes and double-check that he got everything out.

Floyd also said he would meet the big man today—Pascal Cruz. The man sounded real powerful. Maybe Cruz would be his Colonel Parker. The man to recognize his talent and know how to get him exploited. Some people said being exploited was bad, but they were just people no one wanted to exploit. He wanted his face on shot glasses and T-shirts. He wanted people to find the trailer where he grew up and make pilgrimages.

Maybe he'd make enough money to buy that double wide for his mama, a black leather jumpsuit like E wore in the '68 Comeback Special, a classic Trans Am, and a woman to be his Priscilla. That wasn't too much to ask for.

This Cruz dude was his future. At first he wondered about a man who would have such a hard-on for nigra music. But then he thought about it, and realized E did too. Sam Phillips realized E was his man to sound like a nigra. E had taken those old blues songs for his start.

Hell, that was just like Jesse. Runnin' with the blues.

Today, he'd clean away everything that remained of Keith Fields and take his place as Cruz's hit man. Yeah, this was it—the first step of comin' into the sacred loop that E had always promised in the dream.

Jesse looked at his watch and saw he had a little time left. After this, Floyd said he needed his help to get that ole nigra talkin'. Said they'd been screwed again, they didn't get what they needed. Why they didn't just kill that ole man was beyond him. He pulled out a compass, faced due north kneeling, and began to pray to E in the direction of Memphis.

27

"GET YO' ASS in here, boy!" JoJo Jackson said, his voice muffled through the glass of the weathered twin Creole doors. He unlocked a tall door and slowly walked back to the bar. On the shellacked wood lay a copy of the *Picayune*, a cooling café au lait, and a half-eaten croissant.

"They didn't kill you in the Delta?" JoJo said, going back to his paper. He wore a gray sweater over a checked shirt with half glasses pressed against his nose. The gray in the sweater matched the color of his hair.

"They tried," Nick said.

"Hmm."

"You have any more coffee?"

"Yeah, Loretta left coffee and milk on the stove in the kitchen."

Nick walked back and filled a mug with equal amounts of warm milk and chicory coffee. His legs felt shaky from traveling and making love as he returned back to the barstool. He blew on his café au lait and spent the next thirty minutes telling JoJo the whole story.

"Robert Johnson's lost records? Mmm-hmm."

"I think that's why they went to all this trouble to nab Cracker," Nick said.

"Man is black?"

"He's an albino."

"Man is African?"

"Yeah."

"And they call him Cracker?"

"Yeah."

"That ain't right," JoJo said as he slurped his coffee and folded back the Metro page. He slid the paper over so Nick could see the Kate Archer byline on a shooting story.

"I brought a girl back with me," Nick said.

"The redheaded guitar player you tole me about on the phone? Is she any good?"

"She could use a gig."

"That ain't what I asked. I didn't open this bar thirty years ago to get you pussy."

"I was misinformed."

"Bring her in," JoJo said. "You need some pussy."

Nick took a sip of the coffee and asked, "You ever hear of a slide guitarist named Earl Snooks?"

"Earl Snooks. Snooks...yeah," JoJo said, looking away. "Saw him play in a Helena juke back in the late forties."

"Cracker mentioned something about Big Earl not liking people talking about Johnson."

"All those people are older than me. I heard of 'em when I was a kid in Clarksdale but I never talked to 'em. They were kind of like heroes. As far as Robert Johnson, I always thought the man was just a legend like Stagger Lee until I met his stepson. My older brother used to scare the shit out of me, tellin' me the devil was waitin' for me at the crossroads with Robert Johnson.

"One time I was headed home on one of those late afternoons where the sun goin' down looks like a big orange. Anyway, I had to pass the cross-roads at Highway Forty-nine and Sixty-one, where it used to be, and there was this big dead tree without any leaves rustlin' around in the wind. I knew ole Robert was about to jump out and grab my ass...."

The door opened again and JoJo's niece, Keesha, came in popping her gum and waddling as she walked. Her body seemed oddly small, Nick thought, watching her oversize butt. It reminded him of a pack mule's. He thought you could put all kinds of things on that butt: bedrolls, tin pans, mine picks. Nick wondered if she was surefooted.

"Hey y'all," she said with about as much enthusiasm as a dying man asking about tomorrow's weather.

Nick nodded at her. She patted JoJo's back and looked at Nick. No smile. Not a bit of welcome. Maybe she knew about his fascination with her backside resembling a mule's.

When she walked back in the kitchen, Nick leaned close.

"Robert Johnson might have been gone a long time," Nick said. "But three men, maybe four, are dead over those records. I think it's all coming from New Orleans. I don't know yet."

JoJo leaned forward. "Who's dead besides that cop and the kid?"

"Maybe Cracker and Baker."

JoJo slammed down his coffee mug.

"I don't want you foolin' with this mess, no mo'. *You hear me!*"

"Why are you yelling at me all of sudden?"

"*Goddamn it,* Nick, I mean it, this ain't yore business!" JoJo said, his brow furrowing.

Nick laughed, finished his coffee, and stood up.

"I need your help with this one, JoJo. You know a hell of a lot more about the blues scene in the fifties than I do. Of course you have an advantage—I wasn't born yet. All I need is a connection to Snooks."

"I told you, I don't know Snooks."

"You just said you did."

"I'm gettin' old. Now get your ass out of here and leave this mess alone. And think about that ghost story I just tole you. That man has caused a lot of misery."

28

CRACKER'S EYES BURNED somethin' terrible. That hot white light they'd been shinin' in his face made him want to scream. Even when he closed his eyes, the light came through the blood in his eyelids with red-hot intensity. His whole face and body felt red, raw, and irritable. He wanted to find a cool clump of leaves near a tree, where the moss was free to grow, and fall asleep. Wake up when it came natural.

"Wake that old fuck up," a deep, scratchy voice said. It sounded like a white man but when he tried to open his eyelids a little to see who was talking, he had to shut them right away.

"Sir, we want you to go back home real soon," the voice said again. "We'd like you to be comfortable, get a shower and sleep. Hell, we'll even find you a juicy steak and a baked potato. Whatever you want. We just want to know what happened to those records your buddy Robert Johnson recorded. That's it. Very reasonable."

The voice was scratchy and raw from booze and cigarettes but kind of rough and soothing like the ole preacher who left him tin cans of food outside the church. Made him want to sleep.

"Dr. Baker told me you used to work for a

record producer in Texas. Said that man recorded
Robert Johnson before he died and you kept those
records all these years. We know you didn't give
Baker or that deputy the real thing. But I know
what I want, so you can't pass another bad set off.
Understand? Now, we don't want you to be up all
night and that hot ole light must be botherin' you.
What'd you do with those records?"

"You stole my records," Cracker muttered. "I
ain't got nothin' left. You stole 'em, and you kilt
Willie. Damn you sons-a-bitches k-kilt W-Willie."

"Those records weren't worth shit. Most of the
ones you gave Baker were warped like a fried egg.
Almost all the others were a goddamned hillbilly
band, only one blues song."

Cracker could see that fat green moss clinging to
the tree. The shafts of sunlight that cut wildly
through high, leafy branches. The forest, a canopy
over him where he was safe. All that green pro-
tected him from the light and the dirty outside
world. The very thing that killed R.L.

"I can make him say all kinds of shit," a deep
black man's voice said. Sounded like the same man
who found him hiding under the car and tied him
up. Mouth of gold.

Gold mouth found him huddled underneath
that old car in Greenwood. Man took a tree
branch and poked him in the head until he had to
come out. Then a young white boy grabbed him,
tied him, and threw him in the back of a big truck.
They covered him with a plastic sheet and let him
ride on the wet metal for what seemed like days.

"Keep him up," the white man said. "He'll tell
us what we want. If not, tell that new kid to come
in here and keep watching him."

* * *

CRUZ WALKED OUT into the hot August sun from the small brick building near Esplanade where he kept his cars and extra supplies for the Blues Shack. He put on his shades and ran his hands down over his suit to press out the black wrinkles.

"Floyd, this man is old. We don't want him to die. Go get him something to eat and let him sleep a little. He'll come around. But"—Cruz raised a finger—"if he dies without telling us anything, then all this will be worthless."

"Shit, what that ole' fucka want? Chicken or a po'boy?"

"Ask him, Floyd, and give me a call later. I'll be in the office."

"Pascal, between you and me—you bonin' yore secretary, ain't you? That's why you spend all yore time at the club."

"I like to work. That's why I'm successful."

"That ain't no answer," Floyd said. His hair shimmered like a dirty, soaked mop.

"Call me later, Floyd, and tell me where I need to send you next. I don't give a shit if it's damned Tibet."

"Man, I thought one of them records was it, when we started to play that shit, sound like him to me."

"It wasn't Robert Johnson."

"How can you be sure?" Floyd asked, his gold teeth reflecting the sun.

"I just know."

"So we've just bent over twice and taken it in the ass over two collections that ain't worth a squirta piss?...Hey man, you 'memba you wanted to know what was happenin' after Baker showed you them record contracts he found. Them ragged yellow ones from Texas that said this Devlin guy had some studio time with Johnson before he died?"

"Yeah?" Cruz asked, cleaning his sunglasses and slipping them back on.

"Well, I checked out them contracts and they was real. Man I found said he'd have to be a kick-ass forger to fake that paper. You knew that. But I also followed Baker 'round for a few days. Even listen to him bone his old lady from outside his bedroom window. Fine-lookin' white woman with tits like apples. Anyway, I seen him meet a few times in this place called JoJo's down on Conti."

"Yeah, I know the place. Probably be out of business when we start revving up."

"I checked it out. Turns out the old fucker who owns the joint is from the Delta. Real plugged in with that old circuit. Knew all them King Biscuit folks like Sonny Boy and Robert Lockwood."

Cruz stopped and stared at a street painter working. A dying banana-tree leaf touched his cheek. The man's painting was of the same alley where they stood. But there were no cars, no air-brushed signs advertising two-for-one T-shirts, or jumbo cocktails. Only the flagstone sidewalks, the crooked iron balconies above the colonnades, and passing horses. The world is a place of perceptions, he thought.

"Hey?" Floyd said. "See what I'm sayin'?"

29

RANDY SEXTON LIVED in an 1860s shotgun cottage painted a bright yellow with green gingerbread trim, just off the streetcar line in Uptown. On the porch, Randy slumped in an unpainted Adirondack chair as an American flag caught stiffly on the breeze. He sipped on a glass of ice tea. Work gloves lay on the floor beside him.

Randy stood and smiled as if embarrassed by his leisure, then walked down the steps and caught Nick's hand.

It was Saturday morning, but in New Orleans the days of the week rolled by without consequence, Nick thought. Sometimes he felt he lived in the perpetual whirl of a never-ending party.

"Hey man, I'm so sorry," Randy said. "I had no idea about you being in jail until yesterday, and your lawyer told me you were on the way home. Jesus. What happened?"

"Someone killed the old albino man and a sheriff's deputy who was helping me. When I got back to the motel the other night, they thought I was the killer. Man, I'd left them just a few hours before and they were just watching TV, laughing. I should have stayed."

Branches from the hedges littered the stone

walkway to the porch like hair on a barbershop floor. An old plastic radio with a rounded dial was tuned to a classical station playing Dvořák's symphony *From the New World*.

Randy nodded to a chair beside him and took another gulp of tea.

"Would you like some?"

"You have a beer?" Nick asked.

"It's ten in the morni...I'll get the beer."

He returned with a bottle of Dixie. Nick drank it in two gulps. The bottle was cold to the touch and the beer burned the back of his throat.

"Listen, I don't know what to do. This man Cracker had some old records he kept under his porch, said they were old blues recordings from the thirties. He said Baker stole the other half of the records. The ones I saw were all lacquer-coated aluminum. They weren't labeled and we never had them played. Hell, they could have been cows making love. Anyway, they were with Cracker and the deputy, Willie Brown, when I left....Now the sheriff's department people say they can't find anything like them."

"Holy shit," Randy said.

"Yeah man. Holy shit. Brown thought Baker was trying to sell the first set and sent someone back for the rest."

"I don't know, he was too arrogant for that. It's not his style to leave New Orleans in mystery," Randy said. "He'd miss all his waiters and tailors too much. He was a man of routine. You know I could tell you any day of the week what was in Baker's pockets? I could."

"Holes?"

"No, a pack of Doublemint, a money clip, keys,

a handkerchief, and a rusted dime with a hole through it."

"I won't ask," Nick said. "You ever heard anything about Robert Johnson having another recording session? That other tracks exist?"

"Never. You would know more about that than me, man. Is that what you think those records were? Lost recordings?"

"I don't know. Maybe it's just something I'd like to believe. Would be a hell of a reason to kill somebody, maybe the greatest find of this century. Poor Willie Brown, he was a good guy. Kinda reminded me of Jay Medeaux. Listen, I've got an idea of something we can do besides sitting on our hands and recounting the contents of Michael's pockets."

"What?"

"Do you trust me?"

"Yeah."

"That I'd never do anything to embarrass the department?"

"Yeah."

"Let me use your phone. I need to make a few calls."

30

DETECTIVE JAY MEDEAUX arrived red-faced and sweating at the Riverwalk. His tousled mop of blond hair above his boyish face a contradiction to the button-down shirt and candy-striped tie. A beeper hung beneath his big belly, and a Beretta 9mm on his hip.

"The monkey is in the tree," Jay said.

"Watch out for falling coconuts," Nick responded.

Jay sat down and pulled out faxed info and handed him the flimsy pages. Nick knew Jay from his sophomore year at Tulane, where they'd roomed together and shared a common interest in beer and a hatred of authority. Sometimes late at night, after several beverages at JoJo's, they'd call their position coaches pretending to be sportswriters for the *Picayune*, wanting to know about their last bowel movement or the effectiveness of the "thigh master" on college athletes.

Jay never finished college. He left Tulane shortly after his knee turned into a knotted pulp that resembled a rotten grapefruit. It wasn't long before he enrolled in the academy to fulfill his lifelong dream of becoming a cop. He always loved those Eastwood movies.

"There you go, kid's name, date of birth, previous arrest record, and his address in New Orleans," Jay said.

"You're all right, brother."

"Where's my sandwich, *brother?*"

"Easy there, big fella, don't bite my hand," Nick said.

"Well, get that shit out of the way."

He handed Jay a wax-paper-wrapped muffuletta from Central Grocery and a pack of Zapp's chips. The sandwich was stacked with salami, ham, provolone, and olive relish on special Italian bread. Damned good.

"So, what's this all about?" Jay asked.

"I don't know if you want to know."

"I bet I do since I'm risking my ass."

"Risking your ass, that's a little extreme. You remember a colleague of mine, Michael Baker? No? Well, he disappeared while working on a project in Mississippi. When I went looking for him, one of his sources was kidnapped or killed or something while I was there. This kid you checked out for me was the one found dead at the scene with a sheriff's deputy."

Jay stared out at a tourist paddle wheeler playing calliope music and pigeons walking over an indigent girl passed out beside a fountain. Her hair was the color of cotton candy.

"The deputy, Willie Brown, played football at LSU. Ever hear of him?"

"Can't say I have," Jay said. "But of course, football players either study law enforcement or early childhood development."

"Or history?"

"Yeah, sorry Nick. Some of the guys were intellectuals or harmonica players. Heard you were in the pokey. Make any pen pals?"

"How come every time you talk about jail, you have to throw in homosexuality? I'm sure lots of guys leave jail untouched."

"Like I said, make any pen pals?"

Nick opened his sandwich and a bag of chips. As he ate, the oil added fine thumbprints to the papers. He read back through, folded the sheets, and tucked them into his jeans.

"Kid has an address in the French Quarter," Nick said as he scrunched up the sandwich's wax paper. "Why would anyone leave him at the scene?"

"I'd say they didn't have time to grab the body. Probably got scared and hauled ass. Or thought it'd look like he was the shooter."

"I'd like to see his place."

"I'm sure their sheriff's department would want us to check out his pad out. It'd would be real cooperative if the NOPD helped."

"You want an impartial observer?"

"Know any good ones?"

KEITH FIELDS HAD lived in a one-bedroom apartment on the second story of an antique shop that specialized in tin soldiers. The door to the stairwell off Royal Street was unlocked, and they walked up the creaking steps to the unit. The halls smelled like dust and mildew with dark water stains splotched through the white paint. At the top of the stairs, Jay knocked on the door.

No answer.

Jay knocked again and tried the doorknob.

"We really should try to notify any friends and family of the deceased, especially since they might be in danger," Jay said, jamming a tool that looked like a carrot peeler into the lock.

Jay pushed open the door and Nick walked ahead into the apartment. The place was neat: white leather couch, big-screen television, a mirrored coffee table with a stack of *Penthouse* magazines arranged in a fan. In a corner, toward two French doors, Fields had a cheap weight set with several pictures of bodybuilders stapled in a collage on the wall.

"I'll start with the bedroom," Nick said.

Nick pulled out each drawer from a chest and looked not only inside but behind. He went through the dead kid's clothes: T-shirts, red satin underwear, a few pairs of blue jeans, and several pairs of dark black pants.

There was a bedside table but inside drawers were empty. Nick looked under the bed and mattresses and found a few more *Penthouse* magazines, a pack of condoms, and a Polaroid picture of a girl covered in Mardi Gras beads flashing her breasts. There was a golden cross hung on the wall and a Bible on the bedside table.

In the closet, clothes hung neatly on hangers. More black pants and several empty slots. On a shelf above the hanging clothes were two rolled posters of Budweiser girls, a movie poster for a gangster film, a Smith & Wesson still in the carton, and an empty shoe box.

Nick reached down and slipped his hand into the assorted acrid-smelling shoes and found nothing. He reached into coat and pants pockets. Nothing.

"How you doing?" he called to Jay.

"Kid liked beer. Couldn't have been too bad. Seemed to like to bet on sports, not much else. Kept some pot in here. Usual shit. How 'bout you?"

"Either this kid throws away anything personal or we got beat," Nick said.

"Have you found a checkbook or canceled pay stubs? Maybe he had another job."

"I don't think this guy clocked in and out. Can we get a photo of him?"

"He was arrested in Mississippi a few years ago," Jay said. I could have his mug shots sent here."

"That'd be great. Maybe you could call the landlord too."

"Maybe you could kiss my ass," Jay said. "This isn't my biggest priority, ya know? Right now I'm assigned to the rape and murder of an Uptown socialite. Your old friend Kate Archer has been busting the department's ass every day for the last week."

"Please."

"You still hate hearing her name, don't you?"

"Doesn't bother me a bit. I've found someone new," Nick said as he reached deep into a pant pocket. He found a plastic card with a driver's-license-size picture. It was a security ID badge for a local club.

31

SINCE IT OPENED in New Orleans two years ago, Nick had done his best to stay away from the Blues Shack. He had no hatred for it. Or made any kind of high-seated assumption that it bastardized the pureness of blues. He knew the place was all about money. All the public relations bullshit couldn't fix that. The Blues Shack was nothing more than a watered-down version of the real thing for tourists—the putt-putt golf of the blues world.

Fake weathered clapboards and strategically placed rusted road signs on the wall.

As Nick walked through the purposefully crude drawings and tin-shingled doors listening to the tinkling keys of Professor Longhair, he knew he was in Disneyland. Safe, kind, and packaged for mass consumption.

A perky blonde with a bobbed haircut and large breasts smiled at Nick as he walked through the door. An African-style dress hung off her curved frame. She asked if he wanted to sit in the Blues Hall of Fame Room or at the bar. Nick said neither, he wanted to talk to the owner.

She laughed.

"Are you trying to get a bartending job?"

"Far as you know."

"Scuse me?"

"I'm an old friend of his," Nick said. "We shared the same prison shower. He handed me the soap."

Her mouth turned crooked as she cradled a phone between her ear and shoulder. "Is Mr. Cruz in?"

Nick blew his breath out his cheeks and waited. He looked up at the high video monitors playing several historic blues performances. Below, a teenage T-shirt-wearing tourist nodded and laughed at the music being played over him. He had on a pair of sunglasses and mimicked being blind.

It was like watching someone taking a dump in church.

Nick shook his head before the hostess pointed him to a tall, winding wooden staircase to the second floor. The rail was carved to look like a snake and the scales felt smooth underneath his hand.

"Mr. Cruz's executive assistant will wait for you upstairs," she said.

At the landing stood a beefy white guy with a buzz-cut head and thick biceps who wore a radio on his hip. *Executive assistant?* The guy had his hands tucked underneath his armpits and blew a pink bubble out of his mouth. He steered Nick to the twin padded doors, spoke into his lapel, and left.

The doors parted as if in a corny biblical epic.

"YOU'RE A FRIEND of Mr. Cruz's?" a beautiful Amerasian woman asked Nick. She wore a light, flowered sundress and no bra. Must be casual day.

A fattened Buddha statue sat in the hall behind the woman. The rest of the furnishings were a mixture of Scandinavian and Oriental: big black leather couches, chrome racks, curvy floor lamps with tassled rugs, long, rounded pillows, and ceramic elephants.

"Actually, no. I wanted to ask him a few questions about an employee, Keith Fields."

"So who are you?"

"That's a very spiritual question I'm constantly asked. Perhaps a question for Buddha?"

She frowned and stared at the white pages of a leather day planner sitting on top of a glass desk. On her right forearm were four small bruises like an inked handprint.

"Is Mr. Cruz in?"

"He's in a meeting right now," she said.

Nick sank into the black leather couch and lit a cigarette.

"Sir, we don't allow smoking here."

"I'm sorry," Nick said, blowing out a stream of smoke. It was obnoxious, rude, and intentional.

"Sir, I'm going to have to call security."

"Tell him it'll take five minutes."

From a door down the hall Nick heard a rattle and a bourbony laugh. He then saw a short, dumpy man with dyed black hair laugh back weakly as he was followed out by a taller man in an all black suit and sunglasses. The taller man looked over at Nick and put a hand on the other guy's shoulder. He resembled a skeleton with a gaunt face and thin, bony fingers. The black pointed beard jutted from his chin like a dagger.

Nick recognized the shorter guy as a city councilman. The man in black walked the councilman out with his hand on his shoulder the whole way. It looked like he was actually massaging the guy's neck. *Whatever it takes.* Nick stood up, his ciga-

rette dangling loosely in his mouth as if he were
Mississippi Fred McDowell.

The man turned and stared at Nick. "You know
if you did that in L.A. they'd put you under the
jail?"

"I'll have to make a note to myself never to go
to L.A.," Nick said.

"Mr. Cruz, do you want me to call security?"
the secretary asked.

Cruz shook off the question and said, "What
can I help you with, sir?"

"I need five minutes to talk to you about an
employee of yours that was killed in Mississippi."

"Can you show me some identification?"

"You'll have to excuse my driver's license picture, damned guy took it as I blinked."

"You're not with the police?"

"I'm private."

"I see." Cruz snapped his fingers and pointed to
his office with the same hand. "Five minutes."

Nick snapped back. "Got ya, buddy."

Cruz sat at his desk with a picture wall behind
him of quasi-famous people. It was as if they
would somehow support everything this clown
said. Cruz kept on his sunglasses.

"Keith Fields worked for you?"

Cruz shrugged. "We have so many jobs here
Mr. . . . ."

"Travers."

"Mr. Travers. I wish I could, but I just don't
know every person here."

"Who would?"

"Why?"

"I'd like to talk to them."

Cruz took a swig of something in his coffee cup
and turned his head toward a window. Outside it

was dark, and tiny white Christmas lights were strung through an old alley. The crumpled building next door was vacant and Nick could see rotted, empty rooms through the broken glass.

"Mr. Travers, I know you. You're the resident blues historian at Tulane. Right?"

"Yes."

"Oh, I understand, you think what I have here is sacrilege," Cruz said, and shook his head. "You're a blues purist who thinks a California record producer has no business making money off this region's music."

"That's not why I'm here."

"But you don't like it?"

"I really couldn't care less."

"I've lived a long time in Los Angeles but I'm a southerner, grew up in Memphis," Cruz continued. "The Blues Shack is a project that I've wanted to start for a long time. It scares me that if I don't do something to save this music, no one will."

Nick lit another cigarette.

"I'm sorry, but would you please not smoke?"

Nick extinguished the end and slid it back in the pack.

"Black kids in the South don't listen to blues anymore, they listen to L.A. rap or soul—you and I are the last dying breath. The Blues Shack and I know," Cruz held up his hands. "I know you don't like the concept of all the T-shirts and bumper stickers the tourists have...but we have educational programs, and soon we'll have charitable programs for broke blues artists. This isn't a bad thing."

"Did you know Keith Fields?" Nick asked.

Cruz picked up his phone. "Kimber, bring me an employee file on a Keith Fields and a bottle of Beam.

"Are you a drinkin' man, Dr. Travers?"

"I've been known to."

"I think we got off on the wrong foot. Pascal Cruz," he said, extending his hand.

Nick took it. It was wet and didn't let go quickly. Nick didn't know why but he felt an impulse to wipe his hand on his pant leg.

"Didn't you know Keith Fields was shot in the head earlier this week. It happened at the murder scene of a Greenwood, Mississippi, deputy?"

"I had no idea," Cruz said. "I really don't know who he was."

"I'd like to talk to anybody who knew Keith," Nick said.

"Whatever you need."

The door opened and the secretary brought in a file and a gallon jug of Jim Beam. Cruz handed Nick the file, got up, dropped two chunks of ice into a crystal glass, and poured a thick measure of whiskey.

Two hours later, Nick left with a thick head and several useless interviews with employees who barely knew Fields. As he stepped into the Quarter's rugged reality, Nick mused it was like the kid had never existed.

32

JESSE AND FLOYD burst into the old nigra's blues joint off Conti about five o'clock. In the French Quarter, a cold rain hit the hot streets, making steam come off the asphalt like dry ice. The water beaded on Floyd's greasy head and onto a red satin baseball jacket that read GOD FIRST.

No one was inside the old bar except two gray-headed nigras. One carried an armload of colored bottles and the other one leaned over a drink. A ratty houndstooth hat on his head. Jesse didn't like the way they didn't stare at him. He liked people to stare and take notice of his presence. People said when E walked into the room, it buzzed with electricity.

"Which one of you ole fools is JoJo?" Floyd asked.

"Depends on the fool who is addressin' me," the man with the bottles said as he sat them on the bar.

"Don't get tough, ole man," Jesse said, really looking to make his mark. Not let Floyd dominate the show.

"We're closed," the man called JoJo said. His brown eyes hard and flat. The back door was open and Jesse could see a wide concrete loading dock. If Floyd took 'em out, that'd be the way to go.

"Yore do' is open and this man is drinkin'. He ain't a customer?" Floyd asked.

"He's a friend."

The old man in the patched corduroy jacket continued to stare at his drink. Must've been almost ninety, the way he just sat there like he was some kinda bug.

"Hey ole man," Floyd said, handing the seated man his cane. "Why don't you get yo' self outside for a swim. This ain't no show and we is closed."

"Henry, stay where you are," JoJo said.

The old man remained under a faded black-and-white picture of a young black man pickin' a guitar. Floyd took off his jacket and walked behind the bar and grabbed a bottle of Jack Daniel's. He poured a shot, drank it, and licked the inside of the glass.

"Ole man, yo' woman's pussy taste like that? Real fine like whiskey? Bet she's old and dry as cracked leather."

"Listen, you greasy-haired nigger," JoJo said. "You get your trashy ass out of my bar before I shoot you in the goddamned head."

Floyd quickly reached behind his back and pulled out a Glock. He pressed it against JoJo's flat nose. JoJo didn't blink though, had balls like he wasn't scared of Floyd.

"That wouldn't be too smart," Floyd said. "I guess yore woman do have a pussy like cracked leather."

"Nigger, you can't base yore life on what you learn from your mama," JoJo said.

Floyd cracked the butt of the gun against JoJo's nose. Blood spilled on the man's sweater and he fell to a knee with both hands on his face.

"You know a man name Cracker?" Jesse asked,

once again feeling lost. He needed to do something so Floyd would tell Mr. Cruz about his skills.

JoJo shook his head.

"My friend ask a question," Floyd said. "You know a man name Cracker from way back in Clarksdale. I bet you do and I bet you know about the ole man's record collection. Nice one. Bet you know where it at."

JoJo stood. "We ain't got no crack. Now get out. We've got a lot of police that come in here about now. I know they'd love to take you for a ride. Some of 'em even call me Pops."

"Well, Pops, I know 'bout you and them days with those King Biscuit folks," Floyd said. "Some of them knew Robert Johnson. And I know what you tole that black teacher from Tulane about all that shit. I just want those records. You see? That's it. All we need."

"That's way before my time," JoJo said.

The old man seated at the bar scooted back his barstool and whacked Floyd in his head with his cane. His gray eyes surrounded by blood-red whites.

Floyd grabbed it away from him and tossed it behind the bar as this big white dude passed by the window. He knocked on the glass covered in paper ads for shows. Shit, Jesse thought, it was that dude from the Delta, the one that chased his ass through the woods.

Jesse nodded Floyd to the loading dock. Floyd winked back, like he respected Jesse thinkin' ahead.

"JoJo, don't you say shit," Floyd said. "But I'll tell you what. You want to keep this property? Not have it bulldozed like a weak house of mutha-fuckin' cards? You better put yore memory in overdrive. Think about the Delta and all them country folks. Or else I'll be back, with this property paid for, and turn it into a mothafuckin' parking lot."

33

VIRGINIA DARE TUNED her guitar in a white bra and faded blue jeans. Her hair was still wet from a shower as she ran her fingers over her guitar's neck and turned its keys. The tiny hairs on her arms were golden and her stomach was as flat as a porcelain plate.

She dropped her jaw and pursed her lips when Nick slid back the warehouse door. "Hey, I hope you don't mind....I took a shower and cleaned up the kitchen," she said. "Did you realize you had a jar of preserves that had turned to sugar?"

"I didn't know I had a jar of preserves."

Nick sat down next to her. She smelled wonderful. He wanted to take the guitar out of her lap, open the tops of the industrial windows, turn out the lights, and make love to her on the hardwood floors until his knees ached.

"Where you been?"

"Running some errands," Nick said. "Saw JoJo for a while, but he was acting weird so I left. Sometimes he's funny when he's getting ready to open. I don't know, he said he bumped his nose fixing a pipe. His face was swollen and he was grumpy... Before that, I was down at the Blues Shack."

"I would've thought you hated that place."

"I thought it in my best interest to meet the owner. I'm sure he knows a lot."

She put her guitar down and leaned her head back to rest in Nick's lap. He could feel her damp hair against his bare arm. He traced a finger over her right eyebrow and caressed her face with his hand. She had nice dimples, ridges like canyons.

"I'm glad I didn't leave you in that jail cell," she said.

"Although, I was beginning to make friends and get some reading done."

On the coffee table, two of his harmonicas sat out of their cases. Nick carefully leaned forward, not to disturb her, and put the C back in the case.

"I was just playing a little," she said. "You don't mind, do you? It helps me tune."

"No. I guess I'm just not used to anyone being around."

Virginia stretched and put both hands up through Nick's hair. "You sure got a lot of gray in there."

"Someone once told me I was an old Holden Caulfield."

"Who's that?"

"*The Catcher in the Rye.*"

"No, who told you that?"

"A mean woman who left me for an Uptown restaurant owner."

"Is that why you're so quiet? Not telling me anything about you or asking any questions about me? We just make love and eat."

Nick traced his fingers over a few little freckles on her tight stomach. When she breathed in deeply, her ribs showed under the bra. He leaned over to kiss her.

"Sometimes talking spoils it. Besides, I know you. I know you're good. I can feel it."

"Why'd she leave you?"

"She kinda wanted me to get behind the mule. Wanted a little responsibility. A little commitment."

"She wanted to get married."

"Yeah."

"That was it?"

"That and when she decided to come back she found another woman wearing her robe and drinking out of her coffee mug. She just stared at me for a moment and slid that door back. That was it."

"I can promise you one thing, Travers, that's not what I'm looking for."

She kissed him with an open mouth that tasted sweet, like watermelon candy. Nick put his hands under her loose-fitting bra. She moaned softly and kissed him harder. With one eye open, he looked down at his harmonicas littering the table; then he closed his eye.

She tasted too sweet.

NICK RAN THE shower scalding hot and then cold as needles before he roughly toweled off and changed into a clean pair of jeans, a white button down shirt, and buckskin boots. Virginia followed his shower and changed into a form-fitted ribbed T-shirt, black leather pants, and black lizard boots with scuffed toes.

She was excited about going into the Quarter. The last time she'd been was back when she was a kid. So instead of a cab, he took her down Julia to St. Charles and caught a streetcar to Canal. They walked the rest of the way to the Blues Shack.

The neon signs and gas lamps burned in the night sky as if they were a dull flame on a gas stove. A purple dome shone over their heads and there was a strong smell of stale beer, cooked onions, and garbage.

When they reached the bar, a line had formed all the way out the alley entrance and around a brick wall. Nick grabbed Virginia's hand and they walked to the head of the line. A security guard Nick had met earlier nodded them in, and he felt like a cheesy Los Angeles player.

"You really think it's good that we don't know a damned thing about each other?" Virginia asked in the Blues Hall of Fame Room. The video monitors flickered a Muddy Waters concert from the sixties. Waters jammed a little "Hoochie Coochie Man."

"Yeah I do. No jealousies. No pasts. Just feelings. We like each other and leave it that."

"You're all right, Travers. I guess when you know everything there is to know about a person, that mystery and passion leaves your life."

"I agree. So, are you a mystery woman?"

"Maybe. What's in étouffée?"

"Crawfish or shrimp, rice, onions, and peppers. Where were you born?"

"Virginia."

"Makes sense," Nick said. "Your parents alive?"

"You couldn't handle it, could you. My stepfather is. He's a six-foot-five Cherokee Indian named Tom Eagle."

"You keep in touch with him?"

"I saw him a few years ago. He emcees Native American demonstrations for state fairs and things like that. Has a wide pockmarked face that looks like a comical drawing of a moon."

"Is he a good guy?"

"Alright. Alright. This is how it is with me...I gave up that trailer on an Indian reservation a long time ago and have been busting my ass around the bar circuit for almost ten years. I've got thick calluses on my fingers and know how to kick a man right in the balls."

"Have you been dating anybody?"

She threw her head back and laughed.

"I don't date."

"What do you do?" Nick asked.

"When I'm hungry I eat. When I'm depressed I drink. If I feel the need, I make love. When I met you at the Purple Heart, I had the need."

"So I'm a need?"

"Sort of."

Nick looked back down at his menu. He felt his stomach tighten and his head pound. Should have stayed on the original path. He didn't like where this was headed.

"I'm just strange, Nick. You're being too good to me. I'm not used to it. I usually like men who don't treat me well. If you don't love me and treat me like shit, usually I'll hound you. That's just my nature."

"Hmm, who are you? Carmen?"

"C'mon, let's forget this and enjoy tonight. I'm with you now and that's all that matters. We'll eat fatty food, play the blues, get drunk, go home and fuck madly. What could be better? Let's not get ahead of ourselves."

"I guess you don't like greeting cards, long walks in the park, or puppet shows."

Virginia leaned over, the candlelight shining in her sky blue eyes, and squeezed his hand. "I like you Nick...let's just let that be enough."

He liked her mouth, painted the color of Chianti wine, and the way she could twist her jaw slightly to the side. Maybe he'd let the rest slide. He drained half of his Dixie and lit a cigarette.

The conversation swayed, after he ordered Tabasco chicken for him and crawfish étouffée for her, toward blues technique, the difference between Cajuns and Creoles, and Steve McQueen movies. He pounded down four more Dixies and she had a couple.

"Does what happened in Greenwood not bother you? You just block it out of your mind like a dark nightmare?" Virginia asked.

"Something like that," Nick said low as Cruz walked into the room.

His long hair was slicked back and he smiled a toothy grin after seeing Nick. The two flanking bodyguards left and he sat down. He readjusted his black sunglasses, a snake-headed cane in his right hand. Nick wanted to ask him if was going to do a soft-shoe but thought that might piss him off.

"I sure am glad you came. See, it ain't so bad," Cruz said. "I'll tell you what, boy, you sure have some great-lookin' company."

"Mr. Cruz, this is Virginia Dare."

Cruz smiled at her like a dog getting his hind leg scratched. The insides of his nostrils were raw and a bit of ash was stuck in his beard. His breath smelled like an old ashtray—cancerous and dead.

"I hope my waitress told you, whatever you want is on me."

"That's not necessary," Nick said. "Your cook makes a mean peppered chicken."

"Please be my guest," he said, swiping the bill. "I'm just glad you came. It's good to have a purist's approval. Maybe we can sway some of your colleagues that way."

"Yeah, my friend Michael Baker would probably love to meet you."

Cruz turned his head from glaring at Virginia and nodded. "And I him...I did find out about that boy Keith Fields. Seems like we had a bad apple mixed in. We really should do criminal checks on everyone. Boy had committed some serious crimes. I guess I'm too trusting."

"Who's the band tonight?" Virginia asked, coming back into the conversation.

"They have a hip-hop sound mixed with ska and Arabic music. Pretty progressive."

Virginia coughed intentionally and cocked an eyebrow.

"Sometimes you have to bring in what packs the house, so we can get the acts like you would want to see. Unfortunately, there aren't enough people like us. Blues people."

"I thought this was the *Blues* Shack?" Virginia asked.

Nick squeezed her hand.

"Well. I hope you two enjoy the night. Come back anytime," Cruz said. His face formed a smile like a waxen figure.

"Thanks," Nick said as Cruz left.

"That's one slick son of a bitch."

"Ya think?" he asked as he scooted back his chair and laughed until his eyes watered.

34

THE CALL CAME a few hours later.

"This Nick Travers?" asked a hoarse voice that sounded like it came from an old black man. He could hear chattering voices and music in the background as if the phone was in a bar or restaurant.

"Yeah."

"Earl Snooks. Heard you was lookin' for me."

"I don't mean to be rude...but I thought you were dead."

"No one's let me know if I am."

Nick had forgotten about Snooks. Forgot he'd asked JoJo to put the word out on the bar circuit telegraph. He grabbed his watch off the floor and stared at the luminescent dial reading two A.M. Virginia slept naked next to him and he could feel her warm chest rising and falling. Light traffic sounds floated through the warehouse windows on warm summer breezes.

"You want to meet?" the voice asked.

"When?"

"How about now?"

"It's two in the morning," Nick said.

"I'm gonna be in Detroit tomorrow. You the one lookin' for me. Want to know where I'm at?"

"Where are you?"

* * *

ALGIERS WAS NOT the finest place to be early in the
A.M. The pictures of Bosnia Nick had seen while in
jail showed more promise. He drove his Jeep over
the rusting Erector set that was the Greater New
Orleans Bridge as the lights of New Orleans faded
into the blackness of a forgotten city.

Algiers was once a slave port and a refuge for
pirates. Most of the old town burned before the
turn of the century, its apparent age a result of
humidity and neglect. But it was still a world of
smuggling and crime. A dark sister to a corrupt
city.

Nick followed Patterson Road along the Mississippi. To his left sat boarded-up homes and busi-
nesses, their wood rotting and the windows
broken. Derelicts roamed the streets like zombies
as he turned on Verret down to Opelousas Avenue,
passing shotgun cottages painted all the colors of a
Life Savers candy roll.

A faded newspaper blew in front of his car on
River Street and he swerved, thinking it was an animal. He squinted into the darkness, searching for
the part of the levee the voice had told him about.
Anyone could hop in, shoot him, and dump his
body. A disposable world, he thought, driving slow.

There was some comfort underneath his seat, in
the form of a loaded Browning 9mm. Nick hated
guns, but as a tracker it was a necessary precaution. Some might call it callous or even racist to
have fear in poor neighborhoods. But hunger and
meanness weren't a racial problem, they were
damned economic. Besides, he doubted the call
had really come from Snooks. Man was probably
dead. But this was the first tangible lead he'd had
since returning to Louisiana. He had to come.

River Street turned into Brooklyn with the lights of New Orleans over the river, a blurred glow. A few blocks away he could hear the thumping music in a Jamaican nightclub, the drumming sound of cars over the bridge, and brown water churning around a tugboat. He stopped and looked for the house. Nick drove the strip twice before he realized the numbers jumped with only a vacant lot in the middle.

Someone was playing with him.

He looked back at the two shotgun homes on either side of the vacant lot and spit out the window. About thirty yards away lay the rusting gears that hauled people over the river during the World's Fair. Like most things in New Orleans, they were left to disintegrate.

Nick heard a car approach and the square headlights of a van shone into his eyes. It was headed in the wrong direction, right for him. *Idiot.* Nick punched in the clutch and shifted into first. He wanted to get back to Virginia tucked warmly in his flannel sheets. The van kept coming. He let out the clutch and tried to move out of the way, but the van must have been going about forty. He could see a heavy cage built on over the front grille as he took a hard swerve. The van rammed the passenger side of the hood. It was a teeth-rattling, bone-jarring hit that froze Nick's hands on the steering wheel. All he could do was hold on as his Jeep flipped on its side. He felt his shoulder and arm hit hard against rough loose asphalt. A hand and shoulder went numb, trapped between the door and the ground.

Blood boiled in his ears and a pain shot through his arm. He lay there for what seemed like minutes, unable to get up. His body wouldn't respond.

His head pounded and took long swimming strokes. He wanted to close his eyes but he knew they'd be coming for him. Like a snared animal, he used his uninjured hand to try to pull his arm free.

The van idled nearby, its heavy front grille unscathed. Its motor still chugged and headlights burned into the back of his skull. Nick heard a door slam and the crunch of shoes on the gravel-filled road. Two pairs of shoes. French accents. Rough and guttural.

With a soft grunt, Nick pulled his arm free and reached under the seat for the Browning, which had slipped up under the brake. He grabbed it and sighed when he felt the cool trigger underneath his index finger. The men were Haitians. Their coal black Caribbean faces expressionless as they approached. Nick hung sideways, still trapped in his seat belt. He could hear the rolling thick tongues and smell their sharp unwashed bodies.

One leaned down and twisted his head in observation. The other nodded and yelled across the street, "C'mon!" The men went silent as the headlights continued to burn into his eyes. Soon Nick heard another crunch on the gravel and could barely make out the shoes, old-time brogans.

Nick turned his head in pain again and looked up into the face of a gray-headed black man wearing overalls. Must've been in his eighties and wore a corduroy jacket lined with patches like scars. The man stared at him with hard gray eyes and poked at him with a cane.

A face so familiar. So distant. He waited to pull the gun and shoot the man. But Nick knew him from somewhere. He couldn't speak or think. *What about Robert Johnson? What happened to him?*

"Dat 'im?" one of the Haitians asked. His teeth

the color of piss-stained wood. His breath hard and alcoholic, filled with rum. The old man grunted and handed him a couple bills. The Haitians were a couple of cheap hit men. Nick knew of rumors about ex–Tontons Macoutes in Algiers who would shoot their own mother for a quarter.

"Son, this is none of your affair," the old man whispered to Nick as the Haitians got into their van and spun out. "Leave this bidness alone and everythin' will be jes' fine....Remember, Earl Snooks is dead."

The old man straightened up and hobbled back across the street. He climbed into a 1950s pickup truck and drove away with a loose muffler puttering like a machine gun. Nick's arm tingled with numbness. He lay there for a moment just breathing, then unlatched himself from his seat belt and plopped onto the hard concrete. As he slowly got to his knees, Nick reached for the gun and slid it back into his coat.

His old Jeep sat there in the middle of the Algiers street like roadkill. He should have shot those bastards. One half of the Jeep's front end was smashed in like an accordion. Antifreeze leaked like blood onto the dirty road.

Early this mornin'
when you knocked upon my door.
And I said, "Hello, Satan,
I believe it's time to go."

35

JESSE GARON WAITED by the curb of the bus station drawing curvy little patterns with a stick into the gutter grit. It was barely light and he was as tired as a twenty-four-hour whore, but she had said she would come. That little German piece from Memphis was staying in the Biloxi hotel where she said she'd be. She was the one he'd been thinkin' about, the special woman to be his Priscilla. He'd tried to get her out of his mind and get his mind on his killin' career.

But she stuck there with those long legs that could hold him as tight as a boa constrictor.

Maybe he could take some time out from work. He knew Mr. Cruz was pleased with his performance in the Delta. It was like the damned '68 Comeback Special, people all talkin' about his skills. Even Floyd knew he could kick some ass inside that stupid, greasy head of his.

Finally, she stepped off the bus and that buzzin' in his pants started again. Half expected he could break wood with the son-of-a-bitch. There was a good twelve-inch flash of muscular white thigh between her knee-high white go-go boots and a plaid miniskirt. Her blue velvet shirt was wide open at the collar and he could see a white, lacy bra underneath.

I'm just a red-blooded boy and can't stop thinkin' about girls, girls, girls. Help me E. Help me.

Her dark hair was combed straight back. She did a model turn with a little curtsy as she stepped off the Greyhound splattered with dead lovebugs.

"You miss me, no?"

"Hell, I miss you *yes*," Jesse said.

She jumped onto him and wrapped her arms around his neck and her legs behind his back. The tight leather of her boots squeaked as they rubbed together. He fingered the dimple in her chin and just looked at her. She crushed that fat lower lip and stared back.

The bus station was gray and empty. A big, cold cinder-block shed. Just two elderly black women sitting on their luggage. Jesse put his arm around the girl and led her into the men's bathroom. Millions of dust particles caught in a thick slab of sunlight cutting through high windows.

His breath came hard through his nose. The smell of the urinals and the sweet smell of her perfume mixed. His head felt hot and light as he ran his nose down through her chest, chewing at the front latch of her bra. She bit down on his ear now, playful and a little harder, and said things in German to him. They sounded nasty.

A toilet flushed in a stall down the row of paint-peeling dented doors.

He rushed her inside and slammed her back against the cold concrete-block wall. One hand around her waist, the other felt the etched wall's graffiti like a blind man.

Want to be my bitch?

She kicked the door closed behind them.

His eyes shut as he unlatched the front of her bra and put his mouth to her breasts. His hand slid down her flank and found a smooth bare leg and slowly moved upward as she sighed. The lace of her panties felt like hospital gauze under his hands.

"Jesse, before you nail that young girl to the post, there's a little matter we need to discuss," said Puka, who had come to him like a disgruntled Vernon out of the mist.

"SORRY I'M LATE, had a little business to tend to," Jesse said as he dabbed a fork into the last mouthful of eggs Benedict at the Blues Shack Sunday gospel brunch. A choir on the stage below belted out hymns honoring Jesus. "That albino just wanted to sleep. Never had to beat him a bit. That lack of sleep really works, kept on mumblin' 'bout a man name Big Earl. Earl Snooks."

"Snooks? Never heard of him," Mr. Cruz said. His long black hair and beard shone like a raven. Almost blue. "He says this man knows about the real records?"

"He said Snooks told him to guard 'em forever. I think Snooks probably fooled that crazy ole man and took 'em himself."

"When was that?"

"I don't know, sometime in the olden days before E was around."

Cruz leaned over the upper railing and watched the show below. He lit a menthol cigarette. "Kid, I got about a half dozen blues experts who helped me put this place together. Pay them out my ass. They'll find out about this Snooks guy."

"What do we do with the ole man?" Jesse asked, sopping up the rest of the yellow sauce with a roll.

"I don't give a shit. Looks like we're one notch up the fuckin' ladder," Cruz said, laughing smoke out his nose. "You know I got a goddamned empire built here. My own record label, own restaurant. One of the biggest attractions in the French Quarter. All I learned how to do was market a natural commodity. Like corn and cotton. Same damned thing, all in the marketing. Make those yuppie tourists feel safe in a well-lighted area, get a cool logo, have a few bands playing. They go home thinking they had a real cool experience. Sure they were down with the brothers. Why do you think that is, Jesse? Southern guilt? Wanting to be accepted?"

Jesse shrugged.

Hell, he didn't even know what Cruz was talking about, and Jesse didn't care. He just kept thinking about the plan Puka had. Said he shouldn't be payin' no respect to the man who got Keith killed. Wanted to know all about them damned records. Jesse was so sick about people talkin' about that man Robert Johnson and not his own skills that he wanted to puke. But Puka got his attention when he said, *"I got a plan that's gonna make us so rich, them streets of Las Vegas will open up to us covered in green shag carpet."*

His own personal Graceland. The girl from Germany, his Priscilla. Hell, he could take his mama to Wal-Mart anytime he liked. Buy her a new dress, some of that perfume that Charlie's Angel sold.

"I appreciate y'all staying with that albino last night," Cruz said, knocking him out of the dream. "What time did he finally talk?"

"Around six. Floyd's at home sleepin' it off, said you'd want to know."

"Well go home and get some sleep. We might

start getting some heat from the cops about your buddy Keith. I wish you could have gotten him out of there....I understand though. Just stay real cool and keep this all to ourselves."

"Yesterday, when me and Floyd was messin' with that ole nigra, I seen the same man that chased me in the Delta. That big, scruffy white dude with black hair."

Cruz snorted out some more smoke. "His name is Travers." He leaned so close to Jesse that he could smell breath like a cigarette put out in a whiskey glass. "I want you to find his weak spot for me, son. I want you to search it out like flies on shit. See what that sarcastic motherfucker dreams about. What he lives for. Because we might just want to take that shit away to give us some breathing room."

36

VIRGINIA LAY on the couch watching cartoons
when Nick came back from Charity with his left
arm in a bright orange cast. She had on one of his
Tulane Football sweatshirts with a tattered blue
blanket wrapped around her. All comfortable and
at peace with an empty cereal bowl near her as she
giggled at Tom and Jerry.

It was the one at a dude ranch when Tom tries
to impress a cat in a dress and lipstick by playing
his guitar. But really it's just a country-and-
western record that Jerry keeps making skip and
slow speeds.

"Hey," she said as she continued to watch cartoons.

Nick massaged his fingers at the end of the cast
and shook his head. *So much for concern.* He
threw his useless keys onto the kitchen counter and
grabbed a cold Dixie from the refrigerator.

"You don't have to explain to me where you've
been. I know you're a man. Like to roam a little
like a dog....Jesus, what happened to your arm?"

He popped open the top and chased down a
couple of painkillers. God, he felt like some kind of
derelict. Booze, some pills. Party anyone?

"Got in a little accident. I think one of the killers

from the Delta found me. Someone called early this morning and told me it was Earl Snooks."

"They beat you up?"

"They beat up my Jeep."

Nick took another sip of beer and sat down beside her. She hadn't moved, just lay like a kid, wrapped in a blanket on the sofa. The comfort kind of made him mad, like she should be empathizing with him. Move around and fret. Maybe make some chicken soup. She pulled open the blanket wide to offer him inside. He took another sip of beer, leaving it half empty, and set it beside her cereal bowl.

"I'm going down to JoJo's," he said, walking to the door.

"What's wrong?" she asked.

"Nothing."

Virginia jumped off the couch and bounded across the floor to Nick. Hands on hips, jaw a little askew, and staring. Her hair was pasted down flat on her head and she wore no makeup; her eyelashes almost translucent.

"Nick."

"Virginia, please. Let's stay with our pact. Keep the mystery and all that crap," he said, and turned to leave. She grabbed his elbow and walked him in close, then raised up on her toes and kissed him on the neck.

NICK WAITED FOR JoJo and Loretta on the steps of their two-story Creole town house on Royal Street. He knew they were at church and would be back soon. There was never a Sunday that those two missed a service. In their world, it was completely unthinkable not to go, just a mandatory part of life.

He unwrapped a couple of muffins he'd bought at the A & P down the street. Muffins, a bottle of orange juice, and a pack of Marlboros. The sun shone hard in his eyes as he chewed and watched the tourists meandering in and out of the antique shops.

He smoked a cigarette, put it out, then leaned back on the stairs and slept. The dreams came through his mind with force. Random weird patterns. Black-and-white images of searching for Robert Johnson—his music grinding beneath a huge needle. Johnson gagging on his own blood as he vomited. Johnson smiling up at him and telling him, *You're not welcome*. It was the old image from that dime-store photograph now given a face.

You're not a part of this, he said. You're not welcome.

"Nick. Get yo' ass up, boy."

Johnson mouthed the words and then he felt a rough hand shake him awake.

"Lazy ole bum. Actin' like a wino," JoJo said.

Nick squinted up into the faces of JoJo and Loretta. JoJo in a pressed out-of-date blue pin-striped suit with dust-creased knees. Loretta in a long blue silk dress. Her wide, black Eskimo face drawn on with thick makeup.

"Guess I missed church," Nick said.

"Oh my boy, what happened to your arm?" Loretta asked.

"I tried to wrestle a van."

"You all right, kid?" JoJo asked.

"Yeah. Yeah, I'm fine. You should see the van."

"Come on in, son, I'm 'bout to cook a little breakfast for this ole fart," Loretta said sweetly.

"Ole fart. Ole fart," JoJo mumbled as he

ambled up the stairs. His polished black shoes reflected into Nick's eyes.

The last time the Jacksons had redecorated their Creole town house must've been in the late sixties. Velvety furniture with the curves of an Apollo rocket. Black-and-white photos of performances at the Dew Drop Inn and Loretta's album covers hung on the walls. Outside, they had a wrought-iron balcony full of fat asparagus plants and ferns with brown tips.

Loretta went into the kitchen and started banging around. After a few minutes, Nick heard the sound of coffee perking and bacon popping. JoJo leaned into a green La-Z-Boy-style chair, his lower legs propped up in the extension. He pulled a church bulletin from his inside jacket pocket and squinted at the words.

"Band las' night wasn't worth a shit," JoJo said. "Some dumb son of a bitch tryin' to play some old Stax R and B, only he couldn't sing a lick. Tourists couldn't tell but all the regulars walked out. Man, it was embarrassin'."

"JoJo, who'd you ask about Earl Snooks?"

JoJo rubbed a hand over the gray hair on his head and kept his eyes on the bulletin.

"Lotsa folks. I told you I'd make some phone calls."

"Last night, I had a call from a man who said he was Earl Snooks."

"You always have dead men ringin' you up on the telephone?"

"Went to Algiers early this morning to meet him....Well, I don't think they wanted to kill me, just mess me up a little. They rammed into my Jeep. Totaled it and put this silly orange thing on my arm. I feel like a tangerine."

JoJo looked outside at the plants, over at Nick, then back outside.

"I need to know who you called about Earl Snooks," Nick said.

"I wrote down everyone I called at the bar. I'll call 'em back if you think it will help."

"I dunno. You and Randy are the only ones who knew about Snooks. Besides Cracker."

JoJo chewed on a nail as Loretta called from the kitchen, "Y'all get the table outside ready. I'll be done in a second."

JoJo propped open the tall French doors and leaned four ice-cream-parlor chairs forward to drain off the dirty rainwater. Nick took a napkin and wiped off the seats before Loretta came out and set down a hot loaf of French bread in a basket and jam. Nick went back with her and helped bring out three plates of omelettes and thick slabs of country bacon. He clubbed a jar of strawberry preserves in with his cast.

As the food was passed around, Nick watched a van of retarded tourists unload. They were adults with the wonder of children who stared around the brick buildings so old they were turning to sediment. Thick layers of compressed brick mashing hard with the street. For a moment, all the pressure that squeezed out of his mind seemed petty. All of it as unimportant as the thin layer of dust on JoJo's knees.

"You ain't hungry?" JoJo asked, with a mouth full of omelette.

"A lot's been on my mind. Starting to have weird dreams about dead blues singers calling me up on the telephone."

Loretta put a hand on Nick's arm. "Oh, son, you need to slow down some. You keep the weight of the world on those broad shoulders of yours. How's that Virginia treatin' you? Heard she's got the prettiest eyes you ever seen, JoJo. Blue as that neon sign we got out front."

JoJo's face was blank. His food untouched. He looked like he was going to throw up but instead folded his arms across his chest. "I want you to stop lookin' for those records. It's my business," he said. "I'll take care of it."

"JoJo, what the hell is going on?" Nick asked.

JoJo just sighed and shook his head. "I'm sorry, I'm real sorry, Nick."

"I don't believe this. Jesus Christ! I don't believe this. Who was that last night? You know him, don't you? That son-of-a-bitch could have killed me. Did you know about Baker too? Let me tell you, Baker wouldn't have sat down in your bar without wiping off his seat. I've known you...it doesn't matter."

"I can't tell you," JoJo said. "I can't tell you nothin' about..."

Nick pushed his plate away and walked inside, grabbing his blue jean jacket from the old sofa. He bounded down the steps, felt his teeth grind against each other and a muscle constrict tightly in his throat. One of his battered boots slid off the second-to-last stair and he had to grab the railing tightly to keep his balance.

> *My enemies have betrayed me*
> *have overtaken poor Bob at last*
> *An' 'ere's one thing certainly,*
> *they have stones all in my pass.*

37

CRUZ MOTIONED Nick over to the lonely seat where he sat nursing an afternoon Jim Beam on ice. He looked like a blind beggar in the far corner of the Blues Shack bar wearing his black suit and sunglasses. The blond hostess from the other day massaged his neck and looked at Nick with a startled indifference.

"Mr. Travers, grab a seat," he said, gripping the woman's fingers. "Michelle, get us a couple of beers. Looks like my friend has had some bad luck."

She turned obediently as Cruz gave her a gentle pat on the ass. Nick shook his head and sat down. His hand already starting to sweat and itch in the cast.

"I think a black cat shit in my back pocket," Nick said. "Bad mojo."

"Damn, son, what's your pleasure? We got it all. You want a damned bottle in a sack?"

"A cold Dixie would hit the spot."

"Blackened Voodoo in a chilled schooner."

The girl pulled the tap forward, as if milking a cow, with her heavy breast heaving forward in a halter top. Nick watched her turn her head away, bobbed blond hair catching in her mouth. He wasn't in her league apparently, not what she was shopping for—a graying man in a tattered blue jean jacket.

Nick accepted the brownish beer.

"Got in a car smash-'em-up last night," Nick said. "I'm still reeling. Feel like I'm in a bumper car."

"How's that Jeep?"

"Looks like a crushed aluminum can." *How'd Cruz know what I drive?*

"You need a loaner?"

"No. No. I'm fine. Let me ask you something. You've been around. Been in Memphis and all that you told me. Ever hear of a bluesman named Earl Snooks?"

"Have to say I have. Delta slide, popular in the late forties before disappearing. Yeah, I've heard of him."

Cruz turned his head absolutely and completely in Nick's direction. Even though he wore the sunglasses, Nick knew he was listening. The way his neck set, the flared, reddened nostrils. It was like a dog salivating over meat. Pavlovian.

"Ever met anyone who knew him?" Nick asked.

"No. He was old-school. Why?"

"I think he paid someone to hit me. Snooks, mad as hell."

"You're kidding, right? You give him a bad write-up in an essay or something? Make him mad enough to come back from the dead."

The girl set down another round of beers at the table and smiled a coy grin at Cruz before leaving. A not-so-subtle secret between the two of them.

"I've been reading some of your work," Cruz said. "Read an essay last night, you wrote on the migration of the blues to Chicago. We could use a resident historian at the Blues Shack. Benefits, salary. Everything you need. You could play harp for the house band."

"Thanks, but I'm okay where I'm at now."

"Where's that?"

"JoJo's, just down the street."

"Oh yeah. JoJo's. Yeah. Never been there. Heard about that guy. Real showman, JoJo. Talks a good game for the tourists about the old days."

"Yeah...JoJo's been a great friend."

"Well, we'd take care of you here."

"I appreciate that."

The beer was the coldest he'd ever tasted.

JESSE WAS TOLD to take the ole man past the levee on Lake Pontchartrain, shoot him in the back of the head, tie a concrete block to his leg, and kick him in the water. As Jesse was driving down the highway and looking at him in the rearview mirror, the more Jesse thought he was losing his edge. Ole pasty was just starin' at him, lookin' right through him.

Made him feel real creepy, like the guy could read his mind or somethin'. He shrugged his shoulders, took one hand off the rusted station wagon's steering wheel, and rolled up the sleeves of his mechanic shirt.

Striped cloth, real pressed and neat with Crown Electric patch on the breast pocket. Jesse had his hair slicked back today with a little Vitalis, a nice pompadour at the front.

"You just tell us where them Johnson records are at and we'll be done with all this shit," Jesse said.

Ole man just kept starin' at the rearview mirror, his lower lip poked out and quivering.

"You are a goddamned baby, you ole fuck," Jesse said. "Now you hush on up and we'll be fine."

The levee was a long green hump like the spine of a grassy dragon with no end. As he drove, the large houses he passed became smaller—high-life condominiums became crappy apartments until there was nothin' but a few broken-down crab shacks and all-night bars. Jesse took a turn on a dirt road Cruz had told him about.

"I did k-know him," the ole man said.

"Know who?"

"Robert Johnson. I knew him real good."

"I don't care, ole man. I never even heard of the guy 'til I started this mess."

"Yore man Presley wasn't s-shit compared to him," the ole man said. He was crying now, water spilling down his white cheeks.

Jesse stopped the car and rolled down the window. He spit outside, looked into the rearview mirror, and smiled. *I'm gonna enjoy this one.*

A dry August wind ruffled grass as green as the fake kind Jesse had seen on a putt-putt course in Panama City, Florida. He parked the car and came around the side for Cracker. The ole man's hands were tied in front with a thin plastic binder.

"C'mon, let's get this over with. I let you escape me once. It ain't gonna happen again."

The ole man tried to squirm out of the car, but with his hands tied, he just flopped around. Then he tried again to scoot outside with his butt. Jesse grabbed the plastic band tightly and twisted him outside. The ole man fell out to his knees and his face slammed flush to the dirt road. A rusted, torn beer can ripped open his cheek.

Jesse yanked him up again and nudged him forward with the Glock. Jesse smacked on gum as he pushed him forward. He could see where the road opened up toward Lake Pontchartrain. Not a damned thing around but some mosquitoes that started slurpin' out the blood on the man's face. Ole man just squinted into the bright sunset ahead of him, too much to take without any shade.

Didn't matter now.

The clearing's grass was high and brown, and tiny waves rippled toward the shore. All the pebbles worn smooth from thousands of years of constant friction.

"Get on your knees, ole man."

He did without a word, just that blubberin' comin' up.

"You got nothin' to say?" Jesse asked.

"Burn in hell. You shit..."

Jesse jammed the gun into the soft part of the ole man's head and pulled the trigger.

Click.

Click.

"Son-of-a-bitch." Jesse kicked the ole man hard in the back. "You stay down. You stay down."

Ole man looked dead anyway, lying there with a look in his eyes like a deer thrown by a semi. There was drool runnin' down his chin and he was coughin' from the loose brown dirt sucked into his lungs.

Jesse turned and trotted back to the station wagon. Knew he had to have another magazine in the glove compartment, where he'd stuffed that Cajun beef jerky and a pack of condoms—*extra ribbed for her pleasure.*

Must've used up all the bullets when he was shootin' at the passin' driftwood in the Mississippi. He slid into the car and opened the compartment. Yep, two fresh loads. Wonder if he could make it back in time to take Inga and Puka for some dinner. He had enough money to take them somewhere real nice. Like one of them real fancy restaurants in the Quarter where they clean the table before you sit down.

The weeds were to his waist like a field of green wheat and there were a few sailboats far out in the water. Too far to see what he was about to do. As he walked back down the path, three seagulls scattered and squawked away back over the lake. *Shit*.

He picked up the pace, ran to the clearing near the lake, and turned all around in a scouting circle. Goddamnit. Goddamnit. *Ole man was gone.*

Jesse started kicking all through the high grass that spread out for yards all around the lake, shrouding the ground. He started with a large circle and narrowed it with each pass. *Shit*. He widened the circle and followed it again.

"Ole man, you better get your ass out here or I'm gonna start firin' this gun into them weeds. Don't be no fool now. You're dead anyways. You can't make it nowhere. Let me put you out like an ole dog. I won't leave you for long. One shot and them lights'll go out."

Jesse shot three times in sections of the weeded field. The smell of cordite mixed with the deep grass and sour smell of the water. He walked the grass dozens of times, ran through the nearby woods, and drove back and forth all along the highway.

Hell with it, the ole man had to be dead. In his mind, Jesse could see him clutchin' his heart and fallin' out there somewhere. Man was as good as a dog dropped off outside town. That pasty blue-eyed fool was nothin' but roadkill.

38

NICK LEFT the Vieux Carre behind him and grabbed an old olive green streetcar Uptown. He sank into a hard wooden seat and closed his eyes. The rickety old box soothing as it jumbled from stop to stop. He should've talked to JoJo, not just fled like an insolent teenager. JoJo had a reason. If he didn't, the world didn't make any sense.

The one man he believed in more than all others, a common liar? It wouldn't happen. JoJo was a rock of dignity and old-school morals. Besides, he couldn't be tied directly to the records or have any firsthand knowledge about Johnson's death. He was too young. JoJo was born about the time Johnson died.

However, he did know and had known plenty of old-timers. As a kid, JoJo used to spend summers with an aunt in Helena. He'd travel down to the KFFA radio station to watch *King Biscuit Flour Time,* a popular blues show in the forties and fifties. JoJo told Nick plenty of stories about how the great Sonny Boy Williamson and Robert Lockwood, Jr., would send him on errands for whiskey or gathering women. He'd chuckle with an inward gleam in his eye, pleased with the past and proud of his witness to history. For JoJo, it made him feel

more a part of the blues establishment and quali-
fied to comment on what he now heard.

Lockwood was Robert Johnson's stepson. But
JoJo wouldn't have kept a secret for decades only
to let it out to someone like Michael Baker. *He had
to be covering someone's ass.* JoJo's word was a
damned tight bond.

It pissed Nick off that JoJo just shut his mouth
and went silent. Didn't he understand how
damned important this was? This wasn't about
some man cheating with the preacher's wife or
sneaking out drinking. Someone tried to kill him
last night. Smacked into his Jeep like he was nothing. That same person probably shot Willie Brown
in the head and dumped Cracker in the river. *JoJo
and Robert Johnson.* Earl Snooks was that bridge.

Why would someone kill for asking about
Snooks? Nick tried to focus on the face from last
night but it was a blur except for the shoes and the
gray eyes. The man was so damned familiar, like a
photograph not yet developed.

Nick had no destination. No stop. He traveled
way past Julia Street. Just catnapped in the seat as
the streetcar pitched forward and slowed. Stop and
move. Stop and move. Wheels screeched below on
the worn rails. His eyes were closed tight when the
car stopped longer than normal. A woman's voice
yelled back to him.

"Got to get out so they can reverse the seats. Sir,
they gotta reverse, you don't want to ride back-
ward do ya?"

Reverse.

"Yeah, yeah."

Nick got out and stretched his legs and watched
the old wooden seats getting turned back around.
He kicked a rock off the street, then lit another cig-

arette. A black kid, who looked about fourteen, asked him for a smoke. He gave him a couple but decided not to wait. He needed to walk, so he followed the streetcar tracks for about a mile, chain-smoking and thinking. The white paper burned to nubs at the filter tip.

When he reached Tulane, his face and the front of his shirt were damp with sweat, his blue jean jacket tucked under his arm. He crossed St. Charles over into the university and walked into the Jazz and Blues Archives building. No one was in. Randy's office door was locked. He considered calling him at home but decided against it.

Nick had been up too long and his brain felt too thick to recount the last few hours. He decided to go into the office, the one he once shared with Baker, and look around. But it wasn't like the movies where a file was marked SECRET RECORDS or JOJO. The only files he found contained expenses or sheet music. But he went through all of them anyway. Nothing.

He also cross-referenced through the *Blues Who's Who* and *Big Book of Blues* and a few other biography sources. Still couldn't find anything on Earl Snooks. It was Sunday and any calls to other universities would be futile.

Maybe he'd come back tomorrow, call Ole Miss, and start with all of his back issues of *Living Blues*. Or call Jim O'Neal in Clarksdale.

He walked back outside and crossed the street to Audubon Park following the root-buckled path past the lagoon and under heavy branches. At the zoo, he turned back around and walked past a gazebo where a bunch of hippies were banging voodoo rhythms on their drums. Back on St. Charles, he kept to the sidewalks shaded by the leafy canopy above. Absently, he looked high above and saw shiny Mardi Gras beads stuck in the trees.

Near the Columns Hotel, he stopped cold. De-Soto apartment building. His boots traveled back to Kate's place. A serious subconscious move. However, he just stood there dumb and looked three floors up to her screen balcony. All the plants and black wrought-iron furniture still there. She hadn't left. Sunday, she was probably on cop duty for the paper. No lights were on in the windows and he couldn't see far into the apartment.

He imagined her up there with those eyes the color of sunlight hitting morning coffee. He started to whistle for her dog Bud, but didn't. Too much pride. Maybe he'd get a beer at the Columns and see if Cletus was working. See if he knew anything about Baker.

He turned and left.

LORETTA WAS WAITING for Nick at the warehouse. She sat across from Virginia, exchanging pleas-antries. Dull patterns of conversation that echoed through the open space about weather, music, and pretty red hair. Anything but JoJo screwing him over. Virginia listened as she still lay on the couch with a blanket tucked tightly around her. Loretta looked stiff in her Sunday dress with a black leather pocketbook in her lap. She smiled weakly when Nick walked in and stood up.

He felt like a complete asshole.

"He's sorry, Nick," she said. "He didn't mean nothin' by it."

Virginia raised up. "What's the matter?"

She stretched, yawned, and dropped her feet to the floor. All she had on was a sweatshirt and panties. It was sort of embarrassing; she hadn't changed or offered Loretta anything.

"Not much," Nick said. "For some reason, JoJo won't tell me who's trying to take me out. It's a small thing, I know, but to me it's important.... I'm sorry, that was rude.... Loretta, c'mon, let's go upstairs."

Loretta passed him and he patted her warm back. She led the way to the roof with her heels clanking on the stairs like the dull pound of a hammer.

On the roof, the sun was going down. Weak and losing its power, almost white over the Mississippi. The wind blew her stiff black hair as she leaned over the edge and looked at the view.

"Sometimes I think we should move out of the Quarter. Try to get out once in a while. Find some kind of balance from all that craziness. JoJo's been living there ever since he left Mississippi. He was just a shy country boy when we met."

"I know this isn't you. What's JoJo doing?"

She took a handkerchief from her purse and dotted her chest. "He's been under some pressure and didn't want to bother you. You know he...we both think of you like a son. I guess us without children and you without parents just fit. But you're always getting yourself in trouble for other people."

"What kind of pressure?"

"I think he best tell you."

"Loretta, he might not want to involve me, but he should've told me something before I almost got killed the other night or my ass shot off in Mississippi."

"He didn't know. He really didn't. None of 'em did."

"Loretta?"

"He's gonna lose the bar, Nick."

39

THE FLAME REMAINED even though the fountain's water scattered all around it. The whole concept amazed Jesse. A flame still bustin' through all that wetness. How's that possible? Had to be some kind of magic trick, he thought, as he took another swig of his drink.

Big red one full of crushed ice. It tasted like Kool-Aid but sure made the world into a view from a Tilt-A-Whirl. Puka and Inga were with him inside the bar's courtyard sippin' on the same fancy drinks that looked like they were poured inside a glass lantern. Puka kept on tellin' him about the plan and Inga just twirled the silver bar pierced in her navel. She had on another one of them baby-doll shirts she'd cut off right under her tits. Had a picture of a bear right between 'em.

"You just keep actin' like you're part of the program, Jesse," Puka said. "Don't mouth off to any of 'em. Even that big nigra you was tellin' me about."

"How are you gonna sell them records?" Jesse asked. "Mr. Cruz is the only one who gives a shit 'bout them things."

"That ain't true. Plenty care about ole things.

Had a woman from Memphis pay me four hun-
nerd for an ole metal bed. You believe it?"

Puka smiled wide, all proud of himself, with a
row of brown coffee-stained teeth. A couple
missin'. Looked kinda strange in that fancy New
Orleans bar with overalls on, even though he had
changed his T-shirt at the Holiday Inn near the
Superdome.

Jesse was better than this. He'd moved up. He
and Inga had gone to the Riverwalk earlier to
spend some money after he'd left the albino to die.
They'd bought some frilly women things and he
got a real cool black leather jacket, a new pair of
black jeans, a bottle of Vitalis, and a box of pra-
lines. Jesse didn't even think about the old man,
knew he had dropped dead somewhere out in the
weeds.

"You're just pissed at him 'bout Keith," Jesse
said.

"Goddamned right I am! That son of a bitch got
my son killed."

Puka leaned forward, his breath all ragged and
tired, with a face the color of an old beet. Maybe
he shouldn't push it, man might have a heart
attack.

Jesse toed his shoes over at Inga and smiled.
"How 'bout you, baby? What are you thinkin'
'bout this? Wanna take the money and head on
down the road?"

"Thees place scares me. All thees dark corners
and mean people. I don't want to stay here. I want
to see Los Angeles. That place where stars put their
hands. Then we go to Las Vegas."

E did have his Hollywood years. If Cruz ever
found out that he didn't take care of the ole man

like he said, he best be movin' down the road anyway. He'd send Sweet Boy right down on him, real quick-like.

"There you go, son," Puka said. "She's done spoke for you."

A couple guys near the fountain kept starin' over at their table and laughing. At first, he thought it was Puka's overalls, callin' them country hicks and all that mess. He'd heard that his whole life. Reminded him of the time some boys from Ole Miss threw a beer can at his head when he was walkin' on the highway. Called him junior trailer trash.

They giggled again.

Then one got up for a beer and stopped cold in front of him. "You know, little E, that Elvis was just a no-talent hillbilly? That's why he died bloated and fat on the toilet."

The rest of the boys laughed so hard that one almost fell in the fountain.

Jesse felt for his knife inside the leather jacket.

"Naw-aw Jesse," Puka said. "We need you to be cool until we leave here. Think of how you could help your mama with that money. She's always wanted a satellite dish and bills paid some money so she didn't have to work in that Zippy Mart no more."

Jesse pulled his hand back out of his jacket. The boys kept on lookin' over at Inga. And damn if she hadn't sat up straight and started starin' at them. The drunk guy who'd spoke ill of E made a motion for her to show her tits. She looked over at him, lickin' her lips, and cupped a small breast.

"What the hell you doin'?" Jesse asked. "You done gone crazy messin' round in front of me?"

She patted Jesse's leg, got up, and whispered in his ear. "Would you really hurt him for me?"

Inga moved on down the steps and into the night of Bourbon Street. The boy in a sweater with his hair all styled followed. He gave a few high fives to his friends as he left.

"I'll be back, Puka," Jesse said.

"You two kids are sick people. That's the difference between you and my son. You like to hurt and Keith just did his job."

Jesse followed the boy and Inga down St. Peter until they turned at a gas lamp and into an alley without lights. She had her arms around him and looked at Jesse over his back, then moved a hand down and started fiddlin' with his pants.

Jesse thought the veins in his head was gonna bust watchin' that mess.

Like a damned bear cat he walked over to the drunk boy, flicked out his knife, and pressed it tight to the boy's pecker. He held it there like he was about to whittle a piece of cheese and laughed.

"Why'd you call E a no-talent hillbilly? You boys think that's funny? Makin' fun of Him like that? I think He needs a sacrifice. Some type of offerin'. And seein' that you're real proud of your pecker, here you go."

"Please. Please."

"Don't say it to me. Say it to Him."

"Him who?" the boy asked, as he shook in Jesse's grasp. His old pecker had shrunk like a dead worm.

"E. Tell E how sorry you are."

The boy bubbled out some nervous laugher. "My buddies paid you to do this. Like you can rent Marilyn Monroe hookers. Right?"

Jesse cut into the skin, just a bit.

"*Jesus!*"

"No, I said to E. Sorry, remember?"

"E. I'm sorry."

"Holy E."

"Holy E. I'm sorry."

"Sorry for what?"

"Sorry for calling you a name."

"And what?" Jesse asked.

"I won't do it again."

"Do you promise to always respect Elvis Presley, the holy mother Gladys Love, and the great estate of Graceland?"

"I do."

"Then take this small cut as your remembrance of being born again."

Jesse tripped the boy into the hard flagstone, groveling and inspecting his pecker. Jesse grabbed the girl's hand and they skipped down St. Peter to grab Puka and get back to the hotel. He needed to be fresh. Tomorrow was when Mr. Cruz wanted the next deed to be done. *Viva Las Vegas.*

40

NICK WATCHED the twin Creole doors of JoJo's Blues Bar through the front window of a used-book shop across Conti. He thumbed through a collection of Louisiana folk tales called *Gumbo YaYa* and glanced up in spurts. A dull yellow light shone through windows heavily papered with bills for upcoming acts.

He slipped the book back into place and spoke briefly with the store's owner, who offered some bitter coffee. Tasted like burnt motor oil. Nick tried not to make a face before he walked to the other side of the door and pretended to continue browsing. *Still no JoJo.* The coffee made him wince as he looked at a stack of recent acquisitions. No Salinger. No blues histories.

What else was there?

To better read the spines of a flat stack, he knelt and turned his head sideways. Out of the corner of his eye, through the store's barred windows, he saw JoJo emerge and briskly walk down Conti, away from the river. Nick thanked the owner for the coffee, dumped it in the trash, and began pursuit.

Outside, the sounds of the Quarter rattled and drummed in a distant party. Even on a humid Sun-

day night, the conventioneers were going to get
their money's worth.

JoJo wore a blue short-sleeved dress shirt and
black pants, his grayed head like a big Q-Tip walking past colonnades. He moved fast for an old man,
and Nick had to keep his eyes trained through the
milling crowd on Chartres not to lose him.

Where the hell is he headed? JoJo stopped once
to tie his shoe and talk to the bouncer at a bar near
the marble Louisiana Wildlife and Fisheries Building, still an unfinished and vacant shell.

JoJo kept walking, past Bourbon and headed
toward Rampart Street. Now Nick was clueless;
there was nothing on Rampart except a few brave
business owners, hoodoo parlors, illegal gambling
dens, crack houses, fifteen-dollar-whore brothels,
and stained-mattress flophouses.

Rampart was once a moat, a dug pit where
French settlers put raw sewage and other crap to
drive away Indians but instead attracted malaria-
laced mosquitoes. Every time Nick passed the old
street, he thought about what it was like when the
asphalt was a brown bubbling pit of shit.

Not much had changed, he thought, passing a
neon-lit liquor store where they sold Colt 45 in ice-
filled trash cans. Back in the twenties and thirties,
the place was a hotbed for jazz musicians. Now,
Rampart was better known for its crime—the
northernmost point of the Quarter, where no one
wants to be at night.

JoJo passed Congo Square and the giant bronze
statue of Louis Armstrong that played to an empty
park. Nick kept back two blocks from his friend,
his head down and his feet shuffling slowly. Mannerisms tipped people off.

He was about thirty yards behind when JoJo

opened a black iron gate and disappeared. Nick walked faster, head up now, hearing his own boots clop, until he passed a cinder-block wall topped with shards of multicolored glass. The gate swung back slowly almost into its latch.

Nick caught it. Inside a squat moss-covered shack came booming black voices. Friendly sounds. No windows, light coming from an open door. As he peeked inside, he understood—JoJo's cronies sitting on their old black asses passing around a bottle of Jack Daniel's.

Sun Droyton, a bear of a man with a copper complexion, sat with his ham-size arms crossed before him. A straw Panama jack hat on his head. A sliver of mustache and a soul patch on his face. His eyes were hooded and sleepy as he watched JoJo pour a drink.

In another chair was Roland Gooddine, a wiry, scruffy man with skin as black as the baseball hat on his head. He had a hawk nose, small eyes, and laughter that was as constant as a nervous cough.

Nick liked both men very much. JoJo's regulars. Men who always made him feel welcome, yelling his name as soon as he entered the bar. Remembered every sack he had with the Saints. They were the ones that threw him a party on that Monday night. Called him "an all right bastard" for knocking the coach down.

Nick thought about walking right in, but he didn't. He slid from view, sat on a pile of bricks, and listened.

"I gots my car stuck down on Esplanade. Y'all take me back? We need to find somewheres—," Roland began.

"We need to settle this shit," JoJo said.

"I say we kill that son-of-a-bitch that messed with you," Sun added.

"There ain't a thing I can do but go to the police. And they ain't gonna do shit. If they do, those men'll mess with Henry," JoJo said.

"You send them to me and I'll put a mother-fuckin' shotgun in their mouths," said a voice out of view.

"Where them *Playboys* at?" Roland asked.

"Hey, shut up," said Sun.

Nick yawned, brushed the dirt off his boots, and decided to walk inside. All the voices stopped and heads turned. He found a chipped ladder-back chair and sat down. "Yeah, where are the *Playboys?*"

"Nick," JoJo said softly.

"Now I'm hurt, you fellas are having a party and didn't even tell me about it," Nick said. He leaned back in the creaking chair and stared at dozens of water-stained centerfolds that decorated the ceiling. "Oh, there they are, like stars in the sky."

"Get this honky the fuck out of here," said an old man with gray eyes. Even had on the same bro-gan shoes and overalls. There was a small paisley-shaped scar on his cheek.

"You have insurance, Mr. Snooks?" Nick asked, waving his orange cast.

"That ain't Snooks," Roland said as he took off his tattered baseball cap and wiped his brow. "That's just ole Henry."

"Thanks," Nick said.

Roland grinned and nodded.

"You owe me a Jeep, Henry," Nick said. "We'll forget the arm. I've broken it twice before with all my fingers. See how crooked they are?"

The old man thrust his hands deep in his over-alls and spit on the floor.

"I don't owe you shit. You the one come 'round and started fuckin' everythin' up. You stupid white-bread—"

"Hold on, Henry," JoJo said.

"Can we please cut through this immense amount of horseshit? I want to help you guys," Nick said.

"Get him the fuck out of here," Henry said.

"You really make me feel welcome here in the Honeycomb Hideout. But I'm not leaving until you tell me what you guys are up to. Was Earl Snooks a friend of yours? Did he know something about Robert Johnson's death? Is that what this is about?"

"Nick, please," JoJo said. "We'll talk 'bout this later at the bar."

"JoJo, that would've been fine before I dragged my ass all around Mississippi and almost got killed by this crazy bastard in Algiers."

"You shouldn't be here," Henry said.

Nick put all four legs of the chair on the ground, took the bottle of whiskey from Sun, and smiled. "Like I said, I'm not leaving. Who wants to start a little group therapy?"

TWO HOURS LATER, the Jack Daniel's bottle was almost empty, words slurred, and the walls crumbled. To breathe the hot air was to stick your mouth on the end of a hair dryer, and Nick had to intermittently wipe the beads of perspiration from his brow. The inside of his cast felt like a wet sock. Outside, a car rambled down Rampart Street with rap music pounding from its speakers.

Buried secrets seemed out of place with the decade.

Roland made an announcement to everybody

that he was leaving to piss and buy another bottle of booze. "Don't mix up the two," Sun said as his buddy hit his head on a swinging yellow bulb.

"Y'all cough up a little for the fund," Roland said.

Nick gave him a ten.

Henry's eyelids drooped low and he ran a hand over his craggy face as if to remember where he sat. He stared blankly at the mildewed walls of the cinder-block shack and then looked up at the naked women on the ceiling. His weathered face like deeply stained leather.

He had to be at least twenty years older than JoJo.

"Why'd you pay to have me killed, Henry?" Nick asked.

"Shit. If I wanted to kill you, you'd be livin' in a dirt-covered box."

"Why'd you try to kill me, Henry?"

"It's not my fault, Nick," JoJo said. "I started askin' people about Earl Snooks for ya'."

"So?"

"Ole Henry thought you were like that friend of yours, Baker," Sun said. "Baker wanted to know about Snooks too."

"I'm proud to say I'm nothing like Michael Baker," Nick said.

"Motherfucker sold me out," Henry said. "He said we was friends. Said he wouldn't tell nobody. Jes' like a priest is what the man said. Said, get it all out about Snooks."

"Get what out, Henry?"

"I ain't fool enough to repeat myself."

"Son-of-a-bitch." Nick stood up.

"Tell him, Henry," JoJo said.

"Fuck you, JoJo!"

"Henry. Goddamn it!" JoJo said.

"It was a mistake talkin' to that man Baker. Fuck it all!" Henry said as he grabbed his coat and shuffled for the door.

"Did you tell him about Cracker and Johnson's lost records?" Nick asked.

"Bullshit," JoJo said.

Henry stopped and turned. "It ain't bullshit," he said as he ran a fist under his nose and sniffed, then looked at the faces surrounding him. "It ain't bullshit."

And then he hobbled out the door.

JoJo turned to Nick and said, "We just tryin' to protect him. Back in the Delta that man was like an uncle to us all. Used to take us around and introduce us to Sonny Boy and Little Walter. That's how I could get those heavyweights in when I started the bar."

"What'd he tell Baker?" Nick asked.

"Henry say Earl Snooks the one who killed Robert Johnson."

41

NICK COULDN'T SLEEP that night. He was so close to finding another facet of Robert Johnson's life—a discovery that could make a career. It was selfish, he knew, to think in those terms, but it was true. To a blues historian, this was one of those gems only a few had ever found. This was something for Alan Lomax or Samuel Charters, not him.

Those pioneers of blues history were his heroes, etched into Nick's brain from constant readings of their works. They grabbed quotes from the source, not from another's interpretation. Now that most of the original bluesmen were gone, younger historians owed a great deal to those who collected stories at a time when talking to a black man could get your ass kicked.

He removed the coffee from the burner and poured a cup. The sun crept through the high industrial windows and across the wood floors. There was a rustle of sheets as Virginia stirred in bed.

"Are you okay?" she asked, pulling the red hair from her eyes.

"Can I trust you?"

"Well...yeah, of course," she said as she stretched and yawned. "What's wrong?"

"You're not going to turn on me. Be someone else and stab me in the back?"

"Why don't you come back to sleep, Nick?"

"'Cause I'm not so sure about this unknown relationship. Why'd you pick me out in that bar in Greenwood?"

She tucked a pillow under her head and said, "It was really complicated. Every man that I'd met in the Delta was a married farmer. You didn't look like you drove a John Deere."

"What do you know about Robert Johnson?"

She shook her head. "Really, Nick, come back to bed. I think that wreck scrambled your brain more than you thought."

"Do you know why those men were killed in Mississippi?"

"Something to do with that guy you were looking for?"

"No. Listen, I don't want any more secrets. I've had enough force-fed to me lately that I feel like I'm gonna throw up.... There might be some unreleased Robert Johnson tracks. Apparently, the man I told you about, Michael Baker, knew about them. Last night I tried to get his source to talk to me, and he shut me out. And I was just worried."

"Worried that I was after the records too?"

Nick looked down at the sun-painted floor and squinted. "Yeah."

"I love Robert Johnson," she said. "The way he could turn a verse into something so beautiful and tight was wonderful. I really appreciate the man for all that talk about the devil and knobs turning in the middle of the night. But if you did find missing tracks you know it could be more of the same. He could've just redone his basics. You're the one who told me that he liked to play songs the same way over and over again, to get it right. I'm not trying to make you back down, 'cause I know you're the kind of man that's gonna do what he wants. But do you want to get killed for this?"

"Do you know anything about his last recording session in Dallas when he laid down "Hellhound" and "Me and the Devil?"

"No," she said, putting her feet on the ground. Her Scooby-Doo T-shirt wrinkled and one tube sock stretched almost off her foot.

"When he came back to record a second time, he played differently," Nick said. "It was more intense and eerie, almost like he knew he was going to die soon. There are stories they cut the records in the upstairs of a Buick showroom. The producer said it was so hot in Dallas that June they recorded shirtless and had fans blowing on cakes of ice."

Virginia came over and wrapped an arm around Nick's neck and kissed him on his neck. "What's your point?"

"It's eavesdropping. Pure and simple. A record is the only true connection to him. It's his sound trapped in time. And yeah, I guess I'll do what it takes to let it out. To hear some kind of background noise or God willing a new song that could tell us something about his mind-set and music before he died."

"Can I help?" she asked, tousling his black hair.

"Do you like to read?"

RANDY STARED AT Virginia for a moment, his mouth wide open. Then he shook his head, for his gawking, and invited them into his office. For some reason, he wore a long African shirt and leather sandals. His curly hair and wide-eyed smile combined with the clothes reminded Nick of a child in a school play.

"Kunta Kinte, I presume?" Nick asked.

"Very funny. Actually it was a gift from a visiting professor during our African Roots series. You don't like it?"

"It's fine."

"I look silly, don't I? I just thought it looked comfortable and it was hot today."

Sprinklers from the campus lawn tapped at the tall windows behind him.

"Randy, please," Nick said. "This is a friend of mine, Virginia Dare. She's one of the best slide guitarists I've ever seen and she's going to help us dig through the clips."

"Miss Dare, welcome to what some call the most boring job in the world. But to a couple nerds like Nick and me...heaven."

They spent the rest of the afternoon in the archives. They started with thick phone-book-size biography books. There was a born date with a list of recordings but no death date. Snooks would be over eighty.

From there, Randy pulled a very thin file on the man: traditional slide guitarist born in the Delta, did some studio work in New Orleans, played with some big names and then disappeared.

After a couple hours of referencing his names through a small blues library, they started sorting through sets of magazines and newspaper clippings, some as old as the mid-1940s. Randy and Nick also both made phone calls to other universities.

The concrete floors and walls gave the old

archives a pleasant coolness. Outside, the air felt like a bread oven. The disintegrating cardboard of the album covers and the antiseptic smell of the spotless floors soon mixed with a brewing pot of coffee.

Randy poured them all cups and then sat across from Nick at the double-sided teacher's desk. Virginia had spread a stack of clippings on the floor and made notations on a yellow legal pad.

Within two hours, Virginia yelled, "Got him!"

Nick had almost forgotten she was there. She plopped down an open magazine onto the desk with a photograph labeled EARL SNOOKS CIRCA 1947.

It was a black-and-white shot of a young Snooks with a guitar resting between his knees. The face had changed a lot in fifty years, but still had the same eyes and paisley-shaped scar the size of a fingertip.

Randy was quiet while Nick read the article twice. "This is from seventy-four. The article said the man hasn't been heard from since fifty-two."

"Let's look forward for a follow story or an obituary," Randy said.

"No. I got what I needed," Nick said, skimming the article and recognizing the author's name: a southern historian he knew from several conferences and music festivals. He called Auburn University, where the man taught, and left a message with the department secretary.

A few hours later, as they were taking a break and eating fried-shrimp po'boys from Uglesich's, he returned the call.

"Hey, Nick," the historian said. "It's amazing how things hit you all at once. You're the second guy that's asked me about Earl Snooks in twenty years. And the last guy called yesterday. That guy Cruz who owns that big blues chain."

Nick could feel his grip tighten on the desk's edge and his temples throb.

42

CRUZ'S HANGOVER made his body feel as sensitive as a strip of film exposed to the noon sun. The sweat rolled off his forehead and through his sunglasses as the air conditioner blasted through the restaurant. He shouldn't have gotten drunk last night. He'd been so careful about only adding a dash of bourbon to the water, just enough to add color.

But last night he thought, What the hell? He deserved a real generous drink. He poured one after another. The water getting darker and darker. Even had a half-assed idea to see if Floyd would grab some shit and come over and get stoned like the old days in L.A. Back then, he and Floyd would get some hungry wanna-be singer and get her pumped full of juice. They'd tell her what a big star she could be. He'd roll off names of people he'd produced and say she had the same talent. Then he and Floyd would take turns on her, her starstruck eyes watching the ceiling. Didn't matter how old she was; Floyd always said the younger the better.

That wasn't the only scam. Cruz made his way in Los Angeles by pretending to be better than he was. Bigger and more powerful. He could always convince some idiot to sell his home and pay for some studio time. Cruz would pay the musicians below scale and pocket most of the money. When the idiot wasn't picked up by a label, he'd shrug his shoulders and say, "We did our best, they're fools for not seeing your talent."

Cruz had to smile a little at his old craftiness as the cook brought a small plate of red beans and rice, two aspirin, and an ice water. Good man, he thought, adding a few tablespoons of Tabasco and mashing the beans and rice together. As he pressed the fork in the sticky pile, he saw Travers walk through the door. The guy made a grand entrance, swinging both heavy doors wide open like a cowboy in a saloon. Cruz had been expecting this.

"You want to tell me about Earl Snooks now?" Travers asked.

"Could you please watch your voice?"

Several people at nearby tables were staring. Monday's lunch crowd, overloaded with bags of souvenirs and cameras. A short man and his gangly wife leered at Travers like he was part of the show.

"You want to tell me why you lied?"

"I never lied," Cruz said in a muffled voice. "Please sit down."

"Why've you been checking into Earl Snooks's background?"

Cruz laughed and took a self-conscious bite. With food in his mouth he said, "That's why you're mad? 'Cause I called about Snooks?" He swallowed. "I called because I thought it would help you. I was trying to make amends for an employee being an embarrassment to the Blues Shack name. A favor. You're mad 'cause I was doing you a favor, son."

"Quit trying to jerk me off."

"Sit down and I'll talk," Cruz said.

Travers took a seat across from Cruz. Cruz leaned in close and was chomping on gum in a rabid-dog kind of way. *Where the hell is Sweet Boy Floyd when you need him?* He'd ride it out.

"Listen, I know about the story JoJo's buddies concocted about the lost recordings of Robert Johnson," Travers said. "That's a big pile of shit. I can't believe you fell for it. And if you think Michael Baker, who I know sold you on this, is an expert on blues, you're only diddling yourself. That man didn't know Charley Patton from Charlie McCarthy. You got sold a bad deal, Cruz, and that's why you had him killed."

Cruz took a deep breath and pushed the pile of beans away. Heat flushed into his face and he wiped his chin with a soiled napkin. He pulled on his pointed beard and took a swig of cold water. *Where is Floyd?* He tried to get Michelle's attention, but she was off flirting with a new bartender.

"I have no idea what you're talking about," Cruz said.

"I talked to them. I know you promised to spare JoJo's bar if he found the records. He told me a couple guys broke into his place and threatened him. One big black guy with gold teeth knocked him in the face, you asshole. Didn't you get what you wanted from Baker or Cracker? There are no lost records! Johnson recorded twice! That was it! Are you fucking insane listening to that shit?"

"I have no idea what you're talking about."

Travers reached over and grabbed him by the lapels. Cruz did not move; he let the anger pass through him. Cruz imagined a limp rag doll. Travers had a damned crazy look in his eye, like he would tear his head off.

"I know you had those men killed, but it's over now. If anyone even comes close to JoJo's again, I'll kill 'em."

Cruz laughed.

"We're the same, you and me, Nick. Two white men trying to be a part of the blues. Do you think you're better than me? That you have more of a right to those records? It's the same thing. We both want them to make us famous. I doubt if Robert Johnson would've looked either one of us in the eye. So good luck, now we'll just have to see who's faster."

Cruz felt much more bold when he saw Floyd walk into the restaurant with his hand inside his satin jacket. Floyd winked over Travers's shoulder before grabbing him by the arm and nudging a gun in his ribs.

"Good luck, Nick," Cruz said. "May the best pale impersonator win."

THE GRIP ON Nick's right bicep was so tight he could feel his hand go numb. He wanted to jam an elbow into the black man's paunchy stomach, but the gun was a big deterrent. Cruz had had three men killed. Why would he stop with a fourth, who had personally pissed him off?

The back alley of the Blues Shack was filled with heavy green Dumpsters, broken slats of wood, and cardboard packing crates. A brusque wind rushed through the alley with black fast-moving clouds above.

"Heard you went to see my friend JoJo yesterday," Nick said.

"Oh yeah, ole man 'bout pissed all over himself when I bitch-slapped him with my gun. Nothin' but a sorry-ass tramp."

"I've always heard men who love guns and use them for power trips have small dicks. Is that right? You got a Vienna sausage hangin'?"

"Why don't you ask that redhead bitch you been seein'? I bet she could suck it up like a vacuum cleaner."

They've been watching.

"Oh yeah, that's right," Nick said. "I heard you had to take it on the road since your woman seems to keep a steady flow of backdoor men."

The man hit Nick hard in the stomach with the butt of his gun. Nick felt the air expel from his body like a smashed balloon. Through watered eyes, he could see the gun next to his cheek and the shimmering gold smile in the man's mouth.

"Let's see who's hard, man," Nick said as he gasped. "Let's see if you put down that gun could you really kick my ass."

"Shiiiit," he said, clicking on the safety.

Nick swung his cast into the man's crotch and the man fell like a chainsawed sequoia. He groped for Nick's face as he lost his balance, thick fingers plunging. Nick grabbed him by his shirt and slung him five yards. His fat black body thudded into a Dumpster and his eyes rolled back in his head.

In his mind's eye, Nick could see the profile of Willie Brown and the shaky mannerisms of Cracker. He gritted his teeth and water filled his vision. He cocked back his right arm and pummeled the man's metal mouth. Then he popped him hard in the nose with the back of his cast.

Nick hit the son of a bitch until his breath came in choking gasps, blood covering his shirt and the heavy man's eyes twitching.

43

Streaks of lightning cracked in veined patterns in the black sky over Algiers. Nick drove JoJo's '63 Cadillac over the roaring metal of the Greater New Orleans Bridge as he looked at the crumpled map to Henry's house. With the radio clicked off and the windows down, Nick thought of the best ways to ask a stranger to tell the secrets of his life.

Soon he took a left after crossing the brown river and followed a narrow road to Patterson Road, which winds like a snake around the tip of Algiers Point—the opposite side of the river from the French Quarter. JoJo had marked an old Knights of Columbus building and former disco that was now a burned-out shell.

Henry lived in a colorless wooden cottage surrounded by high green shrubs and overgrown with elephant's ears the size of flags. Before Nick walked five paces away from JoJo's car, the screen door flew open and Henry marched out wielding a Winchester twelve-gauge shotgun.

"Afternoon, Mr. Snooks," Nick said.

Henry pumped the shotgun.

"Just want to talk."

Henry aimed the gun at Nick's chest.

"Maybe not."

"What about?" Henry asked.

"Let me come inside."

Henry was silent, then dropped the shotgun and walked back into the house. The screen door banged after him. Nick followed and opened the door to see Henry sitting at his kitchen table sipping whiskey from a cracked fruit jar. A black woman in her fifties rubbed his shoulders and shook her head when she looked at Nick.

Henry turned his head up at her and said, "I'm awright, you go on."

"I'm stayin'," she said.

"I said go on."

She grabbed a purse slung over a kitchen chair and walked out.

"My daughter. She worries 'bout me all the time."

The white surrounding his gray eyes was red and the blackness of his skin looked unreal in the weak glow of a dusty swinging kitchen light. There was a dirty dish in the middle of the table and Nick could smell burnt beans on the stove. Two bottles of pills sat next to another plate, the caps screwed off.

To the right of the kitchen was a wood-paneled sitting room with a ragged green plaid sofa, a ripped canvas chair, and a silent flickering television set.

Henry took a sip of his whiskey.

"On August thirteenth, 1938, I was in Helena pickin' up some tractor parts with my brother-in-law. We stayed at a cousin of mine's house and left the next day. It was rainin' all the way back an' we had to stop in Clarksdale to wait it out. We didn't get home 'til midnight. My wife was there, but she dead now....I got names of folks who can—"

"I didn't ask you anything yet," Nick said.

"I thought you wanted to know where I was at when that Johnson man was killed?"

Nick shifted in his chair. Cool air rushed through the rusted screen door and made it bang against the jamb. Rain started to pat on the wooden porch, which looked like a row of rotten uneven teeth.

"Awe fuck it," Henry said as he poured Nick a full glass of whiskey. "I guess it don't matter none now, you know I'm Snooks. If they want to put me in prison, give me a bunk at Angola. I ain't gonna last long."

He sucked down the rest of his whiskey and looked out the dirty windowpanes.

Nick pulled a pocket recorder out of his jacket and placed it on the table.

"No sir," Henry said. "You want to go back and find what happen, I'll tell you. But ain't no way you gonna record my ass. You hear me? You promise me that this ain't nobody else's bidness?"

"I can't promise that."

"Then fuck it. I ain't sayin' nothin' lessen I have your word, ain't goin' no further. Hear me son? You hear me?"

Nick grabbed the recorder and placed it back in his jean jacket. "You have my word."

Maybe he'd convince him later that the story was too important. But if not, Nick knew he'd have to honor the agreement. It was like what William Holden said in *The Wild Bunch*: "When you side with a man you stay with him and if you can't do that, you're like some animal."

"Before I met Johnson I thought I had the world by the nuts. Had me my own juke, run out the back of a grocery sto' my father left me when he died and made me a nice little profit with all them farmers 'round. Had a good home, near the sto', and .jes married me a fine-lookin' wife. You should've seen her. Had her a Mexican mother and she had these green eyes, long black hair like an Indian squaw, and fine-lookin' body. She was just seventeen years ole and man I was in love.

"Well, Johnson used to come by and play at my juke every few months. Sometimes I wouldn't see him for almost a year and then he would set his guitar down and say he wanted to play. I used to feed him a meal, some whiskey, and let him be on his way. Sometime he'd teach me a few things on the guitar and sometime he wouldn't talk at all. He was real funny that way."

Nick's hands were quivering. This was it. The story men had spent their entire lives waiting to hear. He didn't move a bit. Didn't smile. Didn't frown. It was like balancing a house of cards on your head—one gesture could bring the whole act down.

"Back in thirty-eight, he'd been by a few months before and met my wife," Henry said. "Now I ain't sayin' he was lookin' at her, I mean he 'bout fell over when she come out the back of the sto' carryin' a sack of feed. He said somethin' kinda off color 'bout her backside. And I tole him if he done that again, I done beat him in the head.

"Well he jes laugh and laugh 'bout that, thought it real funny I say that. And soon as he started playin' later that night, he started to sing to her! So now I was mad and tole her to go home. She patted my hand and left. And so did Bob, a little later.

"When I come home from the juke, I heard the back do' slam and seen her button up the front of her dress. She deny it was him, but I knew."

"So when did you see him next?" Nick asked. The words circling in the rotted cottage seemed as unreal as the grainy images from a World War II newsreel. But somehow, he believed them. Somehow it all made sense. The rain patted the house hard now and the thunder shook every loose dish in the cracking wood frame.

"Before he come back that summer, a man come lookin' for him," Henry continued. "Fat white man in a long black Buick, had this little albino boy come with him, carryin' a bottle of whiskey for him like a little slave or somethin'. He tole me he was from Texas and lookin' for a man name Johnson, then he tole me he play the guitar and say what he look like. Say he had this lazy left eye that he kept a tipped hat pulled over."

The bitter whiskey made the acidic bile rise in Nick's throat. He coughed, watching Henry's gray eyes stare into the equally gray rain through the rusted screen door.

"When I heard he was playin' down the highway, I knew he was comin' back. First thing I done is go into Greenwood and send a Western Union message to that fat man."

A truck without a muffler rattled by the house and the smell of burnt beans grew stronger. Henry got up and turned the burner down under a flowered metal pot.

"Fat man's name was Devlin," Henry said, leaning into his kitchen sink, looking deep into the drain and rubbing the stubble on his chin. "Said Johnson stole somethin' that was his. He gave me twenty dollars for sendin' the message when he came the next day. Said he wanted to teach John-son a lesson and ask me to give him a bottle of whiskey."

Another rumble of thunder rattled the whole house and a coffee cup fell to the floor, shattering. Henry opened the screen door and looked out to the Mississippi.

"Later that night, I picked him up outside Greenwood. His suit that was always so neat, all covered in dust like he just hopped off a train or somethin'. When we got to the juke, I served him a drink, ask him 'bout his records and how fine he was doin'. He jes' stared down at the bar, like he didn't care nothin' 'bout talkin', and walked out."

Henry stepped outside, the rain covering his black face, like a drunk man put under a cold shower. Nick followed him and put his hand on Henry's upper arm. Henry jerked away like an angry child and walked out into his yard.

"I didn't mean fo' all that to happen, when Johnson come back he jes sat in the corner of the juke, arms folded 'round his guitar. I knew what that white man done. Johnson had a ash face like a corpse. He was dead already and knew it. Kept on mutterin' that the devil comin' for him, time to give his soul and all that crazy mess. He stayed for a while until his partner, man named Honeyboy, come along and see he jes' wasn't drunk. Two fel-las put him in back of a flatbed truck and I ain't never saw him again. I kilt him though, want for me, that fat white bastard wouldn't know where he been at."

"You didn't kill him," Nick said.

"I kilt him, I kilt the greatest blues player ever lived over a woman who left me six months later for a sour-faced preacher who peed on hisself during Baptist revivals."

"Did Cracker know all this?"

"Me and Cracker's sin is a whole 'nother story."

44

THEY WERE BACK at the kitchen table now, and Nick took another swig of the whiskey. He could feel his hand and upper arm swell in the cast and looked down to his shirt, which was torn from the fight at the Blues Shack. Henry didn't seem to notice. His mind was hundreds of miles and years away.

"After they took Bob, we closed up the juke joint. I was shuttin' all the doors and gatherin' up the glasses when the fat man came back in. Tole me to keep my nigga mouth shut or I'd end up just like Johnson. He stood there laughin' in my own place, sayin' who was I foolin' lookin' all upset about what he done. He said niggas didn't care no mo' about killin' than an animal.

"That's when I hit him with the two-by-four in the head. I was mad at him. Mad at Bob. Mad at the man for makin' me a part of what he done. I couldn't stop and when he reached up under his pant leg I knew what he was lookin' for. I stopped. It just made me madder. Everybody else gone. I'd knocked over a jug of corn whiskey and the tap, tap, tap sound just hanged there like a clock movin' on."

"So you killed him," Nick said.

"No, man sure was about to kill me when that

little albino boy name Cracker walked in and shot his boss man right in the neck and then again in the heart. Lil' boy done fell down on his knees after that. I walked slow over to him, my feet clankin' on the juke's wood floor, and reached out for the gun.

"You gots to understand the mess we was in at the time. A black man kilt a white man might not see the dawn's light. We jes waited there for some white men to bust in the door and string a noose round our necks. But they didn't. The corn whiskey stopped tappin' on the floor and I looked down at that whiskey and white man's blood mixing. It kinda was washin' it away. And I knew what we had to do.

"Tole Cracker get off his knees and clean the man's blood up. And I knew if we dug a grave might make people nervous, so I found a real good spot for the fat man. Problem was that he was so wide it took most all day to wedge him in there. And then right as the dawn was comin' round through the window, me and Cracker took that long black Buick to a deep part of the Yazoo River and let it slide on in."

"And you told Baker everything?" Nick asked.

"He started comin' 'round early this year, askin' me if I knew Robert Johnson. He knew who I was. He wanted to know why I'd changed my name. What it was all about. I guess I got weak. Tole him the same thing I jes tole you. I guess it somethin' with bein' ole and wantin' to confess yo' sins."

"And he went looking for Cracker?"

"Yeah. He say Robert Johnson died about the same time this record producer name Devlin went missin'. Say Devlin might have been the las' person to make records with Bob."

"What'd you tell him?"

"Said I didn't know nothin' 'bout some lost Robert Johnson records."

"Do you?"

"Man had some recordins on 'im. But I'm gonna tell you the same thing I tole that man. Nothin'. What's buried is gone. Even when that man tried to close down JoJo's if I didn't tell, didn't make no difference. You ain't cuttin' into my soul no mo'. Please just go."

THE BLACK CLOUDS had blown over Orleans Parish. Broken shafts of bright yellow sunlight broke through curtained gray clouds like an image from a religious postcard. The rust on the Greater New Orleans Bridge looked almost purple in the splotched light as Nick drove back into the city.

It was exhausting to come back into the later century after hearing Henry's story. But Nick didn't feel superior after hearing a tale told by a man partially responsible for his hero's death. Just sad and tired. What a waste of two lives. Earl Snooks had essentially died a short time after Robert Johnson. His ghost still reaching out after all these years.

There was such an abrupt end to a man who saw beauty in rugged images. Hard, simple words that brought a clarity, color, and feeling to a specific moment. Concentrated like only the best poets could write:

> *When the train, it left the station*
> *with two lights on behind*
> *Well, the blue light was my blues*
> *and the red light was my mind*
> *All my love's in vain.*

Nick exited off Camp Street, then took a left on Julia down to the warehouse and reality. He could see the lights were on in the second floor as he drove into the garage that had once served as a loading dock for lumber. For a moment, he just sat in there and stared at the broken patterns in the brick. He shut off the ignition and walked upstairs.

The front door and the sliding door to his apartment were unlocked. A sad Little Walter tune played low and scratchy on the turntable.

Nick opened the refrigerator and grabbed a half of a po'boy from earlier and a cold Dixie. As he was about to put on some shorts and running shoes for a jog, he noticed a handwritten note placed on his kitchen counter. "Had to get out for a while," Virginia wrote. "Going for a walk in Audubon Park, be back in a couple hours."

Nick grabbed his keys and ran back down the metal stairs. Little Walter's voice and harp played distorted and burned-out under the needle.

45

JESSE WATCHED Virginia standing next to the stone entrance of Audubon Park. She wore a flannel shirt tied at the waist, blue jeans, and cowboy boots. Damn she looked fine, just standin' there face all smooth and body bumpy. He grew hard watchin' her breathe. Most of all he liked her eyes; he had noticed how blue they were when she brushed against him getting off the streetcar.

Blue like E's. She didn't pay no attention to him though, just looked over the park covered in trees and plants like the set from *Blue Hawaii*. Real plushy. Almost too nice to be real.

He was gonna grab the woman tonight anyway but Floyd said he wanted to go along and help. Guess he was mad about that dude kickin' his ass. His face all swollen and puffy as if he wore a rubber mask.

Jesse sat and watched from under a knurled water oak, Spanish moss drippin' in front of his face like a veil. He licked a lollipop Inga gave him, on a low branch shaped in the image of a fat woman's arm. He'd be patient for the right moment to bring her in while Floyd waited in an old Dodge van next to the golf course.

She wouldn't make a scene. He flicked his

switchblade out and shaved the tiny black hairs off his thumb. It would work out. He'd get the dude's woman. The dude would then tell him where the real Johnson records were. Then he would take them and sell them. And he, Inga, and Puka could get out of New Orleans and the South.

Bright light city gonna set my soul, gonna set my soul on fire.

She walked inside the park. He flicked the blade open again and followed, the spidery moss flailing over him in baptism.

THE CADILLAC FISHTAILED as Nick turned onto a partially flooded St. Charles Avenue. He darted through traffic like a scared dog. In and around, he passed a streetcar headed in the same direction. The antebellum and Victorian homes whizzed past in his peripheral vision.

Nick slammed on his brakes and almost ran over a city worker in a yellow slicker. The man held up a caution sign while another man filled a pothole. He drove over the streetcar's neutral ground and headed against traffic as swerving cars blared their horns.

Cruz had been watching him and knew about Virginia. After the fight at the Blues Shack today, everything was out. No more coy games. No hidden agendas. All the bullshit was gone. This was their chance to grab something he cared about and give them an advantage. He was too damn worried about getting the records. So damned wrapped up in the life of a dead man he didn't watch out for Virginia.

So much like him to keep himself in the past while he completely blocked out the present.

He passed the construction and weaved back

over into the right lane. Son of a bitch, they'd been following him and he hadn't even noticed. Probably led them right to Earl Snooks. Goddamn that was soft, didn't take a single precaution for her safety, just skipped around after three men were killed like they couldn't touch him. A tight lump arched in his throat as his mind raced with horrific thoughts of what twisted minds could do to a beautiful young woman.

JESSE TICKLED HIS arm lightly as he followed the path behind the redhead. The light rain must've driven everybody out of the park, just the sound of patting water dimpling little puddles and cicadas grating all around. Jesse stopped as she watched two squirrels tumbling over each other on a putting green as flat and soft as velvet. To the left was a long, flat lagoon.

This place sure was weird. All those twisted trees like they had been here since before Jesus or somethin'. It was damned awesome. After he got what he wanted and killed the woman, maybe he'd take Inga back here.

Maybe they could screw monkey-style high in those old trees. Yeah, they'd climb up there naked and people passin' by wouldn't even know what they were doin'. They'd keep quiet. He'd be a damn ole Tarzan wild man.

When he turned back on the path, he saw the redheaded woman stare at his hard-on like he was crazy.

NICK STOPPED THE car at Tulane and ran across the street, leaving the engine running and the keys in the ignition. He jumped over the stone fence and shouted Virginia's name. The late-day sun heated the pools of water, making steam rise off sidewalks.

There was a mother pushing a stroller of twins and a couple of college girls jogging. No one was on the golf course, and the rest of the park was empty except for a derelict inside a brick gazebo.

Nick asked him if he'd seen a woman with red hair. The white man with a brushy white beard and rancid breath nodded.

"Where is she? When was she here?" Nick asked.

The man's head lolled around and he smiled.

"*Hey*, I said where is she?" Nick said, moving on the step up toward him. "Where did she go?"

"Huh?" the man asked.

Nick kept running forward in the wet grass and began to call for Virginia.

The shouts of her name fell empty.

THE SMOOTH ANDROGYNOUS face, pompadoured black hair, and sideburns—it was like looking at a bubblegum publicity shot of a young Elvis. Even had that same practiced coy grin. Virginia stared at the boy's face before she noticed the knife hanging loosely in his left hand.

His smile turned into a leer and he darted for her. She spun around and ran toward a row of homes bordering the park. Huge, rich-looking ones with high fences. He followed and reached for her, pulling her down by the shirt. She knocked his hand away and kicked him hard in the balls. He grunted with pain and pulled her down by a boot. The deep green juice of the grass stained her forearms and the knees of her jeans as she took off.

She thought about what had happened to the

deputy and the old man in Mississippi and when
someone had tried to kill Nick in Algiers. This
wasn't a time to be tough. She knew the difference
between standing up for herself and stupidity. Virginia tried for the fence of a Victorian home and
could feel the rough wood under her palms. She
tried to gain a foothold as the kid pounced on top
of her and pinned her to the ground. He gripped
her wrists like tight bracelets and bit into his lip
with concentration.

She screamed and tried to knee him in the balls
again but missed, kicking him in the hip. She could
smell his rancid breath as she dug her nails under
the skin of his neck. He hit her hard in the jaw and
pressed her shoulders to the ground before placing
a blade to her throat.

He smiled and said, "You scream again, cry, or
any of that shit, and me and you'll dance later."

The boy thrust his pelvis into hers as his eyes
rolled into the back of his head.

NICK HEARD SOMETHING back toward the golf
course and turned and ran toward the sound. He
was sweating from the humidity and his breath
came in large, hard gasps. The cast made him feel
off balance as he pushed his way through a group
of elderly tourists. They pointed at a map of the
park's trail and one woman called him a rude man.

The sound came from back toward St. Charles
Avenue. Maybe he was hearing things, his mind
becoming a paranoid trap from the day. Could
have been a kid, anything. But he needed to find
Virginia before Cruz did. That line of action
wasn't a stretch for the man, it was the way he
operated. For her to be prancing around smelling
the roses was ridiculous.

He needed to find her and take her to Jay's while he fixed this mess. Damn it, why didn't she understand? She should've known to stay inside and wait. Wasn't that clear?

JESSE HAD A hand over the woman's mouth as they lay flat on the ground. They were against a fence and under some bushes. He could hear the dude shoutin' the woman's name like a crazy man. Ain't no way the big dude could see 'em less he came over and started rootin' round here. It was a little trick he picked up from that pasty ole fool. Make like an animal. Blend in like a rabbit or a monkey.

Jesse had his other hand underneath the woman's soaked flannel shirt and knotted her undershirt so tight around her chest it made her gasp. She needed to know this was takin' care of business. That big dude come 'round here, the deal was done. Jesse was too smart for that.

He would wait until the dude was out of sight, and then crawl under the fence to where Floyd was waitin' in the van. He was probably wonderin' where he was at now, as he bobbed his head to that awful jungle music.

The woman smelled good. Kinda sweet. He licked her face to see what her sweat tasted like. She gasped again on his wet hand and he gripped her face tighter. The big dude just ran on by, none the wiser.

"C'mon. Let's go, baby doll. You're my ticket."

NICK ROAMED THE park for almost an hour. His knees ached from trudging over the concrete in his cowboy boots and his casted hand had turned a bright purple from the earlier fight. He walked the entire perimeter and inside of the park four times. From St. Charles Avenue to the Audubon Zoo.

He sat down on a bench and cradled his head in his hands. He finally called the warehouse and his machine picked up. He called again a few times, then went back to the park.

That was when he saw it. A wadded, soaked flannel shirt. He reached for it and smelled the damp odor of her honeysuckle perfume. But it was the freshly carved letters in a nearby oak tree that made a huge stone sink in his stomach.

In the glow of a high fluorescent lamp, the writing was clear: *TCB*, and a jagged line of a lightning bolt's flash.

46

THE RAIN FELL in a long silver curtain outside the open Creole doors of JoJo's Blues Bar. The reverse neon letters bathed the flagstone sidewalk where a prostitute argued with a bouncer. The woman bit hard on her lip and called him a motherfucker before leaving. Her stance tough, as she hunted for a place to hawk her body. Nick watched the action in a fogged alcohol haze, a mass of empty shot glasses catching a candle's light.

Maybe he felt sorry for himself. Maybe what he was doing equaled crawling into a cave and hiding. But there was nothing more he could do. A few hours earlier, it'd taken five security guards to throw him out of the Blues Shack. Cruz had coolly walked out into the alley where they had him pinned. His thin devil face flushed underneath his dark sunglasses, and he smirked, "You know what I want."

JoJo pounded two Dixies down, breaking Nick's angry thoughts, and joined him. He looked Nick up and down and turned to face his own reflection in a mirror framed in multicolor Christmas lights.

"You call Medeaux?" JoJo asked.

"No," Nick said. "They'll kill her."

JoJo's craggy face twitched in the dim light. His eyes were bloodshot and his hand shook when he turned up the beer. His emotions seemed as brittle as plate glass.

"JoJo, I don't blame you."

"It wasn't yore thing, I've always carried my own water."

"How long you have?"

"Got me a nice eviction notice to be out at the end of the month. Been here for almost thirty years. I'd like to take Pascal Cruz and kick that notice up his ass so far he chokes. That ain't the big worry though."

Nick got up, dropped a quarter in the jukebox for "Walkin' After Midnight," and returned to the back of the bar. Sometimes when you're in love, it's hard to see the woman's face for trying too hard to see every curve and line. Nick could only imagine pieces. Dimples, chin, and a spray of freckles across her nose. Then he saw the gold mouth of Cruz's man and gripped a shot glass hard in his hand. He wanted to take it and throw it into the warped, staring reflection. See all the candied liquor pour out in a sweet mess of color. Nick pulled his hand back as Henry walked in and shook rain from his ragged houndstooth hat.

The old man didn't look back into the bar's narrow corner, just found his stool at the end of the bar, like it was any other night, and ordered a drink. Nick slowly placed the shot back on the bar.

"There might be a way we can save them both," Nick said, his head soft and blurred.

"He ain't gonna tell you where he stashed them records," JoJo said.

"He doesn't have a choice."

Nick walked over to the bar and sat down next

to Henry. The old man just stared straight ahead until Keesha plunked down a tall Beam and Coke.

"You know where they are?" Nick asked.

"I ain't going back to Mississippi," Henry said.

"Can you help me?"

"What? So you can make all that money?"

"Listen to me, Henry. I listened to your story and I appreciated you being honest about what happened on that night in thirty-eight. But if you want a quick shot at redemption, this is your chance. Another man is after those Johnson records and he took a woman who didn't have a damn thing to do with any of this."

"Shiiit."

"They'll kill her, Henry, just like they killed Baker and Cracker."

JoJo moved behind both of them and put his arms around both their shoulders. His soft wool sweater felt smooth against Nick's neck. Fatherly. "Henry, don't fuck with us, if you know about them records. I ain't bullshittin', it's time for you to come through."

Henry took a long pull of his drink and stared at the old photo of himself. He turned back to look at JoJo.

Two hours later, all three were in JoJo's Cadillac headed on a midnight run to a small town outside Greenwood, Mississippi, where it all began.

HOURS LATER, NICK felt the humid Mississippi night air on his face and heard JoJo and Henry mumbling in the front seat. His head pounded as he looked at the luminescent dial on his stainless-steel diver's watch. Past three A.M. The old leather seats smelled of mothballs and faint mildew.

Nick tried not to think of Virginia. When he

did, he became queasy and could see a torrent of hair-pulling and rape. He ground his teeth hard to escape the image and pushed himself up from the backseat to see the flat expanses of harvested cotton now plowed over.

The moonlight kept everything in a surreal coloring like a black-and-white film. Sun-parched clapboard shacks, rusted trailer homes, and laundry still on the lines. A few pine and oak trees. Lonely islands surrounded by the naked dirt. Scenes best accompanied by a lone bottleneck guitar.

"God, I feel like a cat just shit in my mouth," Nick said.

"I wasn't pourin' them Dixies and Jack down your throat," JoJo said, looking back into the rearview mirror and shaking his head. "Henry takin' me the rest of the way to Quito..."

"Turn right over there," Henry said, pointing to a lonely crossroads.

Headlights hit a single dead tree near a cotton field. The tree's sun-bleached branches hung like mangled arms. Nick wondered if Robert Johnson found a similar crossroads to cut his fingernails to the quick and play the guitar until the devil tapped him on the shoulder.

"We gonna go straight for a while," Henry said.

In window glass, Nick could see Henry's gray eyes wide, taking in his home like a man returned from a time machine. A look of shock with a world not quite the way he left it.

"My uncle used to live right there," he said, pointing to a crooked row of trailer homes. "Had him a mule, he used to plow rows of corn by himself. Sweet ole thing. Don't know what happened to him. Don't know what happened to anybody after I left."

The road was the same one Nick had taken with Willie Brown on the night he first met Cracker. Felt like it had been years ago. Too many things clouded his mind in such a short time. He wondered if Brown had a family. If they understood the complexities surrounding a fine man's death. Nick wished Brown was with them now.

"Henry, when was the last time you were home?" Nick asked.

"Nineteen forty-nine."

"Why'd you leave?"

"After years pass, rumor 'comes fact," Henry said. "You know what I mean. It was best I lost myself in the biggest city I know. One day, I pointed my truck south to New Orleans and never looked back."

JoJo looked back and caught Nick's eye in the mirror and winked. First time he'd seen JoJo like his old self in a long time. It was a little redemption mission for both men, Nick thought, as they hit a straight mile of highway with crooked crosses of telephone poles. Nick couldn't help but hear the eerie voice of Johnson sing:

> *You may bury my body*
> *down by the highway side*
> *So my old evil spirit*
> *can catch a Greyhound bus and ride*

47

JoJo TURNED onto a darkened dirt road and followed it for at least two miles before Henry told them to stop. It was silent in the car as dust flew back through the windows. Nick didn't say a word; he wanted to watch Henry's reaction. Henry cocked his head back and searched through the rear-window glass. The taillights glowed red onto the soft dirt.

"Goddamn, it was right here. Right ova here," Henry said as he pounded a fist into the Cadillac's dash.

"Awright, Henry," JoJo said. "No need to be abusin' my automobile."

"Henry, they moved the Three Forks," Nick said.

"Listen, kid, I ain't senile. I know where my store was at."

"That was over fifty years ago," Nick said.

"JoJo, tell this kid to shut the fuck up."

"Where do I need to go, Nick?" JoJo asked.

They followed the dirt road back to the crossroads, where Nick pointed to an old wooden home with a satellite dish on the roof and plastic sheeting for windows. The same house Brown had taken him to, where they sat on the porch and listened to stories about Johnson's exploits. Nick could still hear their laughter and the twittering cicadas.

"That ain't my sto'," Henry said.

"JoJo, let him take a good look."

JoJo turned onto a soft, dusty road in front of the porch. Before he could fully stop, Henry was already out of the car and hobbling up the broken stairs to the porch. A pile of rotted wood and rusted metal scraps lay in a nearby heap.

"He said he wasn't senile, shiiit," JoJo said.

Nick jumped out and followed Henry, who tried to open a chain-caught door. Outside, a yellow light clicked on and Nick could hear the clack of a shotgun loading.

"Henry, *move*, get away from the door!" Nick yelled.

A wiry black man opened the house completely naked carrying his gun in both hands.

"Y'all get the fuck out," yelled Brown's friend James, firing the gun into the air. "Y'all get the fuck out!"

"Listen you little dingdong," JoJo said completely unfazed. "This man right here used to own this here house."

James looked down at his flaccid penis and tightened his grip on the gun.

"I'll give you fifty bucks if yo' cover your ass up and let us come inside," JoJo said. "Can we come inside? Man left something here."

"I ain't no fool, y'all rob me," James said.

"James?" Nick said, stepping onto the cracking porch. "Remember me? I was here with Willie."

James lowered his shotgun and put his hand out. "Nick? Nick? Is that you? Man, I'm sorry. Y'all scared the shit out of me. Been keepin' this gun with me after what happened to Willie and Cracker. Y'all c'mon inside. I ain't got much."

Henry walked ahead of everybody, his gray eyes lit. He traced his hands over the battered molding around the doorframes and stooped low to put his hand on the crooked floor planks. His eyes shut tight like he could still feel the reverberation of a Delta steel guitar.

Planks of wood painted long ago in a seafoam green crudely buckled from the wall. Plywood-separated rooms, hammered lazily with crooked rusted nails. Nick could imagine sacks of feed, rows of fruit jars, and farm supplies lining the old building before it was partitioned. A woman yelled in a back room and two pigtailed little girls stared wide-eyed at Henry.

Henry smiled back and said to James, "You have a pick?"

"Yeah."

"Get them kids out here," Henry said. "What we 'bout to find ain't fo' them."

As James turned, there were heavy footsteps on the porch outside. Everyone stopped cold. Nick walked over and pulled the plastic sheeting from a nail. His breath caught in his throat when he saw who was outside. Sallow faced and dressed in rags paced Cracker.

His weak face drew into a smile when Nick opened the front door. "I was w-wonder...wonderin' when y'all show up here," he said.

"*Cracker,*" Nick said, putting an arm around the old man. "You okay?"

Henry slowly ambled onto the brittle porch and stared at Cracker as if he were a reflection of an ugly woman. He spat on the ground, twisted his head away, then looked back at Cracker, his tired red eyes rimmed with tears.

"Cracker," Henry said, his voice like brittle ice.

"Earl. Earl." Cracker's age fell away and once again he was a scared fifteen-year-old boy. "What are we gonna do? They know? W-What...what we gonna do?"

Cracker got close to Henry and for a moment Nick thought Cracker was going to hug the older man. Nick could imagine the pair of them working in the heat of a Mississippi night to hide the body of a white record producer from Texas.

Henry gave Nick a mean stare, then placed his quivering arm around Cracker's shoulders.

"Jes like I said, Cracker. Every little thin' gonna be jes fine. Jes fine."

AFTER SEVERAL MORE payoffs from JoJo, James finally let them tear the pick into two separate walls at the front of the house. The old two-by-fours became exposed through several layers of wood until there came a loud thunk.

"That's it," Henry said.

Cracker was outside eating some cold chicken with James's children. He hadn't eaten for days and had made his way back to Memphis by the kindness of a white Methodist minister. Then a trucker, on the advice of the minister, took him down to Greenwood. Cracker walked the rest of the way back through the fields and woods he knew so well.

The pick was embedded and Nick strained until he felt his shoulders might leave their sockets again. His cast was a sticky mess and he wanted to cut the thing off. Nick finally dislodged the pick

and then began to pry the wood off the section of
the old wall. The dawn filtered weak sunlight
through the plastic-covered windows. Nick carefully removed sections of the wood, his back and
arm aching.

A large, jagged chunk came away to expose a
human skull and torso. Henry walked outside as
Nick and JoJo stood staring at the upper portion
of the skeleton. Clutched in its arms sat a wooden
crate identical to the one from Cracker's porch.

They'd found the man who'd served Robert
Johnson his last drink.

48

IF JESSE CROSSED his eyes real hard, it made Mr.
Cruz look like some kinda biblical man. Jesus?
Naw, maybe Moses. He kept crossing and trying
different faces until he felt Floyd kick his foot
under the table. He gave one of those "cut that shit
out" looks. Who cared? These weren't his people
anyway and this wasn't what was going to make
him great. This was like Sun Records—a beginning. Hell, the harder he crossed his eyes, the more
Cruz looked like Sam Phillips.

"You got some kinda problem, man?" Floyd
asked. "You lookin' strange, brotha."

Jesse moved his hand up quickly like a draw and
Floyd flinched. He just kept the hand movin' on
and brushed his hair back. Sucker. Still fist-shy
over that ass kickin', he thought as he looked out
the Amtrak train's window at all the Mississippi
scenery rollin' past. Jesse bit down on his knuckle
and hummed a little gospel tune to himself.
*Wouldn't be much longer. Wouldn't be much
longer.*

That mornin' a big nigra in a straw hat came
into the Blues Shack wantin' to see Mr. Cruz. Said
his name was Sun and gave Mr. Cruz a note sayin'
to be in Greenwood tonight. They were supposed

to take that redheaded piece and some kinda paperwork for them ole records. Didn't seem worth the effort. But they sure must be worth an awful lot to Mr. Cruz, since he was pacin' and sweatin' round the train station this mornin' like a rat fuckin' in a wool sock.

Mr. Cruz's flask caught the sunlight just right as he took a sip and made the redheaded woman squint. It hadn't been tough to get her on the train—hell, she was so doped up she'd probably done a striptease in the projects. She'd just walked real cool-like until they got in their train cabin and shut the door. They hadn't messed with her. Floyd wanted to, but Cruz said no way. Not 'til after.

If they got the records, Mr. Cruz wanted all them ole men dead, and the big white dude. What all them didn't know, hadn't a damned idea in their heads about, was that Jesse was gonna take it all and meet Puka and Inga in a suite at the Peabody in Memphis.

He'd be high as a kite and talkin' to the ducks on the roof by midnight.

"Jesse, I sure am proud of what you've done for me," Cruz said. "Must be that good Mississippi breeding. You know I'm a southerner too? Have a little water moccasin in both of us."

Mr. Cruz was just funnin' with him. He must know that he was leavin' them Sun Records days and goin' right for Las Vegas. He and his German woman would start their own shrine there. He'd be E without anyone else.

He'd be E.

E.

Jesse watched the cotton patches, trailer homes, and gas stations roll by.

Tonight was gonna be the first night of forever.

* * *

"HE AIN'T COMIN' and I need to take a shit," Henry said, as he dropped his head and spit on the weathered train station's floor. Nick could tell he was tired of reliving the past and confronting ghosts. The meanness powering his old age taken from him at the Three Forks as if he were a scolded child.

JoJo was indifferent, asleep and snoring softly as Nick looked around the small station. Cracker had a couple of lollipops the kids at the Three Forks had given him. He licked on one as he watched a black man in indigo overalls and an elderly white woman in a faded flowered dress. A steady night heat hovered, broken only by the momentary sweeping arc of a 1950s table fan.

Nick stood and walked back into the station's bathroom, where the cream-colored paint was so thick on the door, it looked like spoiled milk. He checked for feet under the stalls before he inserted the clip into the Browning 9mm and thumbed down the slide release. He tucked the gun back into the inside pocket of his faded blue jean jacket and walked back into the station, wishing he was alone.

None of the men would even listen to his reasoning.

JoJo woke up as Nick sat back on the hard wooden bench and began to rub his fingers hard around his eyes. "Goddamn, I forgot where I was at," JoJo said. "Thought I was dreamin' 'bout all this shit."

"How about we all become Hare Krishnas and play the tambourine on Bourbon Street if we get through this?" Nick asked.

It was a mundane comment, something typical

before a football game, when conversation is as pointless as chewing on a hangnail. A tool to focus away from the energy of an approaching conflict.

"When he gets nervous, he talks," JoJo said.

"Mmm," Henry said. "You good with that gun, kid?"

Nick looked down at the bulky outline in his jacket and smiled. "We'll be fine, y'all just stay cool."

Cracker continued to lick his candy and turned his head as a train whistle sounded outside and a light rumble shook the crumbling brick building.

"What was he like?" Nick asked Cracker.

"Who?"

"Robert Johnson."

"I don't know...h-he use to try to get me to take off from Mista Devlin. Say I...I could do better. Say just hop that ole train son and m-mornin' comes you at where you suppose to be. Neva made much sense. How a train know where I suppose be at?"

"When we get done with this, would you talk to me? Tell me all about Robert. What he played. What he talked about. All of it."

"Yes suh. But I'll t-tell you one thing," Cracker said as they all stood and walked to the platform. "He wouldn't wanna be used like this. Them r-records of his shoulda neva been found. He kept that music with him until the end. Didn't want no one hearin' it."

"Why?"

"He s-say it was all he was," Cracker said, turning to Henry. "W-why you make me think them record were mine. I-I stayed all them years in the woods to protect them and weren't even

R.L.'s. Why you do that, Big Earl? Why you do that to me?"

Henry looked away.

CRUZ STOOD UP and fell forward as the train slowed. "We're leaving the girl in the compartment. Jesse, you watch her, and Floyd, you watch Travers."

Floyd self-consciously touched his swollen lip and agreed. Jesse said he would too, but it wasn't part of his divine plan. He watched the black ovals of Mr. Cruz's sunglasses, but nothing registered. It was just like lookin' at the old wooden shacks slide by the window—shadows the color of old bruises.

"How we know if we ain't bein' screwed?" Jesse asked.

"I'll know," Cruz said, as he dotted the beads of sweat rolling into his eyes. His stiff black suit not much for the heat.

Jesse rolled the sleeves higher on his black T-shirt and tightened the grip on the Glock 9mm. His hands shook a little on the rough handle as the train slowed, still feeling the constant rocking motion of the trip.

"Kid, be tough, remember to hit it like a black man and take no prisoners," Floyd said.

Jesse just stared at him.

The view from the train's open window soon filled with a redbrick train station. Jesse heard the screech of metal on metal braking. He looked down at the redhead, her body as limp as a wet napkin, just lying there with no idea that her boyfriend was about to die. In a way, she kinda looked like Ann-Margret, and he wondered if she could dance like that.

* * *

NICK OPENED THE door for Henry, who held the boxed nine records packed in a moldy red velvet cloth. Brittle as a dried rose petal. JoJo winked at Nick when the train slowed to the platform. A little gesture to let him know everything was going to be all right.

Cracker lagged behind. He hung loose from the crowd, reminding Nick of the omega wolf in the pack. His head down and not looking anyone in the eye. This isn't what he wanted. Nick could tell he felt like he was letting Johnson down. Like he was throwing the very thing he'd sworn to protect into the abyss.

A loose-tied man in a business suit got off the train and trotted inside with a travel bag thrown over his shoulder. A large black woman carried two sleeping children, and a conductor stepped outside with a notebook flipped open.

Last train to Memphis.

"Goddamn, I tole you," Henry said.

Finally, Cruz and the big black man walked off the very last train car. Nick kept his empty hands in plain view as he walked toward them. A smile crept onto his face as he saw the swollen profile of the man, just a beaten dog. He could hear Henry cough and JoJo jingling change in his pocket behind him.

Cruz's face split into a wide grin as he opened his hands like a good host meeting guests on the stoop of his mansion. A dark, heavy silence beat around them in blackness.

"Hello, hello, hello," Cruz said.

"Where's Virginia?" Nick asked.

"Where are my records?"

"Got 'em right here, you sack of dogshit," Henry said.

Cruz's face twitched. Maybe from the comment or maybe from seeing Cracker lagging behind. Whatever the reason, the light went from his face like the last spark from a cigarette butt.

"I guess you know my friend Cracker," Nick said. "Said you weren't too big on the hospitality. Didn't pour him a beer or offer him a job."

"I don't need commentary, Travers," Cruz said.

"Where's Virginia?" Nick asked again.

"Let me see the records first."

"Bullshit, where is she?"

Cruz nodded to the black man, who yelled back into the car. A light flicked on in the window of a train car and a limp Virginia appeared with the kid who looked like Elvis. *Great.* In the shadow, he could see the kid laughing and pretending like they were dancing. The scene framed by the smooth silver car.

Nick whipped out his gun and Cruz's flunky drew his.

"She's fine, just sedated, don't want her stressed out," Cruz said.

The gun looked like a small toy in the black man's huge hands. His biceps bulged and his eyes were flat and hard, waiting to fire. Nick could see the injured pride in the man's reddened eyes.

"Remember, Travers, just a white man trying to carve a little niche from the black man's world," Cruz said. "We're the same."

"He ain't nothin' like you," JoJo said. "You the stink on the bottom of my shoe."

Nick kept his gun trained on the black man as he heard the conductor make a last call. The train whistle blew and the conductor stepped inside.

"Are we going to do this?" Cruz asked.

Henry stepped forward holding the records flat

and in both hands like a holy sacrament before he handed them to Cruz and spit in his face. The white spittle trickled down his bearded chin.

Cruz wiped it off, opened the crate's top, and peeled back the old material. He stared for a moment at the labels marked in faded pen ink. "Until they're played, I'll be taking Miss Dare with me. I've been fucked by these things twice before."

Nick thumbed back the gun's hammer.

"I'm a man of my word, you know that, Travers..."

"Oh. I feel so much better now," Nick said.

The fumes coming from around the station made his eyes water, but Nick didn't keep Cruz's man out of sight. A light went out from the passenger car like an extinguished candle.

"I'm not leaving here without her," Nick said.

Cruz raised his hand, "All right, Floyd, get the bitch."

The train lurched forward and as Floyd turned, a quick double snap came from inside the car. Floyd's head lolled like a drunkard's. His gun raised and came upward spinning in the palm of his hand.

Nick pushed JoJo to the ground and covered his head, the rusted wheels of the train gliding by. A gun exploded and another double pop came from inside the car. Nick saw Henry pull out a revolver from his coat and level it at Cruz, who was looking back into the railcar at the Elvis kid, who'd apparently shot Cruz's bodyguard.

Henry squeezed off four rounds into Cruz. Cruz leveled his gun at Henry and pulled the trigger as they both fell to the concrete.

Through his fingers, Nick looked up again, and saw Cruz lying in a twisted pile with Floyd. The top quarter of his head was blown away and a small bubble of spit and blood formed on his bottom lip.

The records were gone and Henry lay dying on the cold concrete with a hole in his stomach the size of a silver dollar. Cracker was nowhere on the platform.

NICK GRABBED HOLD of the last passing railcar, ran through the baggage compartment, and jumped over suitcases, but when he reached the connecting door, it was locked. He kicked it until his knee ached. The monotonous bump of the train thudded in his ears as the door flung open. He crossed into the next compartment and passed through three more before he was in the same railcar where Elvis had been.

He had left JoJo on the platform to find help for Henry. Cruz and his bodyguard were positively dead and there was no threat to his old friend. JoJo had just yelled to get that kid.

In the first cabin, he found a grizzled woman wearing an Atlanta Braves ball cap and spitting snuff. The next cabin was dark, and he fumbled for the light switch before a fist smashed into his stomach. He lost his breath reaching out for the kid, who ran by him into the hall. Nick lunged for his legs and brought him down. Still out of breath, he held him to the ground.

"Where are they?" Nick yelled.

"Eat me," the kid said, his black hair covering his dark-ringed eyes. His face was as smooth as a woman's. He had to remember the kid just murdered a man before he smacked him hard in the face.

"What'd you do with the records?"

"I ain't got 'em, man. I ain't got them."

Nick punched him again. There were no reservations now. He was so close to hearing the third recording sessions of Robert Johnson. Some punk-ass kid trying to make some cash wasn't going to destroy that. Nick had worked his entire life for this. This was it. There was nothing else. This was it.

The kid tried to knee Nick in the crotch and scratch at his eyes. Nick locked his grip and was about to yank the kid to his feet when two train conductors ran down the hall and knocked him off. They pinned Nick to the ground and let the kid go. Out of the corner of his eye, Nick could see the young Elvis pick up a backpack, wipe his bleeding lip, and flee down the hall.

"Get the hell off me!" Nick yelled. "That kid just murdered a man back at the station."

One of the conductors, a middle-aged white guy with narrow eyes and a stubbled jaw, yelled back to another man to grab the kid, who was already into another car.

They let Nick up, and within a few minutes, four waiters from the dining car tried to wrestle the kid down. The kid shot one of them and jumped off the train a few miles later. No one, not even the police, was even sure where. Nick found Virginia asleep in the railcar and he held her hand all the way to Memphis.

That was the last time Nick saw the kid or ever heard about the lost recordings. The worst of it was that he would never know what filled their lacquered grooves. The sound caught more than fifty years ago had vanished deep into the Delta night.

Epilogue

THE STORY, as Nick read, ended in swirling blue and red lights outside the Graceland mansion in Memphis. A night security guard had called police after he'd seen a white male crawling over the fence and briefly weeping at the Presley family graves. The suspect then broke into the museum where they kept Presley's clothes and gold records.

Jesse Garon, a nineteen-year-old who was wanted for the deaths of a Mississippi deputy and two New Orleans security guards, shattered the glass case containing Presley's "Sun God" outfit. He put on the costume, complete with cape and massive belt buckle, and fled the building.

The security guard, quoted in the paper, said Garon was headed back over the fence when he saw several Memphis police cars outside the gates. Garon turned and ran back toward the mansion, breaking through a back door into the green shag carpet of the Jungle Room.

Police and security officers surrounded the building but didn't try to follow after Garon began shooting at them. About five A.M., the mansion flooded with spotlights from police and news helicopters.

Police tried to communicate with Garon inside the mansion with megaphones, but they got no response. The management of the tourist site threatened lawsuits if the mansion was damaged in any way during a siege for the alleged murderer. They said tear gas could damage the furniture.

A few hours later, the sharp report of a pistol crack came from inside the mansion. The officer in charge gave the order to head in. Team members split up searching the entire home for Garon. Their guns drawn waiting for the killer at every turn.

Instead, they found Garon upstairs, already dead.

Past the red velvet ropes where simple tourists weren't able to go, he lay on Presley's black leather bedspread in a pool of blood. The bullet had made a gaping hole through the jumpsuit's emblazoned sequined sun and right through the kid's heart.

Police later searched the motel where Garon had stayed. But no one ever found a single recording of a blues guitarist who was murdered on a hot August night in 1938. His twenty-nine songs a bible for twentieth-century music.

IT WAS A tattered November night and Nick was back at JoJo's bar sipping on a Dixie. He sat right under the framed black-and-white picture of Earl Snooks. The paisley scar and gray eyes more familiar now. They'd buried him under his real name back in Greenwood. There was even talk of reissuing some of the songs he cut in the forties, due to the press his reemergence attracted.

A writer from *Living Blues* even came to JoJo's a few weeks ago to ask Nick and JoJo about Henry. *Did they have any idea of his real identity?* They both shook their heads and said, he really didn't even seem like a musician. Nick fed him a few nice anecdotes and the guy left New Orleans pleased with the story.

Nick didn't tell anyone except JoJo about the conversation he'd had with Henry in Algiers. About the night Robert Johnson was killed. It was like he was surrounded by this incredible wine of knowledge but couldn't offer a drink. Maybe that's the way Johnson would've wanted it. Forever the phantom poet of Mississippi. Even his death a continuing debate.

After the shooting at the train station, Nick spent weeks in Greenwood looking for Cracker and answering more questions for the Leflore County Sheriff's Department. Some of the deputies knew about Cracker but hadn't seen him. Nick stayed most nights on James's porch at the old Three Forks store hoping he would return. He promised not to tell Henry's story, but he could tell Cracker's.

Nick kept a vigil as the summer warned of a cool fall, the sun turning a bitter harvest orange over the cotton as it had for decades. Their inky patterns quiet and brittle. Wind in the old woods, nothing but a whisper.

But Cracker never returned. His old shack's doors and windows stayed open, allowing leaves to fall inside and mold. His walls, plastered with newspapers, turned brown and splotched, and the deep mildew made the entire shack smell like a decaying stump.

Finally, Virginia came for Nick at his motel one night and begged him to come back to New Orleans. He finally started work again on the Guitar Slim book and the old patterns returned. JoJo laughed, Loretta cooked and sang, and that old deep melancholy feeling came back into the pit of his stomach.

Even having Virginia cradled on his chest with the industrial windows wide open and the soft sounds of an urban night didn't help. He jogged every morning at the Riverwalk, found a battered gym to get the blood flowing in his tired shoulders, and picked up a class to teach in the fall.

So there he was, feeling a nice buzz, his gloved hands wrapped around a beer, when Virginia walked in. She wore an old blue jean jacket and had her guitar and duffel bag with her. Nick turned back to his drink as she punched up "Walkin' After Midnight" in the jukebox.

She sat down and Nick could smell her freshly shampooed hair. Honeysuckle. She touched her palm to Nick's face.

"Time to head on back down that lonesome blues highway. I've stayed too long," she said. "Got a gig in Austin next week."

"I never asked you to leave," Nick said, still looking down at his Dixie beer.

She touched her fingers to his mouth and pursed her lips. Her arms wrapped around his neck. She leaned forward and kissed him deeply.

Virginia smiled and kissed him again. Nick looked into her sky blue eyes and kissed her once on the forehead and then on a dimpled cheek. She pulled up her duffel bag and was gone.

The song finished, and "Last Fair Deal Gone Down" started. JoJo sat down next to Nick, a wet rag still in his hand. He smiled and told Felix to grab them a couple more Dixies.

"Just keep on pluggin' and everythin' always works out," JoJo said, his wise brown eyes soft.

"Remember son, life is easy—livin' is hard."

"I think I've heard that before."

Johnson's voice on the old jukebox was like chilled rain.

COLD RAIN PELTED *the rich Delta earth as a dark figure stumbled upon the old Zion Church. His hands were chafed and his light blue eyes reddened from the whipping cold. He'd walked four days to come back past the trailer homes and shacks strung with fat Christmas lights.*

He had to come back. This might be the final time.

The shadow of the small white church grew larger as he approached the crossroads. The moon was a sliver as thin as a thumbnail in the Delta sky. A beat-up pickup truck passed him but kept going—its twin red lights turning away on another country road.

He removed the wrapped scarf around his head and loped down the weed-covered hill to the cemetery. The whitewashed tombstones were black slabs in the night. He had to feel around, squint. Finally he fell to his knees when he reached the right one.

The pointed obelisk read:

ROBERT JOHNSON

"KING OF THE DELTA BLUES SINGERS"

HIS MUSIC STRUCK A CHORD THAT CONTINUES TO RESONATE. HIS BLUES ADDRESSED GENERATIONS HE WOULD NEVER KNOW AND MADE POETRY OF HIS VISIONS AND FEARS.

Cracker laid some limp purple flowers at the base of the monument and then scrambled to his feet. He picked up the heavy sack he'd toted with him for months and headed on down the highway. R.L.'s footsteps thumped heavy in his ears.

Read on for an excerpt from Ace Atkins's
next book

Leavin' Trunk Blues

Coming soon in hardcover from
St. Martin's Minotaur

IN THE BLACKNESS of a Mississippi night, Nick
watched the Delta landscape roll by from the
Amtrak car window. The barren shotgun cottages,
tired mobile homes, and brittle patterns of dead
cotton fields shot out in strobe-like flashes. He
kicked off his old boots and took a sip from his
stainless steel flask. The thumping metal on metal
pounded a rhythm in his ears.

Kate Archer. JoJo had to bring her up. He just
had to plant that seed in his mind to sprout and
grow until he stepped off the train in Chicago.
What a friend.

Nick had heard she'd taken a job with the *Tri-
bune* after a failed relationship with an Uptown
restauranteur named Richard Brevard, the man
she was supposed to marry. She must've met
Richard shortly after she'd found Nick in bed with
that lanky blonde two years ago. Nick still remembered the vacant look on her face as she rolled
back the old warehouse door. She saw a strange
woman sitting in her robe and drinking out of her
favorite mug.

Kate had shot him a look that wasn't exactly
hatred, just a drained expression of absolute disap-
pointment. There was little eloquent parting con-

versation. Nick recalled her final words as "You are such an ass."

Nick could still feel the heat of her dark skin as they made love in his warehouse with Aaron Neville blaring on the stereo. Both of them loaded with Dixies, whiskey, and blues. The best time he'd ever had.

Maybe JoJo was right. Maybe this whole trip was about her. Some kind of masochism to see if she would kick him in the nuts this time. But she was worth it. If only he could talk to her for a moment and have some kind of ending to the whole thing, he'd feel better. He was never much for closure. In fact, he thought the concept was bullshit. But he needed something...Another screw-you. Another chance.

Shit, he was just bringing hope with him. Bringing a dream of something that could never work out. Nick sipped the whiskey again and stared back at the blues highway and laughed at his situation. He felt New Orleans melt away in the flickering light, the history roll by, and the endless black night reconnect to a past that once showed hope to an entire generation. The train rolled, bumped, and vibrated his back. Thinking about how the old travelers felt made him feel good.

Nick could imagine them now as he turned out his overhead light and pulled down his narrow bed. He could almost smell the past travelers loaded with shoe boxes full of fried chicken and biscuits staring at the same Mississippi night. There were stories of women kissing the floor of the railcar as they crossed over the Mason-Dixon line at Cairo, Illinois. *Trading what was familiar for what could be.*

The journey of the blues started somewhere outside, somewhere in a heated evening about a century ago. The blues was born in the rich, brown earth of the Delta, a region stretching two hundred miles from the Peabody Hotel in Memphis to the edge of Vicksburg, Mississippi. It was once a frontier of mean swamps with bears and water moccasins. A land broken in by blacks who worked from sunup to sundown in levee and prison camps. Sometimes at gunpoint.

From that soul-breaking work came the blues. Like their African forefathers, they used songs to make the work pass—sometimes alone, others in unison—as they picked cotton, unloaded steamship cargos, or beat their tools into the rich earth. Soon, they coupled the hollers with guitars and harmonicas.

The music worked its way into backwood shacks where couples danced, bathed in sweat, as the music brought back the spirit. The early players thumped drum beats on the buckled, wooden floors making the guitar talk back to them. The instruments were just an intimate extension of the players' voices. Blues became a core of Delta life and of the southern black community.

And in the late thirties and forties, blues followed that community. About five million blacks left the south between World War II and 1970 for northern cities, a shift that changed the complexion of America. It used to cost about twenty bucks for a ticket from New Orleans to Chicago on the Illinois Central—about a month's pay for most. Some families, like Old World immigrants, had to split up. They would send money home to bring everyone over to the other side.

In 1943, Muddy Waters told his boss he was sick so he could catch a train to Chicago. He left

with nothing but ambition, a single change of
clothes, and his old Silvertone guitar. He knew
fame was just a trip away.

Nick believed that's when the blues really left
the Delta and started a new life in the Windy City.
Muddy would help mold that country sound into a
tightly-backed band with piano, drums, bass, and
harmonica. Urban blues got a shot in the arm
when Muddy arrived at the 12th Street Station.

When he was finishing his Great Migration project at Tulane a few years ago, he traced the routes
of the Delta greats from the Delta to Chicago. The
change was bone-jarring. The Mississippi Delta
was a fertile oasis. Everything green and alive.
Chicago was industrial. Gray and cold. But for
sharecroppers making inhuman wages, if anything
at all, Chicago was about hope. They'd probably
travel to the depths of hell to escape the poverty
and racial barriers.

Nick imagined folks like Billy Lyons and Ruby
Walker and the absolute loneliness they must have
felt approaching the belching smoke stacks of
Chicago industry. Did Lyons wait for a train in
Clarksdale with nothing more than a suitcase made
of paper and a five-year-old daughter tugging at his
sleeve, as Nick had read? Big boasts to farmers in
Mississippi about how he was going to make it in
Chicago? About how he was going to come back
driving a long, shiny car throwing money out his
window at his country relatives? But when the cold
night cloaked around the train, it must have been
like traveling to another planet. The boast becoming an internal fear.

Bright lights, big city, gone to my baby's head,
Nick thought, closing his eyes.

Today, most of that hope was gone. The 12th

Street Station was now a barren field at 12th and Michigan, and the middle-class South Side world was nothing but rotting slums and burned-out shells. In Muddy's and Ruby's time, Chicago was a place where blacks could make it. Where wealth was as obtainable as someone's work ethic. But today, many blacks were taking that same blues highway back to the Delta. Somewhere, the dream had become an economic nightmare.

The lights of the small towns and lonesome highways scattered across his face as the train rolled through the cold never-ending night. As he fell asleep, his mind dissolved to Kate's face. Brown eyes like sunlight hitting morning coffee. Perfect dimpled chin. Reminded him of a young Ali McGraw about the time of *The Getaway*. He imagined her pulling the brown hair from her eyes and pursing a smile into the corner of her mouth.

I've been gone so long, I know things ain't what they used to be.

IT IS LATE FALL *and the tenements buckle with new arrivals from Mississippi. I want to complain of the filth to my wise-mouth sister but she's so proud of her new home. She washes each dish as if it's a jewel and hangs her husband's ragged laundry outside as if it's a tapestry. Standing on the groaning wooden step, where I smoke my daily cigarette and find occasional peace, the sound of the neighborhood's laundry cracks in my ear.*

By the end of the month, I'm on the street. The husband has taken interest in me and my sister can only imagine my advances. So I take my paper suitcase, my ten dollars in my shoe, and walk. I walk the rain-slicked streets at night. I sleep during the day in vacant buildings.

When I find Dirty Jimmy on Maxwell Street, I haven't eaten for three days. It is only after the third song, that he disappears and buys me a plate of greens and cornbread. I almost choke trying to rush it into my body. Jimmy plays like an angel and we become friends. Half the bucket is mine.

I continue to walk. I find work at a laundry where I get blisters as long as snap peas on my fingers. But it's work and it's more money than I've ever known.

I live at a paper-walled rooming house till Billy Lyons walks over to me and Jimmy at the market. His suit is creased within an inch of his life and his shoes shine like a silver dollar.

He tells me I sing like a man. I laugh and two weeks later I'm in his bed. He pours champagne over my brown body and blistered hands. He makes love to me and leaves flowers by my mouth as I sleep.

The music surrounds me as if I was swimming in blood-red wine. I'm drunk with it.

I sing at Pepper's. The Purple Cat.

I'm at parties at Muddy's house. He's twisted up in a fine suit. He's tellin' me I got something. He tells me he sees something in me like Broonzy saw in him. Spann is there playing a piano in the corner. Drunk. A sombrero cocked on his head, as he pounds out his heart.

The whiskey flows with the blues. I can't get enough. Blackness. Swimming. Blackness, back in the sea. Billy and I fight. He's out whorin'. I'm out workin'.

The world spins and I fall through it. The lipstick on my face is a jagged curve as I trip off the stage in the middle of the first set. I black out. I'm *swimming in Billy's blood. It is thick and I can't reach the surface.*

I'm awake.

A single bulb burns and rocks above my head and I know I've been dreaming again. My sister is dead. Billy is dead. And it's lockdown time. I can hear the locks crack through the concrete walls as I turn the pillow. The guards laugh at our situations. And I close my eyes. Waiting for sleep to come so that I may return to my dreams, and Billy, and my Promised Land.

ABOUT SEVENTY MILES outside Chicago, the Dwight Correctional Center stood like a medieval fortress. Didn't look like a prison. Looked like a mental institution during the Depression or an old college campus. Buildings made of stone with pointed towers. Nick drove a rental car that resembled a white Tic Tac into the visitors' lot and shut off the engine. His back ached from the train and having to bend at the waist for the drive. He finished the cigarette he was smoking, flicked it into the weeds, and walked inside passing through various gates and checkpoints.

The halls echoed with bolts popping and buzzers sounding until he was ushered into a sterile room to wait for Ruby Walker. It was a simple white room decorated with crooked law enforcement posters. The floor was concrete and the door was metal. No windows. Just the annoying burn of the fluorescent lights above.

Prisons were a part of blues, the same way railroads and bars emanated the music. Bukka White was a well-know slide guitarist when he was convicted of shooting a man in 1937. He spent a few

years at Parchman Prison in Mississippi before
meeting Nick's hero, Alan Lomax, in the forties.
Lomax, the first great blues tracker, recorded
White for the Library of Congress.

Lomax also found Leadbelly, who was sen-
tenced to Angola Prison in Louisiana. Leadbelly,
the king of the 12-string, was serving his second
term in prison for murder. Lomax was so moved
by Leadbelly's powerful voice and knowledge of
folk songs that he petitioned the Louisiana gover-
nor for a pardon. In 1934, the big man went to
work as Lomax's personal chauffeur.

Nick was also no stranger to The Farm. He had
interviewed several prisoners at Angola over the
years. This meeting was nothing new. He drummed
his hands on the table and adjusted the cassette
recorder.

The door opened and a white female guard
walked in with a tall black woman. The woman
was lanky and rawboned with darting black eyes.
Her hair was cut short and it frizzed loose above
her ears. She kept her hands in the pockets of her
denim jumpsuit as she took a seat. Her oval face
was still smooth with high cheekbones.

Nick stood and extended his hand and tried to
imagine the Sweet Black Angel from the photographs. Her hand delicately wrapped around a
thick silver microphone, her eyes shut, and her
mouth wide open in song. The slight space
between her teeth and the sheen of her skin speaking of smoldering sexuality.

She did not shake his hand. Nick sat, reached
into his coat for a notebook and fiddled with con-
trols on the recorder. His watch cap and the gloves
laid on the table.

"Uh-uh dude," she said, in a rich, humming

voice. "I ain't putting nothin' on recording. You can stick that thing where it came from. That wasn't part of the deal. You said talk."

"This is for a blues archive. Your own story will be cataloged with your music."

"This isn't for the radio?"

Nick shook his head. Ruby spoke with a defined clarity with only a trace of a Mississippi accent.

"Well alright then," she said, leaning forward across the table. Her voice a husky, growl. The guard behind her blew her nose, coughed up some phlegm, and leaned back against the wall. Somewhere outside, a gate clanged shut. A couple of trusties laughed.

"I read your case."

"It's bullshit."

Nick nodded.

"Aren't you gonna say something about prisons bein' full of innocent people?" Ruby asked.

"No."

"Why not?"

"I'm not here to trivialize your life," Nick said. "You're innocent?"

"Are you gonna ask me why there was blood in my bed?"

"Why was there blood in your bed?"

"After forty years, those things start to rattle in your mind," she said. "You fill your cell with books and your mind with the past. The past becomes like a movie, playing over and over. And this one ain't any good...someone poured that blood on me while I slept."

"Poured?"

"That's what I said, ain't it."

It was going to be one those. Those interviews granted after you listened to some long, hard bull-

shit story of innocence. Most prisoners had spent
so much time alone and in law libraries that they
really believed they never committed the crime.
Nick could play the game.

"Who would want to set you up?"

"If I knew, I wouldn't be here."

"Any ideas?"

She shook her head and looked at her hands.
Short nails. Winter chapped.

"Listen, we don't need to get into that," Nick
said. "I want to know it all. I want to hear about
when you were young, your recording. When did
you come from Clarksdale?"

"Fifty-five."

"How old are you?"

"None of your damned business."

"OK. Why'd you leave Mississippi?"

She rubbed her hand over her short gray hair. It
was if she was searching for the glistening tresses
she once owned.

"Tell me about growing up Mississippi?"

"Why?" she asked. "Nobody cares."

"Because your music is important. People still
listen to it."

"Shit," she said cutting her eyes away.

"They do."

"And you want to hear my story from the beginning. Everything?"

"Yep."

"And you're not messing with me, dude?"

"No ma'am."

Ruby looked down at her rough hands and
inhaled a long breath. She blew it out and looked
back at the masculine guard. The female guard
rolled up on her toes and looked away.

"I was one of nine children of a sharecropper,"

she said. "I worked like a mule from the time I was born. Yes, I picked cotton. People think I'm tellin' a lie makin' it seem like life was hard and that kind of junk. But yes, I picked cotton. My daddy left when I was six and we had to work harder. Never saw the son-of-a-bitch again....I had to clean. I had to cook like the younger children were my own. Cook greens and pork and all that country food."

"Warden said you were a cook here," Nick said. "A good one."

"I appreciate him sayin' that but the food I have to work with is like turnin' dog shit into chocolate pie. Sometimes I feel like that. You want me to go on? Or is that the answer you need, dude?"

"You can call me Nick."

"All right, dude."

Ruby looked like she was relaxing a bit. She looked back at the guard working on a hangnail with her mouth and said, "You listenin' to my story? This is some good stuff, man."

The guard looked away. The man comment didn't go unnoticed.

"So your family were sharecroppers," Nick said.

"Slaves more like it. We worked on a plantation outside Clarksdale. Beautiful place. Still think about it. Can just see the way thunderstorms would roll over the Delta. Looked like big black islands that would beat the dirt for hours. Little thuds turning that dry earth into somethin' we could use. We picked a ton of cotton but at the end of the year, Mr. Williams, man who owned the farm, said 'Miss Walker, look like you're a little short again.' Old withered bastard who wore them old-timey glasses. He had a plantation store where

we would buy seeds and tools and supplies. Flour
and things. And this man would charge us double
what it was worth. See what I'm sayin'? Then at
the end of the year, we always came out on the bad
side of the math. 'Sorry Miss Walker, you're a little
short. Maybe next year.' He said we owed him for
working *his land*. If I got out tomorrow and that
man was still alive, which he ain't unless he about
hundred and eighty, I'd shoot that bastard right in
the head."

The guard looked at Ruby.

"Metaphorically speaking," Nick finished. He
asked her the names and ages of her family members, about her church, and about the house where
she grew up.

"So when did you leave?"

"When I got old enough I was singing out at
juke houses," Ruby said. "You know what a juke
house is?"

"Spent some time in the Delta."

"I would sneak out to the juke houses where
people where drinking corn whiskey and actin' a
fool on the weekends and sing a little bit. I'd hook
up with a guitar or harp player and we'd turn
those folks out. Sometimes they'd laugh callin' me
a bow-legged little girl but I'd break their whiskey
glasses and turn their guts out. Have them cryin'
by the end of the night. All of them men wantin' to
take me home. I knew then, I'd be someone."

"So you took the train to Chicago?" Nick
asked.

"Took a train to Memphis and caught the Illinois Central," she said. "Wanted to be the next
Bessie Smith. The real empress of the blues. Got off
at the station and stayed with my sister for awhile.

Went down to Maxwell Street and caught up with a harp player."

"Who?"

"You wouldn't know him."

"Dirty Jimmy?"

Ruby nodded. She seemed incapable of smiling.

"Maxwell Street is where I met Billy," she said, her thoughts moving on. "He came to hear me sing with Jimmy. Never forget. There I was in my raggedy, old country clothes and him in this long coat, tie, and hat just watchin' me like I was something special. He said, 'woman you sang like a man.'"

Nick laughed.

"I didn't know what to say. Was he making fun of me? Was he trying to put me down? No, he said, he had found a good thing. And from there, he got me into clubs, bought me clothes, a place to stay and put me on records. Said Ruby Walker didn't sound like a blues singer and that's where he came up with the Sweet Black Angel."

"From the song?"

"Yes."

"You and Billy close?" Nick asked.

"You mean were we having sex?"

Nick shrugged.

"I'm not proud of things I did on the outside, but we had sex like a pair of rabbits."

"Can we get some water?" Nick asked the guard. The guard knocked on the door and someone else opened it. She repeated Nick's request. Nick felt like a pervert talking to a gray-headed woman about playing the horizontal hokey pokey.

"So, when did you record 'Lonesome Blues Highway'?"

"You heard it?" she said. She had the straight-
est, white teeth he'd ever seen.

"Of course," Nick said. "*Ain't nobody else
gonna walk it for you.*"

Ruby slapped her knee. "You're *all-right*,
dude."

"Big hit."

"'Blues Highway'? Lord yes...Billy couldn't
keep them stocked. Went straight to the top. You
know that magazine *Cashbox*? They called it pure
gold. Billy couldn't press 'em fast enough."

"You cut how many, four others?"

"No, about a dozen. Only put out about five."

"Which ones?"

"Dude, you're askin' questions from way back.
Let's see, 'Blues Highway,' 'Devil Woman,' 'Cold,
Cold Heart,' and 'Tie Yore Monkey in a Knot.'"

Nick sang:

> "*When you see that woman dressed so fine,*
> *And you got lovin' on your mind,*
> *You better tie,*
> *You better tie,*
> *Your monkey in a knot*"

Ruby nodded to the music.

"Moses Jordan wrote that one?" Nick asked.

"Yeah, Moses wrote most all my songs."

"You still see him?"

"He's come to see me a few times," she said.
"He sent a few letters. But your friends have a way
of forgettin' about you when you're inside. Used to
have this big woman in here who told me that.
Said forget your friends. Forget your family. Only
person you can rely on is yourself."

"What about parole? Seems like you're the

model prisoner. You've cooked, served forty years."

"Yeah, well there was some trouble 'bout ten years ago."

"What kind of trouble?"

"Guard. Man guard was messin' with me. Tryin' to touch me and things."

"Did you complain?"

"Yeah, I complained. I stuck a fork right up his ass in the kitchen. Had to have surgery to get it out and got me in solitary for a month. Had some cross-eyed psychologist tell me I had a problem with men and pointed things. Said I had issues with my daddy. Ain't that somethin'? I never knew my daddy."

"And that was the end of parole?"

"The board told me I was still a threat on the outside. Hell, took me three years just to get back into the kitchen."

Nick looked down at his notes, the cassette recorder whirred in the silence. Nick scratched his cheek and shifted in his chair.

"You want to tell me about Billy?"

"No."

"Elmore King told me you were innocent," Nick said. "That's why I'm here. He said he knew you didn't kill Billy."

Ruby pushed herself away from the table.

"I'm in here. Aren't I?" Ruby stood and nodded to the guard who jangled the keys at her waist. "Jimmy Scott's the one who told the police about me threatening Billy. Jimmy turned on me. When you get accused, that's when you find your friends."

"I can help," Nick said. "If you know something more, now is the time to tell me."

"You want me trust you?"

"Yes."

"Why?"

"Cause I gave you my word."

"Nothin' that easy."

"Is with me," Nick said. "You help me with my research, I'll check out your story. Who should I talk to?"

Ruby shrugged.

"Why did you ask me to come up here then?" he asked. "Why the hell did you send me those picture of you and Billy?"

"I want those back."

"Why even make the effort?" Nick asked. "You afraid I will find out more of the truth?"

Ruby marched over and pressed stop on the recorder. Nick braced himself. He could hear her rapid breathing. He thought she might spit on him. She crossed her arms before her and sat back down. They sat in silence for a few minutes.

"Who do you still talk to?" Nick asked. "Anyone connected to King Snake or the old circuit?"

She finally said: "There's this man named Peetie Wheatstraw. He hasn't done nothin' but suck up every last cent I made on the outside. Said he was my agent. That he'd take care of me and all that kind of mess. We ain't talkin' but Peetie knew all them folks....Slap him in the head for me while you're at it."

"Where can I find him?"

"Last time I heard, he was working at a men's shop on the South Side called Soul Train," she said. "Been doing that ever since he got out of the business."

The guard walked over to the table and pointed at a gold watch on her thick wrist.

"You were convicted in fifty-seven," Nick said. "Why me? Why talk to me?"

"You got the last shot."

"Excuse me?"

She cut her brown eyes away. "I got plans. I ain't stayin' longer than forty."

Nick looked puzzled.

"You'll know soon enough," she said, looking down at her work shoes. "You got till Christmas."

Ruby extended her hand to Nick. Her palm felt wet and small as she squeezed before being led away.

Atkins, Ace
Crossroad Blues

	DATE DUE	
12-6-11	11-19 DA c	

TH
W
to
M
wo
tha

—

CO
W
ho
cu
go
in
ev

—

Pub
P.O.
Ple
$1.
Ser
DIS
Car
Exp
Nar
Add
City
Ple
U.S